WYRDE AND WAYWARD

HOUSE OF WERTH: 1

CHARLOTTE E.

ENGLISH

ONE

The Scions of the House of Werth are all born normal. It is what happens afterwards that sets them apart from the rest of England.

Three years afterwards, to be precise.

No sooner had Augusta Honoria Werth set foot over the threshold of Werth Towers than her name was heard to resound about those ancient brick walls, uttered in the powerfully *resonant* tones of her Aunt Wheldrake. The syllables rolled through the great, craggy pile like controlled claps of thunder, and set the floor a-shake.

'Where,' thundered she, 'is Augusta?'

The importuned lady in question paused to shake the rain from her shawl, a brisk summer shower having caught her unawares as she crossed the park. Werths she saw aplenty, as she swept her calm gaze over the darkly majestic great hall: Aunt Margaret crossing from one side to the other, a pile of linens in her hands; Cousin Theodore wisely disappearing into the library; and Mrs. Thannibour, her elder sister Nell, coming towards her, wielding an ugly but dry shawl with intent.

She did not, however, see Aunt Wheldrake.

'Gussie, how late you are,' hissed Nell, plucking her

sister's delicate, rose-coloured shawl from about her shoulders, and replacing it with the sad, slate-grey substitute. The wool prickled Gussie's bare arms, and scratched woefully, but Nell was deaf to all protests, instead ushering her resolutely towards the enormous, polished oak staircase dominating the central hall. 'Go, please,' said Nell. 'Pacify her, or we shall not have a moment's peace.'

'I do not know what peace is likely to be found on Lizzie's third birthday,' Gussie observed, but Nell was not listening, already hastening away.

Squaring her shoulders, Gussie faced the staircase with resolution, and climbed. 'I am here, Aunt,' she called, just as the thunder began, again, to roll.

Aunt Wheldrake's face, crowned with a gauzy lace cap, appeared over the banister. 'How late you are!' she said, echoing Nell.

'I am very sorry, Aunt, I was obliged to—'

'Never mind that now,' said she, descending with a *whoosh*, and taking a firm grip upon her niece's elbow. 'We are but five minutes from the Great Event, so you see you are just in time, and not a moment is to be lost.' Wisps of roiling cloud swirled about her feet, and then about Gussie's, who lurched unsteadily as she rose into the air. Swiftly was she borne away, sailing through the hall, the library and out into the gardens, where the rain continued, disobligingly, to fall.

'Theodore!' thundered Aunt Wheldrake as they soared past.

'Er,' he was heard to say, followed by the distant snap of a book hastily closed. 'Yes! Coming.'

Aunt Wheldrake cast one dark look up at the glowering clouds, and the pitter-patter of rain slowed. 'Insupportable,' she declared. To the best of Gussie's knowledge, her aunt's stormy powers did not extend so far as to hold dictates over the rain; the coincidence of timing, however, was impressive.

She reminded herself not to be late to any more of Aunt Wheldrake's parties.

On a pretty stretch of emerald lawn, just beyond the borders of Lady Werth's lavender shrubbery, a white pavilion beckoned. Lady Werth herself sat in a cane chair beneath its domed interior, her husband at her elbow, and all the disparate scions of the Werth family line gathered around her. All, that is, save Gussie, and the shabby figure of Cousin Theo marching along in her wake.

'Aunt Werth,' said Gussie, stepping smoothly from her cloud, and bent to kiss Lady Werth.

She was rewarded with a huge smile. 'Ah, Gussie, I knew you would not fail us. What do you think, then, of the birthday girl? Lucretia swears she shall be a mermaid, and indeed she can swim astonishingly well. Cannot you, Lizzie? But for my part I think it a great deal more likely that she shall surprise us all, and turn out a siren, or perhaps a fire-weaver.'

Privately, Gussie knew that Aunt Georgie had the right of it, for the Wyrde, when it came, rarely deigned to manifest in any manner of pattern. Mere mortal expectations were as nothing to it; it always did just as it pleased, and as such made a fitting curse for the wayward Werths.

The hopes of Lizzie's mama must, however, be respected, so Gussie smiled at Aunt Wheldrake and agreed that Lizzie would make a perfect little mermaid.

'What with her golden hair,' said the proud mama, 'and would she not look well all wreathed about in sea-jewels?'

'Very well indeed,' agreed Augusta, happy in her aunt's restored temper. The members of the House being now collected, in an orderly fashion, where the Great Event was to take place, her thunders had departed, together with her mists, and she was able to take her place beside her husband with smiling alacrity.

A chair had been placed upon Lizzie's right hand, undoubtedly designed for Gussie. Someone — Nell, most likely — had piled it high with fat, silken cushions. Being herself of ample figure, she treated her thin younger sister as though Gussie might break in half were she not properly wrapped up, cushioned and cosseted. But such overbearing care had its advantages, and Gussie sank gratefully into the cushions' pillowy embrace as she turned her attention to Lizzie.

The child sat on the Wyrding Chair, so called because the throne-like structure had been wheeled out for every Third Birthday in living memory. Nothing about the chair *mattered*, of course. It was not, itself, Wyrded, nor could it have any impact upon the proceedings. But being oversized, gilded and ornately carved, it offered a majesty and a grandeur to these Great Events (as Aunt Wheldrake would have it) that would otherwise be lacking.

Lord Werth had his pocket-watch in hand. 'And it is time,' he announced, meaning exactly three years, to the minute, since the occasion of Elizabeth Louisa Wheldrake's birth.

A hush fell. Every gathered Werth drew in a breath, and held it, all eyes fastened upon the tiny child shifting restlessly upon her enormous throne.

Gussie felt a moment's pity for the little girl. Long-awaited as her birth had been, she had appeared at last, sixteen years after Lucretia Werth's marriage to William Wheldrake, preceded by only one sibling, who had not survived. Small wonder, then, the weight of expectation that rested upon her; all her parents' hopes must be satisfied in this one little child, for only a miracle would ever bless them with another.

And Aunt Wheldrake had set her heart upon the nature of her daughter's Wyrding. She would be a mermaid in water, and a girl upon land. She would gain in power, and lose nothing, and of course she would be pretty.

Gussie cast up a silent wish of her own, that her poor aunt would not be too disappointed with whatever happened instead. And that she would contrive to control her temper, if she was.

Not that anything was happening at all, yet. Those collective, indrawn breaths were released at length, when poor Lizzie sat unchanged under her family's scrutiny, growing anxious and restless but in no way uncanny.

Then a faint, dry rustling came, a whispering *hiss*, and Aunt Wheldrake clapped her hands together in delight. 'Oh, it is scales!' said she. 'It is her mermaid's tail! Quick, Lizzie, we must get you into the water at once.' And she rose, and bustled forward, ready to scoop up the child and carry her straight to the winding beck that ran, half asleep, through the grounds.

'Stay, aunt,' said Gussie, holding up a warning hand. 'I do not quite think—'

Further words were unnecessary, for a tiny storm caught up the ringlets of Lizzie's golden hair, and whipped it all into a tangle. It was no storm of her mother's, for Aunt Wheldrake's face registered dumb astonishment, and then bleak dismay — for the golden mass shifted, in the blink of an eye, into a nest of slim, gold-gilded snakes. At her approach, all those tiny heads turned as one, and uttered a sibilant *hiss* in chorus.

Aunt Wheldrake came to an abrupt stop, but too late, for one eager little monster lashed out with its ivory fangs, and sank them with alacrity into her wrist.

With a scream, Aunt Wheldrake retired, defeated, from the lists.

The assembled Werths waited to see whether Lizzie's snakes would prove venomous, to be indicated by the sudden and fatal collapse of Aunt Wheldrake.

This undesirable development did not come to pass. Aunt Wheldrake clutched at her injury — but minor, to Gussie's eye, though she keened and bristled as though it had come near to mortal — and gabbled something perhaps only her husband could understand.

'Well,' said Lady Werth into the ensuing silence. 'And we have not had a gorgon among us since Werth's Great-

Aunt Maud. I shall fetch her diaries for you, Lucretia. I am sure they contain a great deal of practical advice upon the management of her hair, and other troubles.' What her ladyship meant by "other troubles" presumably included a tendency to turn living beings into exquisite stone statues; an ability few gentlemen could consider desirable in a wife.

Already, one or two Werths were drawing away from poor Lizzie, as though she might leave nothing of the party behind her but a collection of statuary. Which, of course, she might. Aunt Wheldrake should consider herself fortunate only to have been bitten, Gussie thought, though there was no sign in her aunt's face of any consciousness of a narrow escape.

At length, the disappointed mama drew herself up. 'Mr. Wheldrake,' she said to her husband. 'If you will be so good as to take Lizzie? I believe I will begin upon those diaries at once, sister.'

Lady Werth gave a gracious inclination of her head, and dispatched a hovering footman with instructions to unearth these hitherto forgotten manuscripts. The defeated parents followed, bearing the birthday girl between them, and a silence fell.

At length, Lady Werth sighed. 'And I wish she *had* been a mermaid, for her mother's sake. But for her own, I do not think it at all a bad thing. A gorgon! She will be the quite the terror of society, in fifteen years' time. I look forward to her effect upon the patronesses of Almack's, should the wretched creatures still be in the ascendancy. Only let them tell *her* she is denied entry to their abominable establishment.'

Had she been a man, of course, she might wreak havoc rather further afield, for tales of a long-ago Phineas Werth's services to king and country were legendary at the Towers. He was said to have turned a whole platoon of advancing cavalry to stone, with a single flick of his riotous locks. And he was insufferable about it, too. There was no talking to him at all.

6

As a lady, Lizzie's influence might extend no farther than the elite social establishments of London, but Gussie amused herself very much in picturing the results.

There were reasons, perhaps, why the Werths were not always entirely popular abroad.

Two

Upon Gussie's return across the park, she found a warm welcome awaiting her. Being as it was the kind of welcome born of expectation, she knew she must soon disappoint. Nonetheless, she enjoyed a moment's heart-swelling gratitude upon beholding the familiar and beloved outlines of Lake Cottage, its arched roof and prettily-shaped gables visible from some distance. Lord Werth had granted her residence there only some eight months previously, prior to which she had maintained her abode at the Towers. *Here* she had privacy, and a right to her own style of comforts. Solitude, too, or nearly enough, her uncle's only stipulation being that Someone must live with her, to preserve her respectability. Every other Werth being, at present, suitably disposed of elsewhere, that someone was her former governess, still beloved by Gussie and Nell, and glad of a comfortable situation.

Fortunately for both, she was also excellent company.

'And?' said Miss Frostell, coming out of the parlour just as soon as Gussie stepped into the house. 'How did it all go off?'

Gussie paused to discard Nell's scratchy grey shawl, wondering in the process what had become of her favourite rose-coloured one. She would have to go up to the Towers again in the morning, to enquire after it. 'Considering the hopes riding on Lizzie's birthday, it could only be a let-down,' she said.

Miss Frostell made a grimace of sympathy, and ushered her former charge into the parlour. 'She is not, then, become a mermaid?'

'A gorgon,' sighed Gussie, and sank onto the sofa.

Miss Frostell, a far better needlewoman than any Gussie Werth, and a fine housekeeper too, listened to her recounting of the afternoon's events in quiet sympathy, providing murmured commentary as befitted the extent of the calamity. She was not Wyrded herself, this excellent Miss Frostell, and rather regretted the fact — except that today, a different feeling animated her sweet, thin, withered face. Was that a modicum of… relief, in her hazel eyes? When Gussie was a child, they had speculated together of the gifts for which Gussie wished; of the forthcoming day when the Wyrde might choose her after all, and answer all her childish dreams. But none of those dreams had ever included a head full of snakes.

'That is unfortunate,' said Miss Frostell, when Gussie had finished. 'The poor child. I had thought — well, there have not been so many curses in the current generations, have there? Not true misfortunes.'

'If we pass over Theo, then no. I believe most of us are not too badly circumstanced.'

'Yes, poor Theo,' sighed Miss Frostell, with a degree of tender feeling that might be considered unwise. A woman of quiet habits herself, Miss Frostell saw Theo's bookish tendencies as attractive; in fact, she appeared to find everything about Theo attractive, even his flyaway, rust-coloured hair and his outmoded attire.

Truly, there was no accounting for taste.

'Oh, and now for a surprise,' said Miss Frostell, picking up her embroidery frame. 'A letter has come for you. I have set it upon the table there, just beside you. It has the look of an invitation about it.'

Gussie had not noticed the missive upon coming in, her head full of too many other things. But there it lay indeed, crisp and white against dark mahogany, addressed in a hand she did not recognise. Miss Frostell's hints she disregarded; her governess had Imagination, and a way of wishing on her dear charge's behalf. These wishes invariably involved Gussie's ascension out of the ranks of the poorer Werths, and into great plenty, a trajectory only to be achieved by marriage; and that, of course, required an introduction to more gentlemen. Every letter bearing the name of Augusta Werth was an invitation, but only to Miss Frostell's fancy. Reality was hardly ever obliging enough to follow suit.

But as she unfolded this particular letter, it dawned upon her that Miss Frostell, for once, was right: she was invited somewhere. She, Gussie Werth, least impressive of her line and a poor spinster to boot. In open-mouthed astonishment she read the following lines:

My dear child. You will not know me, for we have never been introduced. I hope you will forgive the liberty I take in thus addressing you, however, for I number your aunt among my dearest and oldest friends, and I am persuaded she would be delighted by the proposal I write to make you.

I shall be holding a little gathering at Starminster. I very much hope you will consent to make one of the party, and give me the honour of your company, for the period of a few weeks.

I trust your esteemed uncle, Lord Werth, will find nothing objectionable...

The letter went on in a similar style for several more lines, and was finally signed, *Esther, Lady Maundevyle.*

Gussie looked up from this puzzling missive, several questions at once upon her lips.

Miss Frostell forestalled her. '*Maundevyle?*' she breathed. 'Lady Maundevyle? Why, is she not a famous hermit?'

'If she is, she must be a *rich* hermit,' said Gussie. 'Without which quality, the world would not find her habits half so interesting.' She read the letter over again, without deriving any particular benefit from the exercise; the invitation still made as little sense.

She set it aside. 'Where is Starminster, Frosty? Do you have your peerage about you?'

Miss Frostell got up at once, and rummaged about among a collection of paraphernalia in the pretty bureau occupying one corner of the room. She returned at last with a small volume in hand, fresh-printed and new, for Miss Frostell liked to keep her peerage up to date.

'Maundevyle,' she said, paging through the book. 'Here they are. Viscounts only — not your dear uncle's equal, then, quite. Principle seat: Starminster, in Somerset.'

Having enjoyed few opportunities to travel, Gussie had yet to venture beyond the borders of Norfolk. Somerset, she knew, was quite on the other side of the country, representing a journey of some days.

Miss Frostell closed the book. 'Your correspondent must be the Dowager Viscountess, Gussie. The current incumbent is named Henry.'

'Naturally I am overcome with joy at her gracious condescension,' said Gussie, but absently, her mind still turning upon the problem of her letter. What could the Dowager Viscountess Maundevyle want with her?

'He is four-and-thirty years old,' continued Miss Frostell. 'And,' she added, with the air of a woman applying the crowning glory to a string of brilliant achievements, 'he is unwed.' She stood, beaming.

Gussie's wandering attention sharpened. 'Unw— Frosty! You are not matchmaking? Again?'

'Why, of course I am. Your aunts may have given up on you, but *I* have not.'

'For shame. Are we not happy here?'

'Blissfully, and I shall cry for a week when you go away. But you are wasted here, Gussie. A woman of your talents—'

'I have no talents,' said Gussie. 'Do not you know it is common knowledge, among the family?'

'I was not speaking of the Wyrde. You deserve a high position, and it is shameful that you should never have had the opportunity to win one.'

'Quite right,' said Gussie, laughing. 'Every woman of moderate beauty, small fortune and little practical use deserves a high position. And how should such a position ever be achieved, except by marriage?'

'Your aunt Werth will support your going, I am sure of it,' said Miss Frostell, affecting not to hear this. 'Her being so old a friend of Lady Maundevyle's.'

'Is she, though?' said Gussie.

'Why else should the dowager invite you, if she is not?'

'Why would she invite me, if she is? We are perfect strangers to one another. Even supposing her to be seized by a sudden freak, and compelled to fill her house with the unremarkable relations of all her friends, why would she choose me? There are Werths enough to satisfy every possible requirement.'

'True,' said Miss Frostell. 'And it does not *quite* make sense that she should not extend the same invitation to your aunt. But,' and here she hesitated, 'perhaps it is your very *lack* of talents, as you put it, or rather your lack of the Wyrde, that encourages her. Not everybody prizes the effects of it as the Werths do.'

'You may well be right, but still it is not quite explanation enough. The world is full of the unWyrded. There are far more of *them,* than there are of gorgons and mermaids and nightmarists. Why, then, me? She must be quite spoiled for choice.'

'I cannot explain it, but I still think you should go.'

'Why, Frosty?'

'Well,' said Miss Frostell, with a shrug of her shoulders.

'Something wonderful could come of it. Who knows?'

'That is like your optimism,' said Gussie, folding up the letter. 'But I am of a suspicious, shrewish disposition, and I say there is more afoot here than is apparent.'

'Do you not, then, wish to find out what it is?'

Gussie sat tapping the letter against her knee, and did not immediately reply. At length she said: 'Well, and why not?' Glancing about at their comfortable, but quiet, parlour, she added: 'Though it will be difficult to tear myself away from the unending revelries of the Towers, I daresay Starminster will contrive to entertain me.'

'No,' said Lady Werth, some two hours later, Gussie having walked back up to the great house to attend at dinner.

'No?' Gussie echoed, too surprised to come up with a more intelligent response.

Lady Werth thrust the letter back into her niece's hands, crumpling the delicate paper in the process. 'Starminster,' she said, with an air of exasperation. Then, abandoning this line of thought, 'Lady Maundevyle is *not* my dearest friend, whatever she may say; we have not spoken in quite twenty years. Why she should suddenly impose upon *you*, well—' She stopped, and looked long at Gussie.

'Yes, aunt?'

Lady Werth swept into the dining-parlour without offering any immediate reply. Only once seated did she say: 'I do not think it suitable for you to attend upon Lady Maundevyle at Starminster.'

'And if that is the case then certainly I shan't,' Gussie said calmly. 'But it does not appear so objectionable to me, aunt. Why should the idea trouble you?'

'You will not be suitably attended.'

'I will take Miss Frostell with me. Lady Maundevyle could hardly object to so proper a measure.'

'It is quite out of the question.'

'Perhaps she would not object if *you* were to accompany me,' Gussie suggested. 'Seeing as she considers you so special a friend.'

'Absolutely not.'

Gussie held her peace, watching her aunt closely. More lay behind her objections than was apparent, that was obvious. She began to feel quite tangled up in secrets, and the feeling did not please her at all.

She was not strictly obliged to seek her aunt's or her uncle's permission, being six-and-twenty years of age, and possessed of her own independence. But living, as she did, in one of her uncle's cottages, and so often attending upon the family at the Towers, any outright defiance would be both unwise and unbecoming.

She did not mean, however, to be kept forever at home.

'I should like very much to go,' said Gussie, after a moment. 'I have barely stirred beyond the family grounds. If I do not travel when I am granted the opportunity, then I will never see anything of the world.'

'The world,' said Lady Werth shortly, 'is vastly overrated.'

Lord Werth, having made his appearance at table, now interrupted his wife. 'What's that, Gussie? Are you asked somewhere?'

Gussie explained, aware of her aunt silently fuming beside her as she did so.

Instead of leaping at once to her defence, as Gussie had hoped, and immediately offering her the use of his carriage, Lord Werth looked at his wife. Their eyes met, and something Gussie could not read passed silently between them.

'You think it unwise?' said Lord Werth.

'You know that it must be,' came the reply.

Lord Werth submitted. 'Perhaps another time, Gussie,' he said, kindly enough. 'I am sure there will be better chances to see something of the world, than to be walled up at Starminster.'

Gussie gazed helplessly at her well-meaning protectors: at her aunt in her lavender silks and her elaborately arranged hair, perfect and composed and utterly unmoved; and her uncle, never unkind, but with a will to match the iron hue of his hair.

'Why?' she said.

Her aunt was startled into meeting her gaze. 'Why… what?'

'Why do you object? What is the real reason?'

Lady Werth looked away. 'How fanciful you are, my dear.'

Gussie gave it up. This conversation had been conducted before an audience of attentive Werths, but one glance at their rapt faces — Cousin Theo at her elbow the only exception, intent upon a wholesale rejection of his food — convinced her that they could not intervene, nor were they inclined to try.

With a soft sigh, she turned her attention to her own dinner, and tried to console herself with ragout of mutton, and herb pie.

THREE

Upon the morrow, after the sad duty of answering Lady Maundevyle's invitation in the negative, Gussie busied herself with the myriad duties attendant upon so large a gathering of Werths. It was a pleasure to see Nell, whose residence some distance away with her husband and four children kept her too busy for regular visiting.

Gussie found her in the garden pavilion, enjoying the late morning sun. She was alone; Mr. Thannibour had elected not to attend Lizzie's Great Event, and her children remained at home with their nanny.

In Gussie's private opinion, Nell was hugely enjoying the respite.

'Gus,' said she upon her sister's approach, looking up from the book spread open in her lap.

Gussie sank into the pretty cane chair opposite, her glance falling briefly upon the Wyrding Throne. The servants had not yet removed it, and it loomed still, all the more terrible for its emptiness. Gussie would never admit to having taken a seat there herself, on more than one occasion since her own, failed Wyrding. As a three-year-old, she had proved herself the only Werth in living memory passed over by the Wyrde. At ten, she had proved it again; and at fifteen, and one-and-twenty…

'I came looking for my shawl,' said Gussie. 'And also, my sister.'

'The pink? I believe I left it in the cloakroom.' Her own gaze wandered to the throne. 'You're lucky, you know,' she said. 'Though I am sure you don't feel it at the Towers. The Wyrde is… troublesome.'

Gussie recognised the book she was reading. It was a book of spectres, penned by a long-ago Werth, and added to by later generations — including Nell.

'Perhaps I am better suited to a life outside the Towers,' Gussie agreed. 'But that, it seems, I am not to have.' That piece of fortune had fallen, instead, to her sister. She had found in Mr. Thannibour a man who did not mind what she did in the night, and who was unruffled by the shades that wandered into Fothingale Manor, bent on having a comfortable cose with his wife. Such men were not often to be met with.

'Your chance will come, Gus,' said Nell, with a look of sympathy.

'Oh?' said Gussie. 'When?'

Nell shrugged, and closed her book.

'Do *you* know why my aunt and uncle are so set against my going?'

'They think it unsuitable, did they not say that?' said Nell, frowning.

'An explanation not much to the purpose.'

Nell's frown deepened, and she turned upon her sister a troubled gaze. 'Gussie. Have you not sometimes wondered…'

'Wondered what?'

'Have you never *noticed*?' said Nell.

'Noticed? What am I to have noticed?'

But Nell would not be drawn. 'No,' she said thoughtfully. 'How could you have? And perhaps they are right, after all.'

'Nell! If you, too, are keeping secrets from me, I swear

I shall — why, I'll tell Great-Aunt Honoria what became of the fur tippet she left to Mother.'

Nell gasped. 'You would not!'

Gussie subsided with a sigh. 'Probably I would not. I am nowhere near evil enough.'

'She was delighted about Lizzie,' Nell offered.

'Well she might have been. You should stay here to keep her in line, or she'll be haunting the poor child quite until she is grown.'

'I cannot,' said Nell, not without regret. 'I must leave tomorrow, as planned, or heaven knows in what state I shall find Arthur and the children.'

'They can manage very well without you, I am sure.'

'*They* may, perhaps. The spectres, I am persuaded, are most unlikely to leave them alone.'

Perhaps that was what Nell meant, when she called the Wyrde *troublesome*. And a fair observation at that.

A flicker of movement caught Gussie's eye. She looked up, and beheld the distant figure of Cousin Theo, recognisable by the shock of red hair blowing in the wind. He was red elsewhere about himself, too, in places he rather ought not, and Gussie averted her eyes.

'Oh, is that Theo?' Nell sighed. 'Someone ought to break him of those habits, or he will never find a wife.'

'Perhaps he doesn't want one.'

Nell's brows rose. 'That can hardly be permissible.'

'Whyever not?'

'Well — look at him, Gus. Did you ever see a more total figure of helplessness?'

Theo was, at that moment, engaged in stalking across the distant grass, a book tucked under one arm and something red and glistening clutched in the other hand.

Gussie began to laugh. 'I doubt the woman exists who could make Theo respectable.'

'I would settle for tolerable,' said Nell.

'Well, and from tomorrow,' said Gussie lightly, rising from her chair, '*you*, at least, will not have to tolerate him at all.'

Nell waved this away. 'I love Theo,' she said. 'Even with all his... quirks. And I love you, Gus, even if you are boring and ordinary—' She squeaked as Gussie swatted at her hair, and ran away, laughing. 'The Towers may be as mad as it gets,' she called back, 'but I miss it, all the same.'

Gussie was left to ponder her own and her sister's very different fates: in being trapped at the seat of the Werths, Gussie had learned to resent it; and in having left it, Nell took every opportunity to return.

The scent of an impending storm reached Gussie's senses, and a chill wind swirled about her feet.

Thunder growled as Aunt Wheldrake wafted by.

'Oh, Lord,' said Nell, coming up again. 'Is she going Theo's way? I believe she is.'

'Better stop her,' said Gussie, and away ran Nell again.

Great-Aunt Honoria's head appeared. 'And how is my darling grand-child— oh! Was not Lucretia here? I quite thought she was.'

The head was uncomfortably solid-looking, complete with a bloom of health across the thin cheeks. Her hair was piled high in the fashion of some decades before, and bristling with ornaments. Honoria might still have been alive, were it not for the fact of having mislaid everything of herself below the neck.

Gussie merely pointed.

Great-Aunt Honoria gave a sigh, and disappeared.

Gussie took the opportunity quietly to withdraw, and return to the tranquillity of her own, spectre-free house.

A haphazard, rambling place some centuries old, Werth Towers covered a great deal of ground. Many successive generations of Werths had altered it, and added to it, until it sprawled across the parkland as though thrown there by a careless child, gables and chambers and chimneys scattered every which way. The main house had originally been built in Elizabeth's time; a later Werth had added a set of towers, and accordingly changing the name; another had expanded the stables, and the coach-houses. Yet another had indulged a passion for architectural symmetry by building a new wing in the modern style, a confection of chalky limestone and pilasters far out of step with the rest of the pile.

Gussie thought its eccentricities charming — from the outside. Inside, the house was a perfect maze of passageways, staircases, towers and garrets, halls and parlours, bedchambers and salons. Many years' residence there had been insufficient to make her acquainted with all its nooks and crannies; moreover, she suspected the Towers — or its spectral occupants — of occasionally changing things. A door removed; a staircase turned about; a window shifted or a trapdoor barred; such minor alterations might never occasion any remark, but could nonetheless cause considerable inconvenience. Indeed, no one could claim to have seen the south-west tower in several years.

'It will come back,' was Lady Werth's comfortable prediction, and Lord Werth seemed hardly to regard the matter at all.

An unladylike curse or two might escape Gussie, however, as she navigated her way from the rear entrance adjacent to the kitchens, through the utility rooms and the servants' halls, up past the drawing-rooms and the best bedchambers, up again past the second-best bedchambers, around a winding mess of corridors and at last into the east tower, presently termed Theo's. The door to his private chambers was, as usual, firmly shut.

Gussie tapped upon it. 'Theo?'

No answer.

'Theo,' she called, knocking again. 'It's Gussie, and I have need of you. Will you let me in?'

The silence continued, and Gussie wondered if she had calculated wrongly. Theo's schedule tended to be regular: he had his hours in the library, his prowlings in the gardens, and his (typically reluctant) presence at family meals. The rest of his time was spent closeted in his rooms, where he did not like to be disturbed.

Gussie had only once ventured to seek him there, and did not lightly do so again. A small part of her felt relieved at her mistiming, for it meant that she need not—

The door swung open, yanked with some force from the other side.

There stood Theo, pale and frowning. 'If this is about the rabbits again—'

'It is not.' Gussie smiled, and endeavoured to look like a person come on no excessively troublesome errand. 'May I come in?'

Theo's frown relaxed, and he stood back to let Gussie pass. She swept into the airy, well-lit room, took up a station upon a crimson carpet in the centre of it, and mentally prepared her speech.

Theo did not encourage her by any word or gesture. He merely waited. A tall man a year or two younger than Gussie herself, Theo had inherited none of his mother's delicate, fair prettiness; he was his father's son through and through, lean of figure, with that wild rust-coloured hair and remarkably white skin.

A spray of blood had discoloured his carelessly-tied cravat, a diamond pin making an incongruous ornament in the midst of such a mess.

Gussie averted her eyes from it.

'You see, cousin, it is like this,' she began. 'You have heard, I imagine, about my invitation to Starminster?'

Theo looked blank.

'Seat of the Viscounts Maundevyle,' Gussie supplied. 'In Somerset. The Dowager Viscountess begs the honour of my company.'

'Maundevyle,' said Theo. 'Right.'

'And, well, my aunt and uncle will not give me leave to go.'

Theo said nothing.

21

'They say it is inappropriate in some fashion, though I do not know why, for I cannot feel that it is. And — and this is where I was hoping you might help me, Theo. For it cannot be inappropriate if I take Miss Frostell with me, and — and you. Now, can it?'

'Me?' blurted Theo. 'Somerset?'

'Your being Lord Bedgberry, I mean, and quite able to go wherever you please. Your father and mother would not interfere so in what *you* chose to do, would they?'

'But I don't choose,' said Theo.

'It would only be for a week or two,' said Gussie. 'And I am sure there are rabbits aplenty on the Starminster estate.'

Theo folded his arms. 'Cousin,' he said. 'Being among the least intolerable members of my family, there are numerous ways I would gladly contribute to your comfort. But this is not one of them.'

'But—'

'I cannot leave the Towers. Certainly not to spend a week or more as the guest of a perfect stranger, who is not expecting me, and could hardly want me.' He punctuated this depressing speech with a gesture at the drying blood upon his cravat, which was eloquent enough.

Gussie, deflated, had nothing to add. She had known it to be a gamble, approaching Theo. And she knew he was right in his objections. An hour ago, pacing about the parlour of her little cottage alone, she had persuaded herself that Theo could contain his odder qualities for a week or two, and pass for a respectable gentleman; that the viscountess who was so eager for *her* company must be flattered to receive that of the much more important Lord Bedgberry, also; and that a possible future lay before her in which Theo himself might be amenable to it.

Even as she had toiled up the stairs into the east tower, her certainty on all these points had been declining. Now she saw all the folly of it, and wondered that she had ever thought it likely at all.

'You are right,' she sighed. 'Your cousin is a pot-bound fool of a Gussie, so desperate for novelty as to importune a poor Theo over it.'

Theo, arms still folded, subjected her to a hard, cold-eyed stare.

Gussie's spirit rose under this ungracious treatment. 'Well, but was it so bothersome a request as all that?'

'Maundevyle,' said Theo again. 'Is that the Selwyn family?'

'I do not know what the family name might be.'

'I knew a Selwyn,' said Theo. 'School-fellow.'

Gussie wondered if this might be the Henry who had since succeeded to the Maundevyle title, but before she could enquire Theo added, 'Charles was the name.'

'Edifying,' said Gussie.

'Hated him,' said Theo.

Gussie blinked.

'But I think it odd,' said Theo next, 'that Mama should object. Especially if you are to have Miss Frostell with you.'

'Yes!' said Gussie. 'And when she and Lady Maundevyle are such old friends, at that.'

'Are they?' said Theo, visibly losing interest in so insoluble a problem. His gaze wandered; Gussie knew he would be looking for the book he had doubtless placed down but lately, somewhere easily to hand, where he would in no wise be unable to find it again half an hour later.

'It is on the window-sill,' she said with a sigh, pointing to where a large folio lay, drenched in morning sunshine.

'Hard luck, cousin,' said Theo, drifting that way. 'But there is no persuading Mama, when she is fixed upon something.'

Gussie only sighed, and withdrew.

She wandered slowly downstairs again, all the way down and around and down, until she emerged into the sunlight, blinking in the sudden glare. Instead of returning by way of the kitchen-adjacent entrance, as had been her intention, she had, in the abstraction of her thoughts, wandered out of the great front door instead.

In the drive-way stood a carriage. Gussie, regarding it in confusion, noted firstly that it was not one of her uncle's equipages; secondly that it was a great, lumbering travel-coach, a little out of date, but excessively handsome; and thirdly, that the driver sat still upon the box, as though only just arrived.

She had not known that her aunt and uncle were expecting any visitors, and she had passed nobody on her way to the door. Her curiosity piqued, she went around the side of it, to see if she could catch a glimpse of any arms emblazoned upon the gleaming black paint.

The side-door opened in a rush, and somebody barrelled out.

'Oh!' said Gussie, and jumped back.

'Beg pardon,' said the visitor; a gentleman, by his attire, but the voice was light and melodic.

'There is no earthly need,' said Gussie. 'For if I *will* blunder into the way of the door, it is quite my own affair if—'

This speech was destined never to be concluded, for to Gussie's stupefied surprise, she was seized by a pair of thin, but strong arms, lifted off her feet, and borne in the direction of the waiting coach.

'What in the—' Gussie spluttered, and recovered from her surprise so far as to writhe like an animal in an attempt to free herself.

'Oh, but don't spoil it!' said her attacker, in tones of exasperation. 'Otherwise I shall be obliged to call Charles, and that would be *very* tiresome, for he *said* I could never manage it alone. You do not want to prove him right, do you?'

Gussie spread out her arms and legs, making each limb an obstacle to her being stuffed through the beckoning doors of the coach. 'It is the outside of *enough*,' she gasped, 'to be expected to collude in one's own abduction, for the sake of proving a gentleman wrong!'

'Don't think of it as an abduction, then,' said her abductor, whom Gussie was now quite sure was in fact a woman. 'Call it a pressing invitation, if you will.' By some agility beyond Gussie's comprehension, the insufferable woman contrived to thrust Gussie's arms into the coach one by one, and soon afterwards she fell all the way in, landing face-first upon somebody's booted feet.

'Steady on,' said another voice, certainly male, and Gussie looked up into a man's face, young and sharp-featured, with chestnut-coloured curls and vividly green eyes.

Without troubling herself to venture any reply, Gussie picked herself up, thrust her head in the way of the rapidly closing door, and drew in a great breath. Her mouth opened; and in a vast scream borne of fright and indignation both, she cried: *'Great-Uncle Silvesteeeer!'*

The door then colliding smartly with her face, Gussie fell in a senseless heap upon the coach's floor.

FOUR

Contrary, perhaps, to appearances, Lord Bedgberry was not an unfeeling man. If asked, he would not hesitate to declare himself fond of his family; yes, even of thunderous Aunt Wheldrake.

However, in his general view, relatives were best enjoyed from a comfortable distance; and no circle of hell could be considered deep enough to receive those who interrupted his reading.

All of this being the case, the appearance of Great-Aunt Honoria in his quiet tower-room could fill him with nothing but a mild wrath.

'And I have but *just* got rid of Gussie!' he said, snapping shut his book.

'But that's just it!' gasped Great-Aunt Honoria's head. 'We *have* got rid of Gussie! And in a shocking fashion, too! I have been trying to tell you.'

It distantly filtered through to Theo — his head full of J. Barber's treatise on the nature of the constellations — that Great-Aunt Honoria did not ordinarily manifest in the east tower. Nor was she normally observed to be screaming at such unladylike volume, nor pouring quantities of ethereal blood from the stump of her (apparently) severed neck.

'Something has upset you,' he observed.

This silenced Honoria altogether, though only briefly. 'Theodore,' she said severely. 'I tremble to think what is to become of Werth when your poor father dies.'

'Nothing in particular, I should think?' said Theo. 'Why, is something likely to happen?'

'Something *has* happened,' said Honoria. 'Your cousin! She—'

'Which cousin?' enquired Theodore politely.

'*Augusta.* As I have just told you — really, did you not hear a word of it? — your unoffending cousin Gussie has this moment been snatched from the very doors of Werth! By a pair of unscrupulous villains!'

Theodore, his thoughts and his gaze having wandered back to his book, looked up. 'What?'

'Snatched!' proclaimed Great-Aunt Honoria.

'Gussie?'

'Carried off! Overpowered and borne away!'

'Abducted?' Theo said. 'Gussie? Are you sure you've got it right, Aunt?'

'I saw it with my own eyes!'

'Perhaps you mean Nell,' said Theo helpfully. 'Or m'father. Really, who could want Gussie?'

Great-Aunt Honoria swelled with the sort of rage that could only presage another explosion, and Theo had suffered quite enough unscheduled noise already. He held up a pacifying hand. 'All right, I can see you are serious about it. But what can it possibly have to do with me?'

'Why, you must instantly go after her! She must be retrieved!'

A notion wandered through Theo's thoughts. The notion was this: in the general way of things, he was not the person to whom crises were brought.

It also occurred to him that he ought vigorously to object to such treatment of his family. Indeed, if Great-Aunt Honoria's report were not a mere nothing, why then

27

he *would.*

Regretfully, Theo set down his book.

'Did you chance to observe who these blackguards were?' he asked.

Great-Aunt Honoria had not. But she had noticed a coat of arms emblazoned on the side of the coach which had carried off his cousin; and when Theo heard her description of this symbol, and discovered that he recognised it, he did not pause to listen to the rest of Honoria's diatribe. He was out the door and halfway down the stairs in an instant, his feet pounding heavily upon stone, a slow fury burning in his heart.

He found his father and mother lingering over the breakfast table. 'That cur,' he announced, 'has made off with my cousin.'

Lady Werth looked up from her plate of eggs. 'Which cur?' she enquired.

'Which cousin?' said Lord Werth.

'Gussie, and the cur is Charles Selwyn! I always knew he was no good, and now he has taken Gussie!' Theo said this with the feelings of one vindicated, for had he not always detested the Selwyn boy at school?

'Selwyn?' said Lady Werth, setting down her knife and fork. 'You cannot mean—'

'Lord Maundevyle's younger brother,' supplied Lord Werth. 'But there must be some mistake, Theo. How could Charles Selwyn come upon Gussie at all, and what cause could he have to carry her off?'

'He is brazen enough for anything!' said Theo grimly. 'He has come right up to our own door, if you please, and snatched her off the doorstep. And there is no mistake, for I have just had it from Great-Aunt Honoria, who was there.'

Lord Werth exchanged a look with his wife. 'My dear?' said he. 'Perhaps you can shed some light upon this?'

Lady Werth had more than once behaved mysteriously regarding Gussie, intervening in her life in ways she did not seem minded to do with Theo's. But she had been close-lipped about why that might be, and Theo had not the smallest idea what might motivate such treatment.

Nor was he destined to find out, for Lady Werth appeared to be in the grip of some strong emotion. Her eyes stared; her mouth opened in shock, or perhaps fright; and she swelled with... rage? Indignation?

'My dear,' said Lord Werth, laying a hand over hers. 'Calm yourself. I am sure this is all a mistake, and will soon be resolved—'

Ice-crystals formed in her ladyship's hair, and frost bloomed in her horrified eyes. A flurry of freezing snow burst into the air, liberally covering the table, her husband and her son in a small blizzard.

'Mother,' said Theo, wiping snow from his face. 'Pray remember to breathe—'

But with a *crack* and an unpromising splintering sound, Lady Werth succumbed. In her chair sat a statue of her ladyship, worked in icy glass, still clutching her silver knife. The detail was truly extraordinary.

Lord Werth sighed.

'Any chance she'll recover inside of an hour or two?' said Theo, without much hope.

'I should think there is almost no chance of it,' said his father. 'I have never known her to reanimate under two days.'

'Last time it was above a week,' said Theo gloomily.

'Do you think there is anything in this absurd tale of Honoria's?' said his lordship.

'If there is I won't have it. I mean to find out what has become of that coach.'

'I imagine Gussie has the matter well in hand,' said Lord Werth, returning, unruffled, to his breakfast. 'But if you are going, you had better do so without further loss of time.'

His hopes dashed as to the likelihood of his father's preparing to wade into the fray, Theo was very ready to obey this parental edict. The sooner he left the Towers, the sooner he could come back again; and if he was prompt in pursuit of the coach, no doubt he could overtake it upon the road, at only a little distance away. He and Gussie might be home in time for tea.

But having given orders for the horses to be put to and the carriage brought round (in a clipped tone expressive of his general feelings), every pleasant prospect of the kind was done away with.

'*All* the wheels?' Theo repeated in disbelief. 'All? From every vehicle?'

Jem Coachman, clad in his driving-coat ready to depart, gave a miserable nod. 'All four, sir, quite off his lordship's coach, and the barouche, and my lady's phaeton as well. Ned came to tell it to me hisself. I can't think how it came about, only if I weren't to be thought fanciful, sir, I'd say as it looks like—'

'Sabotage,' said Theo grimly.

'Aye, sir. But who could have done it, 'round here?'

Theo did not trouble to enlighten him. Later, he would enquire (through Nell) of the Towers' various spectral inhabitants, if anyone had observed the sabotage being done. No one had; except for Cornelia, who swore to seeing a gentleman saunter into the coach-house as casual as you please. But since poor Corny had died before she had reached her eleventh year, she was not much attended to at any time.

Obliged to await the coach's repair, Theo consoled himself with a fresh rabbit — just the one, it would not do to over-indulge before a journey — and waited.

In the end, there was a delay of some six and a half hours before he could at last follow the cooling trail left by the Selwyns' equipage. At such a distance of time, word of the occurrence, and of Theo's meditated response to it, had spread across the Towers. And the end of *that* was, that Theo found himself with an unwelcome but persistent travelling companion.

'I am afraid it is of no use to remonstrate with me,' Miss Frostell declared, climbing resolutely into the carriage. 'You cannot imagine I shall sit at my ease when Miss Werth is in trouble, and we shall have Honoria, you know, by way of companion.'

'Honoria...!' stuttered Theo, appalled at the twin vision of Miss Frostell ensconced within the very carriage he meant to drive, and the severed head of his great-aunt opposite to her. Both ladies considered it unnecessary to say any more, but only looked at him, calmly certain of his acquiescence.

Theo was left with a choice: to haul both women out by the hair and hurl them into the dust, before driving off as fast as he could without them. Or to submit to the inevitable, and hope that the presence of Miss Frostell in particular did not cause him more difficulties than might be acceptable, in consideration of the cause.

Fool, Theo thought, and savagely slammed the door upon them both. Very well, if they would have it so. On their own heads be it.

***

Sense and feeling returned in an unwelcome rush, for Gussie's head ached fit to burst. She sat slumped upon the plump, upholstered seat of a swaying coach; straightening, she risked opening her eyes, and at the fresh stab of pain thus provoked, quickly shut them again.

A brief glance had revealed to her the figure of the chestnut-haired gentleman, seated opposite her, and by his side a second person. This additional creature had swept off the tall hat she had worn, and let down the auburn hair previously concealed beneath it. The hat lay on the seat beside Gussie, a mute reproach for having been so easily taken in. The woman's features were by far too feminine ever to be taken for male; in fact she was ravishingly pretty. No mere hat ought to have so lulled her good sense, Gussie thought; but then, for all the oddities one expected to encounter at the Towers, a woman clad in the garb of a man was not typically to be counted among them.

'You would be the Selwyns, I suppose?' said Gussie, without opening her eyes. 'I have just been hearing about a Charles Selwyn. Quite detestable, I am told, and since you, sir, are both detestable and a Charles, I cannot think it a coincidence.'

She heard amusement in the rich voice that answered her. 'And what have you to say of my sister's conduct? I assure you, it was all her idea.'

Gussie half-opened one eye, and regarded the sister in question sourly. She received in response a winning smile. 'A diabolical pair,' she pronounced. 'And when my head has finished aching quite so badly, I assure you I shall do everything in my power to escape.'

'Oh, please don't!' begged the lady. 'When we have gone to so much trouble to rescue you!'

Gussie's eyes opened all the way. 'Rescue me?' she repeated. 'From what?'

'Why, from the tyranny of your uncle and aunt! We *knew* they would refuse to let you visit us. They did, didn't they?'

'That can hardly be termed tyranny,' Gussie retorted. 'And I do not remember mentioning any opposition from Lord and Lady Werth, when I declined your mother's invitation. Not that you can possibly have received my letter yet.'

'Well, but why else would you decline?' said Miss Selwyn.

Since they had, by accident or shrewdness, hit upon the exact truth, Gussie gave up arguing the point. 'You must take me back,' she said coolly. 'It would present so very odd an appearance, you know, if you were to make a habit of abducting your house-guests by force.'

'Then we shan't make a habit of it,' said Miss Selwyn. 'Just this once, I cross my heart.' She did so, marking the outlines of a sacred cross over the black expanse of her coat.

Gussie said nothing for a moment, engaged in listening. Was that a scraping upon the roof, perhaps a half-caught glimpse of a flickering shadow beyond the window? She could not convince herself of it.

'Besides,' said Gussie next. 'My family will be frantic with worry when they find me missing, and that is unkind.'

'They won't notice for some time yet,' said Miss Selwyn airily, rather to Gussie's indignation.

'And we have sent a letter,' put in Charles, who hitherto had watched the play between his sister and Miss Werth with a gleam of silent amusement, and said nothing.

'Yes, so they will know where you are, and shall not be concerned for you at all.'

A terrible suspicion struck Gussie. 'Did *I* write this letter?'

'You dictated it to my brother's secretary,' said Miss Selwyn with aplomb. 'He has particularly fine handwriting.'

Gussie looked at Charles.

'Her other brother,' he supplied.

Gussie's heart sank. Was the whole family complicit in this bizarre scheme? What manner of woman was she to find in Lady Maundevyle?

Resolved upon one last-ditch attempt at reason, she sought desperately for another rational objection (all the self-evident ones having failed to move the Selwyns), and at last fixed upon saying: 'Had you really to whisk me off alone? If I had accepted your invitation, I was to have brought Miss Frostell with me.'

'And who is Miss Frostell?' said Miss Selwyn. 'Is she amusing?'

'She was my governess.'

'*Not* amusing, I collect,' said Miss Selwyn, wrinkling her perfect nose. Her eyes widened in realisation. 'Oh! But you shall have no need of a chaperon, Miss Werth. You will have me.' A seraphic smile punctuated this statement, and Gussie began to wonder, with a distant flicker of alarm, whether there was any madness in the Selwyn family.

She did not really believe herself to be in any danger, despite appearances. Neither of the Selwyns had offered any direct harm; the blow she had taken from the door had been an accident of her own causing. Nor did the siblings have the air of ruffians, or dangerous villains. They had more the manner of overgrown children, spoiled and wilful, unable to comprehend why their mother's chosen toy — or perhaps, their own? — had not chosen to come and play with them. She ought, she thought, to be equal to such a situation: peculiar, but in no real way threatening.

Still, they proved resistant to her sensible objections, and with every passing minute the coach barrelled farther away from Werth Towers.

And if Great-Uncle Silvester had heard her plea, he was being awfully quiet about it.

By the time the coach finally drew to a stop at a wayside inn, several hours had dragged joltingly by. Gussie had given up hope of Great-Uncle Silvester, or of drumming any sense into her new *bosom-friend* either (as Miss Selwyn insisted on calling herself, before kindly offering her the gift of her Christian name: Clarissa).

Gussie's attempts at persuading the Selwyns to turn the coach around, and deliver her back to her home, had universally failed. So had her enquiries as to the *reason* for her abduction; 'Word of my wit and vivacity has spread as far as Somerset, I suppose, and naturally engendered in you a burning desire to enjoy my company?'

'You have hit upon the very truth of it, Miss Werth,' drawled Charles, a sardonic glitter in his eye. 'We have never known anything half so entertaining at Starminster, I assure you.'

Clarissa delivered her brother a thumping blow upon the shoulder, which he swatted away, muttering, 'Really, Clara, if you will not be more feminine we will never be rid of you.'

'That is a good thought,' said Clarissa, arrested in the middle of whatever she had been going to say. 'I shall marry the first man I see.'

'John Coachman, I collect.'

'Except John Coachman.'

'Ahem?' said Gussie.

'Oh! Charles is quite right,' said Clarissa hurriedly. 'We were anxious to make your acquaintance, and really, what with Mama and your aunt being so thick with one another, we are practically family. Are not we?'

Gussie had longed to observe that family were not ordinarily inclined to abduct one another, not even among the peculiar Werths. But she had seen enough of the Selwyns to realise that theirs were different rules of conduct altogether, and held her peace. She was not to receive an explanation en route, it appeared.

By the time the inn was reached, she had abandoned thoughts of escape. Partly because she was road-weary and sore, and eager to seek her bed. And partly because, though the manner of her journey was somewhat... unorthodox, and she felt some apprehension at the prospect of making so odd an appearance at Starminster, she could not feel an absolute disinclination to go along with it. For to go there coincided exactly with her wishes, however the means.

And her curiosity was piqued. Whatever reason the Selwyns had for forcing her compliance, it could have nothing to do with anything so absurdly simple as a desire of making her acquaintance. And though she prided herself a little upon her wit, she could not for a moment believe that fame of it had spread as far as her aunt's old connections in faraway Somerset.

No, the Selwyns must have another reason for bringing her to Starminster. And Gussie, alive with curiosity, was determined to find out what it might be.

FIVE

Miss Frostell took her time getting down from the coach. Theo, travel-sore and suffering a powerful thirst, gave up waiting for her to overcome her scruples, or whatever might be causing the delay, and strode into The Red Lion coaching inn by himself.

'I require two rooms and a private parlour,' he informed the landlord, noticing only that the man was short and as thin as a reed before he resolutely turned away his gaze, and regarded instead the portrait of a fat woman in a great wig that hung over the fireplace.

The landlord bowed low. Theo never troubled himself to dress to suit his eminence; nothing about his dusty driving coat, with its meagre two capes, could have provided any real clue as to his status, nor the favourite old hat crowning his unbrushed locks. Still, innkeepers had a special sense for such things, he supposed, for somehow his status was always found out.

The fellow hesitated. 'I am sorry to disappoint your lordship,' said he. 'My two best bedchambers are yours, but at present I have no parlour available—'

Theo favoured the hapless landlord with a stare. Then, a slow smile.

And the landlord stepped back, as they always did, his eyes darting away from the glint of Lord Bedgberry's teeth. He swallowed. 'I was mistaken,' he said hurriedly. 'A private parlour, and two bedchambers.'

Theo put his smile away. 'I am much obliged,' he said affably. 'And I should like a good dinner for one person to be set out in it, in half an hour's time.'

'One, my lord?'

Theo heard Miss Frostell's measured steps approaching, and her light voice as she addressed some remark to Great-Aunt Honoria. 'One,' he said firmly. 'Whatever is most like to please the lady.'

The landlord coughed. 'You shan't be joining her, my lord?'

'I shall have other arrangements.'

The landlord paled. Behind him, a pair of begrimed maids hovered in a doorway, staring at Theo and crossing themselves.

No; not at Theo, for sailing off to the fireplace went Great-Aunt Honoria's head. Not, at this time, attended by a trail of fresh blood.

'Lord Bedgberry's aunt,' explained Miss Frostell in a kindly tone, answering the unspoken question in the landlord's face. 'For really, it would never have done for us to take to the road without her. Have you bespoken rooms, my lord?'

'Yes, yes,' said Theo, on his way to the door. A mere, spindly landlord he could withstand, but the presence of two vibrant maids, glowing with life and blood, was too much to be borne. 'This fellow will see that you are fed.'

'How obliging,' murmured Miss Frostell.

As Theo stepped out into the dust of a hot afternoon, he heard the landlord saying, in a quiversome way, 'W-will her ladyship be requiring dinner?'

'Lady Honoria?' said Miss Frostell, her voice receding with every stride of Theo's. 'I believe she sups on terror, sir, and I can see she is already being well provided for.'

***

They were three days upon the road, wending slowly westward across the country. Clarissa had had forethought enough to bring extra supplies for Gussie, in the way of nightgowns and tooth-powder, but Gussie soon tired of wearing the same dress. It had not been intended for travelling in the first place, and the light, rose-coloured muslin, while becoming to her pale complexion and dark hair, was ill-suited to the road. Moreover, she had come out without bonnet or spencer either, being engaged in only a short walk across the park in the height of summer.

'Do not concern yourself about it, Miss Werth,' was Clarissa's airy reply. 'You will find everything you could require at Starminster. We are very well prepared for your visit.'

This turned out to be the literal, extraordinary truth.

In the midst of a hot afternoon upon the third day, the Selwyn family's travelling coach drew up at last before the elegant façade of a house so grand it bordered upon palatial. Gussie, too astonished to remember her dignity, stuck her head out of the window, the better to look her fill at Starminster. The house dated from a similar period to Werth Towers, she judged, but was in a different style altogether. It bore none of the rambling eccentricity of her own family's home, none of its patchwork peculiarity and mismatched design. Starminster made an imposing presence, built as it was entirely from a pale, honey-coloured stone and positively bristling with big, bright windows. Huge double doors, gilded in gold, guarded the entryway; a myriad of little turrets and spires and battlements crowned the roof; and the lawns surrounding this majestic abode were arranged with a perfection only a small army of gardeners could achieve. Starminster, in short, reeked of money.

But it would not do to act too much the country mouse, and gawk at such splendour with round-eyed astonishment. Gussie withdrew her head, and composed herself to behave as though she had visited dozens of palaces.

She did not fool Charles, who smiled at her with a kindness laced with malice. 'Charming little place, is it not?' he said.

'Don't torment our guest, Charles,' said Clarissa, too impatient to wait for the footman to open the door, and throwing it wide herself. 'Or she will abandon us before the day is out, and *then* you will be sorry.'

'She can hardly do that without stealing Henry's carriage,' said Charles. 'And I am persuaded Miss Werth's manners are far too good to permit of it.'

'I should hesitate to steal a carriage, certainly,' said Gussie, emerging into the bright air of the afternoon. 'But I am sure your brother would not mind my *borrowing* one, for he could never wish to keep me here against my will.' She held Charles's gaze as she spoke, hoping to provoke some telling reaction from him. But he only smirked, and strode towards the glittering doors that were already swinging open. Servants poured forth, and converged upon the carriage, bent upon divesting it of luggage, cushions and other what-not before its return into the coach-house.

Before Gussie could collect herself, and will her stiff legs into movement, she was accosted by Clarissa and swept into the house.

'I am putting you in Adley's charge,' she declared. 'You'll like Adley, everyone does. A dear old creature, quite devoted to the family, and I assure you she has the *strictest* instructions to attend to your every need.'

Adley turned out to be Mrs. Adley, the housekeeper. Gussie's impressions of housekeeper and house were brief and muddled: she was marched through the hall too quickly to discern much about it, save that it was enormous and echoing, honey-coloured and cool, and hung all about with tapestries and paintings. Mrs. Adley escorted her up a wide, white stone staircase clad in scarlet carpet; grey-haired and comfortably proportioned, with her plain garb and welcoming manners, she proved something of a foil to the breath-taking splendour of the house. While Gussie mildly resented the cavalier treatment of Clarissa, she soon warmed to Mrs. Adley, just as Clarissa had said she would.

'I will show you to your room,' Mrs. Adley said. 'Doubtless you'll be tired, after such a long journey, and wanting a bit of rest.'

'I am very much in want of rest,' Gussie agreed. 'But more in want of a washstand, and a change of gown.'

'Of course, my lady,' said Mrs. Adley. 'You will find everything awaiting you in your room.'

'It's just Miss Werth,' said Gussie. 'Shall I indeed find everything? Gowns too?'

'I believe you will be pleased, miss,' said Mrs. Adley. 'Her ladyship has gone to a great deal of trouble to secure your comfort.'

Gussie, mystified, did not know what to think. Some part of her felt a little compunction, upon hearing this, for her family's easy dismissal of the invitation. It was rare that anybody had gone to so much trouble purely for the sake of Gussie's comfort — indeed, no one ever had — and she could not help being gratified by such attention.

But her ladyship had been so discourteous and high-handed as to compel Gussie's attendance upon her, and for reasons that remained unclear. Under such extraordinary conditions as *those*, a close attention to her needs was the very least she had the right to expect.

Furthermore, for a lady to arrive at a house unattended by any relative or companion, or even by her maid; unencumbered by any luggage, and wearing a gown wholly unsuited to the occasion; these were the heights of impropriety, by anybody's measure. Nobody appeared to regard it at Starminster, however, not even the servants. Either they had expected it, and saw nothing to question in her ladyship's importing her guests by force; or they were too well-trained to betray any condemnation or surprise, and contented themselves with despising her in secret.

Gussie held up her chin, and swept up the stairs with all the implacable hauteur of a duchess.

She was taken aback upon reaching her room, and finding that the term had been misleading. A whole suite of rooms was assigned to her use, of sufficient grandeur to flatter the consequence of a princess. She had a handsome salon, fitted with elegant, low divans and mahogany tables; a bedchamber so enormous she might lose herself in it, the four-poster bed hung with velvet drapes; a reading room, small, but amply provided with books and upholstered chairs; and a dressing-room. This last Mrs. Adley ushered her into with a smile, pointing out a fine porcelain wash-basin upon a marble-topped table, and the great mirror that hung above both.

She then proceeded to throw open the doors of the closets, and Gussie gasped at the array of garments waiting inside. Gowns aplenty, sewn of fine muslins and silks; spencer-jackets and an embroidered pelisse; stockings and half-boots, dancing slippers and shawls; and a handsome pearl-grey cloak. She had never worn clothes so fine in her life.

'Why,' she gasped. 'I believe they mean to keep me here forever.'

'You're to be paying us a long visit, miss?' said Mrs. Adley. 'I thought her ladyship had said as much.'

'No,' said Gussie. 'Not so very long a visit, in fact.' Only as long as it took her to unearth the motive behind such peculiar treatment, so inexplicable a mix of consideration for her comfort, and contempt for her will. 'Where did all these come from?' she said, gesturing at the astonishing array of garments before her. 'Her ladyship might have been preparing for my arrival for a twelve-month.'

'As to that, I do not know,' said Mrs. Adley, serenely untroubled. 'Some arrived only this morning. Others were gathered from somewhere or another about the house. Her ladyship will be able to explain everything to you, I am sure.' Upon which helpful note, having enquired as to Gussie's further requirements, Mrs. Adley excused herself, and left Gussie to wash and change her attire in peace.

For some moments, Gussie eyed the handsome gowns with something approaching trepidation. She felt ushered into a jewelled trap, replete with every comfort but freedom. As though, like Persephone in the Underworld, she might be condemned to remain forever, were she so foolish as to partake of any of the proffered delights.

But that was foolishness. They could not confine her at Starminster forever; her family would have something to say about it, in due time. And she still had not quite given up hope of Great-Uncle Silvester.

Besides, what reason could they possibly have for doing so? For clothe her in luxury as they may, feed her on sweetmeats and beguile her with flattery, she remained a mere Gussie Werth, of no particular distinction.

Perhaps it was odd to be so comforted by a recollection of her own insignificance, but Gussie launched a foray upon the closets with renewed confidence. She selected for her immediate use a gown of sky-blue muslin overlaid with white gauze, and a fine, pale-gold shawl to throw over her elbows. She had thought, upon taking them down, that they must prove too large for her; but when she donned the gown, and tied the drawstring of the neckline over her stays, it proved to be perfectly suited to her figure, as though sewn especially for her use.

Thus attired, her complexion refreshed by the contents of a porcelain water-jug set upon the wash-stand, Gussie prepared herself to venture downstairs.

It was only as she was passing back through the bedchamber and her salon, that she was fully struck by the nature of the contents. For the rooms were arrayed in dusk-rose and ivory, accented in delicate silver; and it had only just at that moment struck her how odd it was, that her assigned chambers should happen to be decorated in all her favourite colours.

SIX

Clarissa awaited her at the foot of the great staircase. She had changed out of her gentleman's attire, and now wore an unexceptionable gown of figured muslin, trimmed with lace, and with a shawl similar to Gussie's own cast about her arms. She beamed up at Gussie as she descended the stairs, and said: 'Well, and while the rose is a *shade* more becoming with that hair, the blue really looks very well indeed.'

'How kind,' Gussie said tartly. 'I should be ashamed to look anything but my best, indeed, when on the point of being introduced to my chief abductor.'

Clarissa tutted, and presumed so far as to tuck her arm through Gussie's, in the friendliest — and most familiar — manner. 'I *wish* you would not fix so upon this notion of abduction!' she said. 'While I own that we did not *precisely* ask your permission, still, you cannot pretend not to be delighted to find yourself at Starminster?'

'Who could be anything but delighted, indeed?' Gussie agreed. 'I daresay nobody in history has ever been provided with so luxurious a prison.'

Charles's voice intruded from somewhere across the hall. 'There is nothing to be said in defence of our rudeness, Miss Werth, I quite agree. You were not in so very great a hurry to escape, however, were you?'

'Would it have been of the smallest use to attempt it?' Gussie countered.

Charles appeared to be giving the matter serious thought. 'I am not perfectly certain,' he said. 'Clara? What is your opinion?'

'Not the least use in the world,' she said merrily, and steered Gussie towards a door at the rear of the hall, that led into a short passage. 'Now, Miss Werth, if you do not object, Mama is quite wild to meet you.'

'And Lord Maundevyle?' said Gussie.

'Henry, too,' Clarissa agreed. 'Though I do not know if he is about the house, at present. He is given to long walks, you know, and might rather be on the other side of the park.'

'That is as it should be,' Gussie murmured. 'When one has been kidnapped, you know, it would be the heights of rudeness to expect one's presence to interfere with the regular habits of the household.'

'Exactly!' said Clarissa.

'Such exquisite manners these Werths possess,' said Charles from somewhere behind. 'I am quite put to shame.'

'Why,' said Gussie, 'I think it even possible that my aunt has never abducted anybody in her life. The thought has never even crossed her mind.'

'A pattern of good breeding, to be sure,' said Charles — no, it was not Charles. Clarissa had, by this time, propelled her along the somewhat dark passage leading off the hall, and through a white door standing ajar. On the other side of it was a pretty receiving-room, all decked in frothy gauzes and silk upholstery, and the room proved to contain two occupants.

The Dowager Viscountess occupied the best of the chairs. The majesty of her posture, together with the sumptuary she wore, identified her at once. She sat in a pool of sunlight filtering through a great window, the frondy vegetation of a shrubbery visible beyond. The light turned her grey hair silver, and glittered upon the heavy jewels she wore.

The one who had spoken must be Lord Maundevyle, the third of the peculiar Selwyn siblings. He stood before the window, previously engaged in looking out over his domain; but he had turned his head to observe Gussie's entrance, and stood regarding her, rather expressionless. He was as tall as his brother, and had a similar colouring; only his hair was darker, and he had the appearance of a man several years older. He was dressed expensively, but soberly, in a dark blue coat and plainly tied cravat, and wore no ornaments about himself at all.

'Mama, Henry,' said Clarissa, drawing Gussie forward. 'Look! We have brought you Miss Werth!' She spoke like a small child, eagerly showing off its latest accomplishment, in the happy expectation of receiving great praise.

'I hope you were not put to any great inconvenience by the journey, Miss Werth?' said Lord Maundevyle.

Gussie blinked at him in astonishment. 'Not the smallest inconvenience, I assure you,' she answered. 'Indeed, how could I be so ungrateful as to be aware of any?'

He frowned slightly, and said no more.

'Miss Werth,' said the dowager, and everything that was forbidding in her appearance melted away as she smiled. 'We are *greatly* honoured by your visit.'

'Thank you,' said Gussie coolly. 'I am very sensible of the honour of your... invitation, I am sure.'

The dowager rose, and came forward, hands extended to take Gussie's. 'I trust you will forgive us,' she said. 'It was *unconscionable* treatment, and I sincerely beg your pardon. But it was a matter of such very great importance, you know. I quite thought your dear aunt would sympathise, but I could not help fearing the reverse.'

'I believe she was concerned for me,' said Gussie. 'Not,

47

it seems, without good reason.'

The dowager's eyes opened wide. 'But you shall not come to the smallest harm at Starminster! You shall not do anything that you do not like, and we shall all be quite *devoted* to you.'

Gussie, rapidly learning where Clarissa had got her extravagance of manner, permitted herself a small smile. 'Nothing I do not like? And if I do not like to stay, ma'am?'

'Then of course, you shall go home,' said the dowager soothingly. 'But will you consent to give us a trial, first? A day, perhaps two? If you find you truly *cannot* like us, then we shall not stand in the way of your going.'

'How obliging.'

Lord Maundevyle spoke. 'Am I to understand that Miss Werth has arrived here against her will?'

Clarissa looked daggers at her brother, and drew herself up. 'Anyone would think it a punishment to be here, the way you are all carrying on! Do not you know how many there are who would *kill* to spend a week at Starminster?'

'Miss Werth, however, does not appear to number herself among them,' said Lord Maundevyle. 'Mother, you cannot have condoned this.'

'I am afraid it was all my idea,' said the dowager. 'Do not blame Clarissa, Henry.'

Unable, or unwilling, to take his mother to task in front of a guest, Lord Maundevyle subsided into glowering silence.

Gussie's attention being at that moment distracted, she missed whatever passed next among the Selwyns. A flicker of movement attracted her notice, much as she had thought she'd seen upon the journey: a fleeting, *whisking* movement, and perhaps an unusual depth of shadow in a corner of the ceiling. A glimpse, even, of granite?

Did she deceive herself?

Nothing more occurred, and she returned her attention to the dowager. 'Why, ma'am?' she said, interrupting

Charles in the middle of some drawling speech.

The dowager blinked, her mouth slightly open. 'Why?' she repeated. 'Why what, Miss Werth?'

'Why was I brought here? Neither Miss Selwyn nor Mr. Selwyn has seen fit to explain it to me, and I *do* believe myself entitled to an answer.'

The dowager looked at Clarissa, then at Charles, the latter of whom shrugged.

Some silent communication passed between the group of them, but Gussie could not read it.

Then Clarissa said, in a whisper meant to be beneath Gussie's comprehension: 'She does not appear to *know*, Mama.'

The dowager reeled back, as if struck a physical blow by surprise. She said nothing more for a moment, but her eyes widened, and then narrowed, as she visibly thought something through.

'And nothing… happened, upon the journey?' she said. 'Nothing — untoward?'

'Nothing whatsoever, Mama, as you see.' Did Gussie imagine it, or was Clarissa's tone one of disappointment?

The dowager's smile returned, if a forced one. 'Ring the bell for tea, Clarissa,' she said. 'You must all be parched with thirst, after your journey.'

The conversation following being little to the purpose, Gussie finally left the dowager's presence burdened with a renewed sense of frustration. Whatever her aunt had been so reluctant to tell her was known to the dowager *and* her children, and yet still eluded Gussie.

Having successfully requested letter-paper and a pen from her hosts, Gussie returned at once into her own rooms, and sat down to write to her aunt. In her letter, she outlined the whole, strange sequence of events that had led to her taking up her abode at Starminster, knowing that in so doing she would be contradicting whatever had been the contents of the fake letter sent in her name.

I trust you are will not be too angry with me, Aunt, she continued. Though I had, I own, considered defying your authority, I had not finally resolved upon doing so. In fact, that choice was imposed upon me.

I now find myself in a situation of some difficulty. I cannot but be perfectly aware that there is some mystery surrounding myself, the solution to which is most likely known to you. Also, it appears, to the Selwyns; and whatever it is must be of great interest to them. They want something from me, and I cannot doubt that you know exactly what it is.

I cannot know your reasons for keeping this secret from me, but I must beg you to share it now. One way or another, Aunt, I will get to the bottom of this. If that means I remain at Starminster until the matter becomes clear, so be it. But I had far rather hear it from you.

I remain, your affectionate niece, etc,

G. Werth

PS: If Great-Uncle Silvester is discovered to be missing from his customary perch, you may rest assured that all is well, for he is (I think?) with me.

This letter she placed into Lord Maundevyle's hands, in the hope that he might be prevailed upon to send it. She encountered him on his way out into the park; destined for one of his long walks, she supposed, for he had donned a wide-brimmed hat to keep off the sun, and a lively hound frisked about his ankles.

'May I rely upon you to serve me in this errand?' said Gussie, having explained her request. 'For my aunt and uncle have been deceived, and they must not be longer left in ignorance of the true circumstances of my absence.'

Lord Maundevyle bowed. 'It shall be as you say,' he promised. 'I shall see that it goes to the post without delay.'

With this Gussie had to be satisfied. Seemingly indisposed for further conversation, his lordship made his polite excuses, and left. The dowager having retained her state in her receiving-room, and Charles and Clarissa being departed to unknown parts upon mysterious errands of their own, Gussie considered herself fully at her own disposal.

She instantly resolved upon making free with the contents of so fine a house, by conducting an exhaustive exploration of it. Who knew but that somewhere in the building, there may not be some clue to be gleaned as to the mystery that so weighed upon her?

Off she set at once, and spent a happy hour in rambling up and down stairs, through galleries and salons, drawing-rooms and libraries. Unmitigated opulence met her eye everywhere she stepped: marble and gilt, velvet and silk, mahogany and jewels, there seemed no end to the perfections and delights that only great wealth could bring. Gussie might have imagined herself cowed by such majesty and splendour, or likely to be so, for the contrast could hardly be the greater, between her own ordinary self and the extravagance of Starminster. Such a person might feel herself diminished to nothing amidst such an array. Gussie found herself quite equal to it, however, and even forgot her quest, for some little time, in her frank curiosity about everything she saw, and the composition of a few amusing daydreams, in which she was not merely a poor scion of a grand family, but a great lady in her own right, walking through luxuries of her own possession.

She was adrift somewhere upon the upper floors, her legs growing weary from so much upping-and-downing of stairs, and beginning to think of returning below, when a pronounced scraping sound interrupted all thought of refreshment, and caused her to look sharply up. She knew that sound: it was the grinding, unpleasant *scrape* of rough granite against some solid surface.

Halfway down a wide passage was she, passing yet another long window framed in silken drapes, the ancient wooden floors creaking under her feet. Ahead of her, something swooped and dived, wings akimbo, and there she beheld the coarse, grey form of Great-Uncle Silvester.

'Uncle!' she cried, delighted and relieved. 'I thought I had seen you before now, but I could not be sure.'

'Hush,' said the gargoyle, the one, gravelly word all he seemed inclined to utter for the present, for he perched but briefly atop the nearest door-frame, and then took off again. Gussie interpreted his movements as an invitation to follow, and did so with alacrity, trotting eagerly in his wake through a series of passages and rooms she had not yet explored. A final corner was turned, and in stepping through another door Gussie beheld a long gallery, the ceiling rising to great heights above. Polished floorboards bore a set of carpet runners unspooled all the long way down the room, and wherever the walls were not lit with windows, there hung paintings. So closely crowded were they, and in so great a quantity, that little of the figured wallpaper behind them could be discerned.

This, it appeared, was what Great-Uncle Silvester wanted her to see, for he flew straight up towards the ceiling, and took up a perch at the top of the door-frame. Gussie turned, saw him hunched over her head in his customary crouched posture, his large ears twitching but his ugly face otherwise stone-still.

'Thank you, Uncle,' she said.

One long, stone ear quivered.

Gussie returned her attention to the gallery, and began a slow perusal of the portraits upon the left-hand wall. These were the oldest that the family possessed, she judged, for they were age-begrimed, and hung in heavy, carved wooden frames that could only belong to a bygone era. Immediately her attention was arrested for, having passed two unremarkable paintings of long-dead ladies in elaborate head-dresses, the third stopped the breath in her throat, and held her motionless in shock.

Whether the gentleman depicted there was the first Lord Maundevyle was not indicated, but Gussie guessed that it must be so, for he had all the arrogance of an aristocrat, and his attire was so replete with velvets and jewels as to indicate that the Selwyn wealth was of no recent date. What interested her far more than any of these things, however, was the fact that this early Lord Maundevyle was unmistakeably Wyrded.

It was his eyes that first gave her the clue, for they were too pale, and as hard as ice. His complexion, too, was bloodless and pale; he looked, she thought, as though he might be quite dead, only that he bore too much animation of expression for that to be possible. She could not tell from the portrait what manner of Wyrde he possessed, but that he was no mere ordinary mortal was apparent enough.

Gussie passed on to the next portrait, and the next. Not every painting showed a Wyrded Selwyn, but many did. She saw a lady in red velvet, a multitude of birds nesting among her garments and in her hair; another lady in a great ruff of a collar, a living flame erupting from her raised palm; a gentleman who might, she thought, share the same Wyrde as Theo, judging from the prominent fangs revealed by his rather sinister smile. One Selwyn ancestor had a head full of snakes, like Lizzie; another had the claws of some great beast, and the teeth to match, and looked caught in the process of some transformation.

Gussie walked on and on, until she had reached the end of one wall, and begun upon the next. The same array greeted her wondering eyes, the portraits becoming more recent as she progressed. And, she realised, more unobjectionable, for by the time her weary feet brought her near to the entrance once more, and the Selwyns depicted displayed the fashions of only the preceding century, the signs of the Wyrde faded. The last portraits were of the Dowager Viscountess and Lord Maundevyle himself; like the four portraits immediately previous, they bore no signs of Wyrde whatsoever. These pictures might take up their place in any great house in the country without occasioning any comment, even those who detested and feared the Wyrde.

Paused in thought, Gussie let her eyes wander, half-seeing, over Lord Maundevyle's composed features. He, then, was just a man, as had his father been before him.

The Selwyn family, the Lords Maundevyle, had once been as liberally touched by the Wyrde as the Werths. But something had changed, and they were not now.

That explained Lady Maundevyle's close friendship with her aunt, to a degree: with such ancestry, her ladyship could never have been among those who scorned acquaintance with so peculiar a family. But it explained little else.

Was it that they welcomed the change in their lineage, preferring their unWyrded status? Might that be the reason why they had so singled out Gussie, when they might have had any number of Wyrded Werths to stay?

But, no. The explanation was insufficient, for why had they invited any Werth to Starminster at all? What advantage did they expect to derive from having done so?

SEVEN

'Well found, Uncle Silvester,' said Gussie. 'Though I confess myself unable to understand the import of all this, just yet.'

The grinding rasp of stone against stone answered her. The gargoyle rumbled, from some undetectable spot in the gallery: 'Little Bella Selwyn. Charming girl. Turned into stone when she was vexed, but I always thought that rather an advantage to George.'

Gussie searched the ceiling for some sign of her great-uncle, but found none. 'I do not understand your meaning, Uncle,' she said. Silvester was not much given to coherence, it was true, but such a pronouncement defied all comprehension. 'Who is Bella Selwyn?'

A shadow shifted on the far side of the gallery. Gussie saw a dark, whip of a tail hanging down in a curl, partly obscuring the tall hair worn by a grand lady in a portrait there. She approached, and beheld again a picture she had only briefly glanced at before: a lady long dead, having lived rather more than a century before. She had a lively expression and a great many jewels, and her eyes looked shaped from sapphires. 'Is this Bella?'

Great-Uncle Silvester, crouched atop the frame like a

pint-sized curse, swished his tail. He did not answer in words, but Gussie took this for assent.

'And who is George, if you please?'

'Used to put frogs in my boots,' ground out Silvester. This memory did not please him, for his claws tightened upon the frame, and the wood groaned in protest.

'That sounds like something a mere child would— oh!' Gussie saw it in a flash. 'You grew up with George, did you? Why, then he must have been your brother. And if Miss Selwyn's proclivities had the power to affect him in particular, why then, there must have been some enduring connection between the two. They were married, were they?'

Great-Uncle Silvester's granite tail swished, swished.

'So the Werths and the Selwyns have some long-ago connection,' Gussie said thoughtfully. 'I suppose they must have, if both families were among the more Wyrded in the land. Such an alliance must have been reckoned as sound good sense.'

A horrible thought then occurred to her. Was she, Gussie Werth, invited here because Lady Maundevyle sought to renew this age-old family connection? Was she chosen for being unwed, and intended to pledge herself to one of the Selwyn sons?

Hideous thought! For Henry was cold, and Charles cruel, and while Clarissa could be engaging, Gussie did not relish the thought of a madwoman for a sister-in-law. All the innocent pleasure she had taken in her daydreams of an hour or so before now returned to reproach her. Delightful and splendid the house may be, but she did not in the smallest degree wish to possess it on such terms as that! Or any terms at all. She missed her cottage, and Miss Frostell, with a sudden fierceness, and experienced a moment's regret at being lured beyond the doorstep at all.

But, no. She had wanted to travel beyond Werth Towers, and now she had; and what did it signify, if the experience brought its own dangers? She was equal to any match-making scheme of Lady Maundevyle's.

Gussie drew herself up, lifted her chin, and swept towards the gallery's doors. 'Thank you, Great-Uncle,' she called back — and a moment later regretted it, for standing just beyond the door's frame, on the point of entering the room, was Lord Maundevyle.

'Ah,' he said, his gaze moving from Gussie's face to the room behind her. He was searching for something. 'That creature is yours, is it? I had concluded as much. I do not see how any great-uncle of yours could contrive to turn himself into stone, and yet remain animate — remarkable. But the Wyrde, I suppose, is equal to anything.'

'In fact, sir, he is dead,' said Gussie haughtily. 'Has been these many years, I believe. At present he is haunting a cathedral grotesque. It is its very ugliness that amuses him, I am sure of it.'

'I see,' said Lord Maundevyle.

'Before that, it was a rock.'

'A rock?'

'A mere ordinary rock, such as one might pick up on any country ramble. It was found in all sorts of odd places all over the Towers, and I believe it took my aunts some three years to understand its provenance.'

'It did not speak much, then, this rock.'

'I conclude not, sir. It is the lack of a mouth, perhaps. In which respect, Great-Uncle Silvester's current choice must be considered superior.'

'A mouth,' said Lord Maundevyle, once again searching the room behind Gussie. His eyes narrowed. 'And wings, and I am sure I perceive a set of horns?'

'Yes, sir. Positively devilish, I know, but then I have never received the impression that Great-Uncle Silvester was especially a religious man.'

Lord Maundevyle searched Gussie's face, as though he might suspect her of amusing herself at his expense.

Gussie mustered her most charming smile. 'What a coincidence it is, that you should come up here at the very time I was exploring. I had thought you gone out into the park.'

'You must have been exploring for some time,' said Lord Maundevyle. 'For I have had my walk, and come back. My mother sent me in search of you. I believe it is time to dress for dinner.'

A glance out of the nearest of the long windows confirmed this thought: so absorbed in her discoveries had Gussie been, she had failed to notice the lateness of the hour.

'Surely a servant might have been better employed upon such an errand?' said Gussie. 'It demeans Lord Maundevyle, to chase about the house after an errant guest.'

She meant to poke his lordship into giving away some inkling as to his mother's notions — and perhaps his own. Had Henry been sent up as part of a general scheme to throw them together?

But Lord Maundevyle was as unruffled by this as he seemed to be by everything, for he merely said: 'I found myself at leisure, and had no objection.'

'So fine a collection of paintings,' said Gussie next. 'I found myself quite absorbed. Your family has a history as colourful as my own, I observe.'

'My mother is very proud of it,' he said. He stepped back from the doorway as he spoke, and gestured for Gussie to precede him. 'I do not doubt she will be enchanted to meet your great-uncle.'

'Silvester is almost as sociable as he is religious,' said Gussie, sweeping past him into the passage. 'And I am afraid his speeches are infrequent, and generally incomprehensible.'

'I do not imagine that will much disconcert Mama.'

Gussie could well believe that little disconcerted Lady Maundevyle.

Before she had gone more than halfway down the passage, Lord Maundevyle called her back. 'Miss Werth?'

Gussie turned.

'I have ordered that the carriage should be brought round at an early hour in the morning. If it pleases you, you shall be taken straight back to Werth.'

Gussie regarded him thoughtfully. She could not determine whether the gesture was made in earnest; had he truly known nothing of his family's scheme, or was he set up in apparent opposition to it, in order to win her approval?

Common sense decided that the point was immaterial; she was not going to marry him either way, and it must be perfectly apparent by now that while she objected greatly to the *method* by which she had been brought to Starminster, she had evinced no particular distaste for the prospect of remaining there.

'I am grateful for such attention,' she said, which was true. 'But I shan't need the carriage just yet.'

Lord Maundevyle's eyebrows rose. 'I had thought you resentful of my regrettable brother and sister's treatment.'

'And I am. Their conduct was indefensible.'

'Why, then, would you not seek an early removal?'

'Because some mystery is apparent in all this, and I can hardly be expected to feel no curiosity about it, can I?'

'You are quite as bad as Clarissa,' he said.

Gussie's mouth opened in shock. 'How ungenerous! I am persuaded no one has ever been as bad as your sister.'

He surprised her with a swift smile, soon gone again. 'She would be delighted to hear you say so.'

'Then I shall make a point of keeping the thought to myself.'

He bowed.

'Lord Maundevyle,' she said.

'Yes?'

'Do *you* know why your mother wanted me here?'

He studied her. 'It pains me to admit it, for my sister at least is clearly in my mother's confidence. But she has not seen fit to confide in me about it.'

59

If it was a lie, it was smoothly said. If it was not... did her ladyship fear that her son would disapprove of her scheme, whatever it was? As the current Lord Maundevyle, he *was* master here.

'I will find out what it is,' she vowed.

'I can see that my mother can be no match for you, Miss Werth.'

EIGHT

Silvester defied all of Gussie's expectations. When she entered the dining-hall an hour later, escorted by an obliging Lord Maundevyle, she beheld her disgraceful ancestor seated atop a vast silver epergne occupying the centre of the table. He sat tall (or as tall as his diminutive frame permitted), and alert, as though he expected to enjoy an entertainment of no common order.

The epergne being not wholly dissimilar in hue to Silvester's own grey, and possessed of a variety of flourishes and extrusions besides, nobody save Gussie immediately registered the presence of the grotesque.

Except, perhaps, for Lord Maundevyle, whose lips formed a small, half-suppressed smile as he bowed Gussie into her seat, for which she could not otherwise account.

'I trust you have passed a pleasant morning at Starminster, Miss Werth,' said Lady Maundevyle, upon the commencement of the meal. She sat at the head of the long mahogany table, surrounded by festoons of napery, fine porcelain and silverware. Gussie she had caused to be seated on her right hand, next to Lord Maundevyle. The other two Selwyns occupied the two seats opposite to their brother and their guest, Clarissa a restless vision in ivory silk, Charles a monument to boredom in an exquisite green coat. Gussie felt thankful for the presence of Silvester, if only for his disruption of a family party she might otherwise find a degree *too* cosy.

'Quite pleasant, thank you,' said Gussie. 'Finding myself not, after all, confined to the dungeons, I undertook to go all over the house, and poke my nose into a great many things not at all intended for my amusement.'

'Why, I wonder that you can still walk!' said Clarissa. 'You cannot have gone over *all* the house in an hour or two, surely?'

'Oh, no,' said Gussie, dipping her spoon into her bowl of creamy soup. 'There is plenty left for tomorrow.'

'I found her in the long gallery,' said Lord Maundevyle.

Lady Maundevyle looked sharply at Gussie. 'Then you have become acquainted with our sorrow.'

The words were spoken with a heavy emphasis; were the words written down, Gussie would certainly expect to see *sorrow* spelled with a capital *S*. 'I do not believe I am, quite,' said Gussie. 'Do you — do you refer to the prevalence of the Wyrde among your ancestors?'

'Oh, no!' said Lady Maundevyle, shocked.

Lord Maundevyle had spoken of his mother's pride in her lineage, but Gussie was still surprised. A family of such consequence might more naturally regret such a heritage; many an aristocratic family in England would. In fact, many did. Only the Werths insisted on celebrating their many, many, *many* peculiarities, a tendency the more generous of their critics sometimes termed "making the best of a bad lot."

They had company among the Selwyns, it seemed.

'You observed, perhaps, an alteration in the character of the paintings, among those more recently taken?' said Lady Maundevyle.

'I did,' said Gussie. 'Not a grotesque in sight, nor a gorgon either.'

Lady Maundevyle sighed. 'The Wyrde has forsaken us,'

she lamented. 'Not a single Selwyn has enjoyed its eldritch touch in quite two generations complete, and in Old Lord Maundevyle's day — my father-in-law, you know — it was only his sister Gertrude who could boast of it. She had a Voice, Miss Werth. Sang like the very angels themselves, and I assure you it is no mere figure of speech.'

'A siren, of sorts?' said Gussie. 'One of the more favourable Wyrde-curses, that. I believe we had one ourselves, somewhere around the time of old King Charles.'

'A curse!' said Lady Maundevyle. 'Do you call it such?'

'Why, do not you?'

'Never! Who that enjoys such powers could ever call it anything but a blessing?'

Gussie shook her head. 'I think you would not say that if you knew my cousin Theo.'

'Tell us, then, Miss Werth,' said Clarissa, eyes alight with interest. 'What of this mysterious Theo? Is he handsome? And is he *very* tormented?'

'Neither,' said Gussie brutally.

'You crush me.'

'And that is not to mention poor Lizzie, who stands in danger of turning her every future beau to solid stone. No, the Wyrde has many drawbacks. I find myself quite content to have been passed over by it.'

Clarissa exchanged a *look* with her mother, and Gussie felt again the insidious pressure of undisclosed secrets. 'You are not the slightest bit Wyrded yourself, Miss Werth?' said she.

'The Wyrde has never so much as glanced in my direction. You have selected quite the least interesting Werth in existence, I am afraid.'

There, let them fully understand her prosaic nature; see if *then* they were still minded to keep her.

This gambit failed. Charles said, in his drawling way: 'But you have other qualities, Miss Werth, have you not? A *wit*, I believe, was prominently mentioned.'

Remembering the rambling way in which she had so recently addressed Lord Maundevyle, Gussie could not presently flatter herself she possessed any such talent.

Thankfully, Great-Uncle Silvester chose that moment to expose himself. The grotesque fell off the epergne in a spray of lily-petals, landing with a spectacular *crack*; and, unperturbed, knocked the head off a nearby porcelain figure. Gussie thought the insipid thing rather improved by decapitation, but when Silvester opened his maw impossibly wide, and inserted the porcelain girl's head intact, she could not but feel a moment's mortification.

The grotesque's jaws snapped shut with a *crunch*, and a spray of shattered porcelain erupted in a puff of white dust.

'Oh, dear,' said Gussie. 'I am so sorry. I had no notion he was so fond of statuary.'

An appalled silence followed.

Then, surprisingly, Charles began to laugh. 'An adept illustration of Miss Werth's point,' he said. 'You were not too attached to the thing, Mother, I hope?'

'Gracious, no,' said Lady Maundevyle calmly. 'It was Grandmother Totton's, and of no value at all beyond the mere sentimental.'

Gussie's heart sank. Charles's snort proclaimed his mother's words either a polite lie, or a sarcasm to rival any of her son's.

Still, as Great-Uncle Silvester's chosen means of expressing his sense of obligation to the Lords Maundevyle, it was not unfitting.

Lady Maundevyle had nothing further to say upon the subject of the porcelain nymph. Instead she said: 'You say you found Miss Werth in the long gallery, Henry. I trust you enjoyed a pleasant conversation?'

'Perfectly,' said Henry, without looking up from his soup.

'And did anything of any… import, chance to happen?'

Gussie looked up, sharply, at her ladyship. Heavens,

she was not suggesting her son might have felt disposed to make an *advance* upon their guest? She was but barely acquainted with him! She opened her mouth, minded to express her precise feelings upon such disgraceful notions at once.

But Lord Maundevyle said: '*No*, Mother,' in such a tone as to quell all further comment.

Lady Maundevyle subsided.

'Well,' said Clarissa brightly. 'It has been scarce half a day, yet. We must not expect any very great attention from providence, Mama. It has been ignoring us these fifty years, at least.'

Gussie could make no sense of this speech, and her look of enquiry was answered only with an airy smile.

'Besides,' Clarissa went on, 'there is always the ball.'

'Magical occasions, balls,' said Charles. 'There is no saying what might happen.'

Coming from Charles, the words were probably meant to provoke, and they certainly provoked Clarissa, who — judging from the way Charles jumped, and scowled — proceeded to kick him under the table.

Did they possess a kernel of some imagined truth, in the minds of these peculiar Selwyns? Was Gussie meant to be so overcome at the sight of Lord Maundevyle in his formalwear as to fall in love with him directly?

Was he meant to feel any such sudden passion for her?

Gussie's indignation swelled to such a height, she did not immediately recollect the simpler peculiarity of there being any ball to raise such expectations. A minute or two passed before she was able to enquire: 'Is there to be a ball, ma'am?'

'Naturally there is to be a ball,' said Lady Maundevyle with asperity.

'Tomorrow night,' put in Clarissa helpfully.

'But— but—' Disparate thoughts whirled around Gussie's head, most of which she could not, in any politeness, express. Was not her ladyship a famous hermit?

How, then, could she consider anything *natural* about hosting a ball at her own home?

And was this on Gussie's account? If so, it must have been planned some way in advance. Just how long had Lady Maundevyle been harbouring designs upon Gussie?

'I hope you are not ill disposed for a dance, Miss Werth?' said Clarissa, with a smile of glittering mischief. 'Mama, you see, has quite set her heart upon it.'

'Oh, no!' said Gussie. 'When I have come into Somerset with no other view!'

'Miss Werth's motives become clear,' said Charles. 'You have anticipated her wants exactly, Mama.'

Under different circumstances, Gussie might indeed be positively inclined towards a ball, for she had never in her life attended anything but a small, impromptu dance among her own family. Some part of her might, by the morrow, feel delighted at the prospect — were it not for the utter strangeness of such an event's being held under such conditions at all.

'I have never been more than passingly fond of asparagus,' said Great-Uncle Silvester, apropos of nothing.

'Then we certainly shan't serve any,' said Clarissa without turning a hair. 'Besides, Charles hates it above all things.'

When Gussie retired at last to her bedchamber, she was in a state of muddled confusion she hardly knew how to resolve. She had been treated all evening as an honoured a guest, as though the circumstances of her arrival at Starminster counted for nothing. When Lord Maundevyle and Charles had joined the ladies in the drawing-room, the former had made not the smallest effort to distinguish her; in fact, he had not spoken more than three words to her from the moment of his entry until the moment of her departure. Even Charles had been more civil than that.

One might have imagined Lady Maundevyle to object

to her son's cool treatment of Miss Werth, but she had not seemed to notice. The only intervention she had made was on the occasion of Henry's sitting down, quite on the opposite side of the room from Gussie.

'Why, Henry, you will give Miss Werth a conviction of your disliking her,' she had said, and waved her son to a chair at Gussie's elbow. 'Do, pray, try to be an amiable host.'

The tightness around Lord Maundevyle's mouth had declared him less than pleased, but he had made no objection to the alteration, and had spent the rest of the evening seated next to Gussie. In silence.

Gussie had at last excused herself, claiming weariness after her journey. It was true that she was inordinately tired, though not because of the morning's travel. Rather because of everything that had happened since, and the impossibility of making any sense of it afterwards.

She missed Miss Frostell's observations. In all likelihood, her governess would have something to say of it that would make everything clear, or at least tolerable. Gussie could only console herself with satire. She lay in her bed, listening to the faint sounds of Great-Uncle Silvester consuming some other trinket of priceless worth and questionable taste, her mind turning upon the peculiarities of the Selwyn family until she fell asleep.

NINE

Gussie woke in the morning to the extraordinary sight of the very Miss Frostell of her plaintive imaginings. Her friend, unquestionably many miles distant the night before, was seated in a deep chair on the far side of her bedchamber, rapt in the enjoyment of a steaming cup of tea.

'Frosty?' she said, sitting up.

'Good morning,' smiled Miss Frostell.

'But— but surely you are a dream! I had no notion I had the power to conjure up visions. How curious that I should never have happened to do it before.'

'It would please you to no end if you could, no doubt,' said Miss Frostell. 'But I am not a vision. I have this moment arrived, and probably woke you as I came in, for which I am sorry. It is past eleven o'clock! You must have been excessively tired, to sleep so long.'

'Don't reproach me!' Gussie begged. 'I had quite the day of it yesterday, I assure you.' She got out of bed, drawing her shawl around her shoulders, and advanced upon Miss Frostell with the purpose of satisfying herself as to her friend's solidity.

'I am quite real,' said Miss Frostell.

'I see that you are. But how came you to be here?'

'Why, I came after you, of course. Lady Honoria observed what happened to you, and raised the alarm, and after that it was no very difficult task to trace the passage of the Maundevyle coach. Though we were delayed in setting off. By some unaccountable accident, all the wheels had come off our carriage, and the repairs were not speedily accomplished.'

Gussie thought of Clarissa at once. It would suit her idea of high adventure and conscienceless mischief, to discourage any possibility of pursuit. Not that Gussie had had any idea of there being any. 'You mean to say you came all this way alone?' she cried. 'Across half the country?'

'No, not alone. Your great-aunt Honoria is downstairs, and Lord Bedgberry. I believe he and Mr. Selwyn must possess some prior acquaintance, for they did not greet each other with any very marked friendliness.'

'Theo declared him to be detestable,' Gussie confirmed. 'I have never heard what Mr. Selwyn's sentiments might be towards Theo, but I collect it is mutual.' She looked about for her gown and stays, but could not remember where she had deposited them the night before. 'Did Great-Aunt Honoria come? I am astonished. I never thought it likely she would leave the Towers.'

'Or Lord Bedgberry, either,' said Miss Frostell drily. 'And he is not half sour about it, I can tell you.'

'I am sure he is perfectly savage,' Gussie agreed. 'But then he need not have come. What can he have meant by haring after me in this fashion? Quite as though I were not fully capable of managing my own affairs.'

'The circumstances were unusual, you must own,' said Miss Frostell.

'We are Werths,' said Gussie. 'The merely *unusual* comes as a matter of course.'

'I shall leave you to dress,' said Miss Frostell, rising

from her chair. 'I came up to help you with your packing, but I see I am too precipitate. The horses must be rested a while before we can depart, of course, so all of that may be done later.'

'But we are not departing just yet, Frosty,' said Gussie, espying her gown thrown in a disgracefully untidy heap over the silver-gilded dresser, and her stays on the floor beneath. 'Lord Maundevyle has already offered to send me home, and I declined, for I am not at all ready to leave.'

'I know you wanted to accept Lady Maundevyle's invitation,' said Miss Frostell. 'But surely there can be no call to remain here upon such disgraceful terms?'

'But I remain here upon excellent terms. The manner of my arrival notwithstanding, I have been treated with the greatest kindness. *So* great, dear Frosty, that I am persuaded some powerful motive must lie behind it, and until I have uncovered what it is, I must beg you not to carry me off again.'

Miss Frostell only sighed, being accustomed to Gussie's stubbornness, when once she had got hold of an idea. 'I shall tell his lordship,' she said, and took herself and her tea-cup out of the room forthwith.

Gussie was not afraid of encountering much opposition from Theo. He did not like to be away from Werth Towers, this was true, but she had only to show him the library at Starminster to reconcile him to the prospect of a short stay. Once absorbed in a book, he would quickly grow oblivious to every other consideration.

And seeing as Starminster turned out to have such a long history of Wyrded ancestors, she did not imagine the current inhabitants would be too much discomposed by Theo's peculiarities, either. Really, it was all quite perfect.

Gussie made herself respectable as quickly as she could, and hurried downstairs to enact her plan upon Theo's peace with brutal alacrity.

She found Lord Bedgberry standing in the hall, surrounded

by Selwyns. Miss Selwyn had been the first to accost him, Gussie judged, but her brothers had not been far behind. Clarissa might be said to be doing her best to be fascinating; she seemed turned from her usual brash self to an adorable, kittenish creature, quite overcome by the excitement of Lord Bedgberry's presence. Theo was patently more interested in Mr. Selwyn, who was prudently stationed behind his sister, and regarding their unscheduled visitor with a satirical eye. Lord Maundevyle stood near the door, watching the proceedings with a quiet intensity, though without seeming minded to interfere.

The air crackled with animosity, and Gussie perceived that Theo and Charles might easily come to blows if she did not intervene.

'Theo!' she said, sweeping into the hall with Miss Frostell at her heels. 'What *can* you mean by coming so far? And without an invitation!'

'*You* did not precisely receive an invitation, cousin,' Theo said curtly, and without taking his eyes off Charles.

'Why, but I did.'

'And declined it, did you not? But a lady's wishes count for nothing with *some*.'

'Yes, and another time I will hope not to be bodily picked up, and thrown into a coach without so much as a by-your-leave. But since it has all turned out for the best, you need not trouble yourself about it. Has my aunt Werth received my letter?'

'I doubt it,' said Theo. 'She was in no state to receive much of anything, when I left.'

Gussie, who knew perfectly well what that meant, winced. 'Was it news of me that did it? How inconvenient for Aunt Werth. And, for that matter, for me. Clarissa, please,' she added, as Miss Selwyn began, in a loud voice, to compliment Theo's dress. 'This is hardly the time.'

Clarissa cast her an anguished look, which Gussie, rather to her confusion, took to mean that she was *dying* of love for Lord Bedgberry and quite wounded by her bosom friend's lack of support.

Play-acting, Gussie perceived. Clarissa did seem addicted to the art, and no one could genuinely languish away over her awkward and dishevelled cousin.

Having thus dismissed Theo from all possible notice, Gussie said: 'Do say you will go away again, cousin? As you perceive, I am unharmed, and quite in my element.'

'Do not say you are determined to be rid of *me,* as well?' murmured Miss Frostell beside her.

'Never,' said Gussie. 'Though I do not think it precisely necessary for you to have come here, either.'

'Cruelty, thy name is Augusta,' said Theo. 'The devotion of her loyal companion means nothing to her.'

'Nothing at all, today,' Gussie agreed. 'Tomorrow I daresay I may think differently.' She pressed Miss Frostell's hand as she spoke, for really she was touched by her retiring governess's daring ride to the rescue. Why, she had volunteered herself to be closeted with Lord Bedgberry *and* Great-Aunt Honoria. For days!

The said Lord Bedgberry, plagued by the beseeching regard of Gussie on the one hand, and Miss Frostell's calm certainty that he would instead do as *she* wished, knew not how to reconcile these competing claims, and retired into a distracted silence.

Gussie noted the way his attention lingered upon Clarissa. Clarissa noticed it, too, and preened; but Gussie did not imagine the girl understood the real reason behind his lordship's regard.

'Cousin, have you… breakfasted?' she said hastily.

Theo did not look away from Clarissa. 'No.'

'All the more reason to take your leave at once!' she proclaimed. 'Miss Frostell, I believe you must by now be familiar with my cousin's requirements. May I leave him in your capable care?'

Miss Frostell responded with a glare. 'And leave you here, I take it?'

Gussie smoothed her gown. 'I shall do very well here.'

'There is not the slightest need for anyone to leave,' said Lord Maundevyle unexpectedly, rousing himself from whatever silent study had hitherto occupied him. 'I have no doubt that my mother will be pleased to extend Miss Werth's invitation to include her cousin and her companion, and naturally I shall not oppose her wishes.'

This was not quite the same thing as a hearty declaration of welcome, but Gussie perceived that Miss Frostell was perfectly willing to take it as such.

Theo's fixation upon Miss Selwyn did not abate.

'Lord Bedgberry and Miss Frostell will find ample refreshment laid out in the dining room,' added Lord Maundevyle.

Gussie exchanged a look with Miss Frostell. 'Ah,' said Gussie. 'I believe my cousin would prefer to take a turn about the gardens. Would not you, Theo?' Upon which words, she advanced upon Lord Bedgberry and bodily shoved him towards the doors. Halfway there, he blinked and shook himself, as though surfacing from a trance.

'Get you gone, Theo,' Gussie hissed. 'Or you *know* you will disgrace yourself.'

'But—' said Lord Bedgberry.

Gussie expelled him from the house via the expedient of one final, hearty shove. 'Miss Selwyn is supremely irritating, I grant you,' she said, a trifle breathless from her exertions. 'But she is *not* to be breakfast.'

Theo sighed, and turned away.

'I sincerely hope you did not avail yourself of Miss Frostell, either!' Gussie called after him. She had surreptitiously surveyed Miss Frostell for signs of interference, and had, to her relief, perceived none.

His lordship did not dignify this parting sally with a response, and disappeared into the sunlit garden without a word.

Gussie spared a brief moment's sympathy for any unwary creatures that might be ambling about Lady Maundevyle's shrubbery, before dismissing the matter from her mind.

She returned into the hall to find Miss Frostell departing in the direction of breakfast, under Lord Maundevyle's escort. To her mild unease, there was no sign of either Mr. or Miss Selwyn. She hoped they had not taken it upon themselves to pursue Lord Bedgberry into the shrubbery.

But, that was Theo's look-out. Gussie could not be expected to solve *every* problem single-handed, especially not when she was so ferociously hungry. Dismissing Lord Bedgberry and the Selwyns from her further notice, she followed Miss Frostell in to breakfast.

***

Theo was halfway through a fresh rabbit when he discovered himself to be under surveillance.

It must be Miss Selwyn. She had shown tiresome signs of wanting to attach herself to him, despite his attempts to glower her out of her fancy, and he imagined her both bold and shameless enough to follow him out into the gardens.

It was a pity she had found him. He ought to have gone farther away from the house before he caught his breakfast; he had known it at the time, but the creature had darted into his path as though sent for the express purpose of quenching his appetite, and hunger had defeated him. Really, it was tiresome in the extreme to have to catch one's own food. He did not at all understand why coaching inns did not offer an alternate menu of fresher fare, nor why the dining-parlours of the great and wealthy were devoid of such accommodations.

Miss Frostell had attempted to defend all these disparate souls with a singular argument. *'Why, the trouble is that you are unique, my lord,*' she had said, some way through one of the interminable days of their journey hither. '*If there is another man or woman in England with your particular dietary interests, I should be surprised.*'

The reflection offered Theo no comfort at all, and only depressed him, so he did not think of it much.

He stood on the far side of an immaculate shrubbery, a wide lawn opening at his back, crimson droplets pouring down his chin and the limp corpse of his breakfast clutched in both hands. A compromising situation, but Theo felt no personal sense of shame. If Miss Selwyn did not like it, she and her witless relatives ought not to have made off with Gussie.

But it was not Miss Selwyn. When a pair of laurel bushes parted and the figure of Charles Selwyn appeared, Theo began to wish rather that it *had* been the sister after all. She at least seemed disposed to approve of him, however absurdly and without cause.

Charles had no such positive feelings. He regarded the vision of a bloodied and feasting Lord Bedgberry with distaste, and stopped several feet away, as though unwilling to taint himself by a nearer proximity. 'I did try to dissuade Mama from this mad plan of hers,' he said, his conversational tone at odds with his demeanour of icy disapproval. 'No good can come of mixing with the Werths, and so I told her. But she is used to command, and my brother did not exert himself to oppose her.'

Theo did not immediately lower his breakfast. He rather amused himself by taking another lingering bite, relishing in the ensuing spurt of blood. Only when he felt himself reasonably replete did he set the small corpse aside, like a man pushing away his emptied plate, and smiled at the infuriating Charles Selwyn.

The man gratified him with a grimace, even a flicker of fear, and he took a small step back.

His cravat being somewhat disarranged, Theo neatened it, aware that he was thus transferring the blood from his fingers onto the snowy white linen. 'And what is the "mad plan"?' he said. 'I remain determined to escort my cousin out of here, before the morning is gone.'

'You may do so with my goodwill,' said Charles. 'I should think it wiser. But you will not so easily gainsay Mama. No, not even you,' and he grimaced afresh at the sight of Lord Bedgberry's bloodied linens.

He did not seem either shocked or horrified, which interested Theo, accustomed as he was to such reactions. From this, he concluded that the inhabitants of Starminster were better informed as to the Werths and their Wyrde than most.

What did they imagine they knew about Gussie, that might explain their behaviour?

'And how long does her ladyship mean to keep Miss Werth?' said Theo. 'Is she never to be released back to the Towers?'

'Oh, not much past tonight, I imagine,' said Charles carelessly. 'Once the ball is over, there can be scant reason to want her, for either Mama's point will be gained, or it will be apparent that she is to be disappointed.'

Theo did not waste his time enquiring again into the nature of "Mama's point". It was evident that Charles meant to goad, and was being evasive on purpose. Theo would not gratify him by pressing for an answer.

Still, the situation irritated him immensely. He did not doubt his ability to gainsay Lady Maundevyle, if he so chose, regardless of Mr. Selwyn's words; he had methods at his disposal that had never failed to carry his own point, whenever he chose to employ them.

But Gussie, now, that was a different problem. For if she did not choose to leave, could he compel her? Yes, without a doubt; but *would* he? For if he had so condemned the Selwyns for hauling her off without her leave, what right had he to do the same? He was not, after all, her father, or her husband. His authority over her did not extend so far.

Besides, Gussie might herself possess no particular Wyrde, but she had other powers. Not the least of them being the ability to make the journey home *deeply* miserable, were she displeased.

Theo resigned himself to an overnight stay and a forced attendance at a ball he would much rather miss. He need not do more than put in a courtesy appearance, however; the rest of the event would be better spent in a long ramble over the grounds, for the night-hours were ever more productive for hunting.

And then he, his cousin and Miss Frostell would depart bright and early upon the morrow.

Reassured upon all these points, Theo abandoned Charles Selwyn without a syllable, and stalked away towards the house. His appetite being, for the present, sated, he ought to make some small effort to keep Gussie in some kind of order, before she created some manner of incident at Starminster. His mother would have a great deal to say to him, if he did not.

As he passed under the lintel of the great front doors, the scrape of stone met his ears, and a grinding voice said: 'I should not myself favour hair-powder above a plain, cropped head, only it does cover all manner of sins.'

Theo gave a sigh. 'Thank you, Silvester, that is a great help.'

Ten

Gussie was far more fond of Great-Aunt Honoria than the lady's abrupt manners and unprepossessing appearance might strictly warrant. However, she did rather wish her esteemed ancestor would contrive to control her mischievous impulses a little better.

Breakfast proceeded at a docile pace and in a serene silence, Miss Frostell choosing to devote herself to the benefits of toast and coffee, declining for the moment to harangue Gussie any further about a prompt departure. Lord Maundevyle, as appeared to be his habit, was taciturn. Gussie, regarding him thoughtfully over her own repast, did not find his silence forbidding. Rather, he had an air of abstraction — coupled, admittedly, with a supreme indifference to company — that suggested his mind was simply elsewhere.

'And what are we to expect at tonight's ball, my lord?' said Gussie after a while.

Lord Maundevyle looked up, blinking, as though surprised at hearing anyone speak. He did not appear displeased by the question, and might even have answered it, had not Great-Aunt Honoria chosen that moment to manifest above his lordship's plate. She refrained from streaming blood, to Gussie's relief; her neck-wound was quite dry; but the ghoulish expression she favoured on such occasions was more than enough to disconcert even the calmest of men. Gussie had seen it happen, more than once.

His lordship did give a start, spilling his chocolate. He stared at the severed head before him (Gussie had never been able to determine whether Honoria was a spectre, exactly, or whether she was simply not more than half dead), and he was observed to swallow down a cry, perhaps, of revulsion.

Then he said: 'Good morning, Lady Honoria. You do not find anything to your liking?' And he gestured at the array of breakfast-dishes, unruffled and undeterred.

Great-Aunt Honoria cackled. 'It is as well,' she said. 'Any man who has care of my great-nieces and nephews ought to have a strong stomach.'

With which pronouncement she whisked away to the window, and faded through it into the golden morning beyond.

The ensuing silence was broken, after a few moments, by Lord Maundevyle. 'I wonder what she was like in life?' Gussie was almost sure she perceived his mouth twitching, as with suppressed amusement.

'Much the same, I understand,' said Gussie. 'How she contrived to detach her head from her neck with such ease, or to restore it afterwards, was beyond anybody's comprehension. And there has never been another Werth with quite such a Wyrde, that I recall.'

'Such is the nature of the affliction,' said Miss Frostell lightly. 'No one chooses the nature of their Wyrde, and in my experience the grotesqueries do seem to be more common. Though Lady Honoria does not appear to be displeased with hers.'

'Oh, no,' said Gussie. 'She has always been unbecomingly delighted with it.'

'You are not Wyrded yourself, Miss Frostell?' said Lord

Maundevyle.

'It is a great relief to me that I am not, my lord,' she replied. 'Nor Gussie either. We are much more peaceful at home as we are, I believe.'

'But furnished with far fewer opportunities for engaging mischief,' said Gussie. 'Uninterrupted domestic harmony has its drawbacks, on occasion.'

'And what manner of mischief might you like to commit?' said Lord Maundevyle. 'Had you been Wyrded, like the rest of your family.'

Gussie, unprepared for the question, had no ready answer to give. She had spoken flippantly, out of fun; not once had she ever given serious thought to what might have been, if she had inherited the curse of the Werths. Not since she was a child, anyway, and those flights of fancy had been just that — daydreams.

'I do not know,' she said. 'I could not wish for Theo's, certainly, nor do I quite have the stomach for Honoria's. And while I am sure Lizzie will make a splendid gorgon I cannot but be relieved that I have all my own hair.'

'Lord Bedgberry shall not be too inconvenienced in remaining here for the ball, I trust?' said his lordship.

Gussie recognised this as a form of subtle enquiry into Theo's particular affliction, and did not choose to gratify his curiosity. Let her cousin remain an enigma for as long as possible. Lord Bedgberry took some getting used to. 'I am sure he will manage,' she replied. 'He always does.'

Lord Maundevyle cast a glance out of the window, as though reflecting on the precise ways Lord Bedgberry might be *managing* at that moment. Wisely, he did not enquire.

'And where is Lady Maundevyle this morning?' Gussie said. 'I should like to ensure she is amenable to the presence of Miss Frostell and my cousin.'

'My mother has not yet come down,' answered Lord Maundevyle. 'But do not trouble yourself over the matter. She will not contradict me.'

This bordered upon a rather repugnant self-satisfaction, though it was uttered without undue pride. Gussie decided she had had enough of the Selwyns for one morning. If her hosts did not require her company, she could easily furnish herself with more agreeable activities.

'Come, Miss Frostell,' she said, rising from her chair. 'If Lord Maundevyle will excuse us, it is time to see whether my excellent closet can supply us with suitable attire for a ball.'

'It is a costume ball,' said his lordship, as Miss Frostell rose, obedient to Gussie's command.

'Oh?' said Gussie. 'There are to be masks and intrigue, then, I collect?'

'Certainly the masks. As to the intrigue, I cannot say.'

'I should think it inevitable,' said Gussie. 'There is mystery enough surrounding the event already. Masks and secret identities were all that was wanted to make it quite perfect.'

Lord Maundevyle looked at her. Perhaps he was deciding whether or not she was in earnest; she could not tell how he got on. 'You are amused by mystery?'

Gussie merely smiled.

Miss Frostell gave a somewhat unladylike snort of laughter. 'Consider her mere presence here, my lord. Your mother offered her a mystery, and Gussie, as you see, cannot let go of it until it is solved. It was quite the perfect way to ensure her compliance, whether her ladyship knew it or not.'

'Then I see my mother has chosen the nature of the ball with similar luck,' said his lordship. 'Or skill.'

Gussie also wondered which it was. Lady Maundevyle appeared to know more about Gussie than Gussie did herself, which was disconcerting.

But it was also a situation which could not last beyond the evening, so she repaired to the door with a cheerful spirit, having made her courtesies to her taciturn host. 'How shall you be dressed, my lord?' she called back, as a parting sally. 'Some dark and gothic character would doubtless be suitable?'

'Naturally I cannot tell you before the ball, Miss Werth,' he replied. 'That would be to wholly spoil the fun, would it not?'

'Well, Frosty, and how shall *we* appear?' said Gussie ten minutes later, having arrived once more in the relative sanctuary of her own rooms. No Clarissa had waited for her en route, ready to jump out unannounced with some fresh scheme of high drama. Nor had she seen anything of Mr. Selwyn, which also pleased her.

Theo, she did not consider for so much as a moment.

'I believe *I* should like to be some dark and gothic figure,' said Miss Frostell. 'If Lord Maundevyle is not going to claim the role.'

'A white gown, perhaps,' said Gussie, walking into her dressing-room. 'Signifying virtue and innocence, all ready to be outraged by some depraved villain—' She stopped, for two sets of matched garments had already been laid out by some unknown hand, and that they were intended for the ball could not admit of a doubt.

The first set consisted of a gown of shimmering blue-green, the colour of the sea, sewn from exquisite silk and adorned with myriad pearls and other gems — what Aunt Wheldrake would have described as "sea-jewels", in fact. A crown of pearls and sea-spray gauze had also been provided, and a quantity of silk ornaments she collected were meant to resemble ocean weeds and blooms. The mask matching this array was of soft golden silk, like sunlight on the water, and presented a striking appearance with its silver and blue-green embroidery.

The second costume was some mythical creature; a dragon, perhaps, for the gown was of heavier substance and bore the appearance of delicate scales. A pair of cleverly-contrived wings was attached at the back, borne up and out with some manner of hidden construct, and the headdress and mask and other ornaments were all of dazzling jewels; a veritable dragon's hoard. Eyeing them, Gussie could not quite convince herself that they were only of paste. Surely the Selwyns had not given over *real* jewels in such quantity?

'One of us is to be a beautiful mermaid, I perceive,' said Gussie. 'And the other a fire-breathing monster out of legend. Which shall you prefer? For my part, I think the latter role perfect for you.'

Miss Frostell declined this honour. 'I have not the spirit to carry it off, my dear,' she said. 'It must be all for you.'

Gussie gazed mournfully at the vision of shimmering silk and gauze claimed by Miss Frostell, and heaved a sigh of resignation. 'Then it falls to me to wear all of these jewels,' she said, picking up the crown. Diamonds and emeralds were set in gold, and interspersed with sapphires. *Paste* diamonds, surely. 'I wonder why these costumes?' she said, trying the crown against her hair. The mermaid sent her mind winging back to Lizzie's Great Event of only a few days before, and all her poor aunt's dashed hopes. 'We have not had a mermaid in the family for several generations, and I never heard that we ever had a dragon at all. The Selwyns might, perhaps, be misinformed.'

'It may not be intended to bear any reference to your family,' suggested Miss Frostell, and Gussie felt a fool for not having considered that possibility when she had seen every portrait at Starminster. Had there been any mermaids or dragons among them? She did not recall, having taken in far too many portraits too quickly to remember the details of them all. But it was possible. Perhaps that was the theme of the ball: hearkening back to a Wyrded past that Lady Maundevyle evidently regretted losing.

And Gussie was here as the representative of a family that had lost nothing of theirs at all.

Considering Lady Maundevyle's accepted status as a recluse suspicious of general company, Gussie was expecting a modest affair. The family; herself and Theo and Miss Frostell; some few of the Selwyns' immediate neighbours; that would make up enough for a respectable ball, but without too far violating her ladyship's preferences. Even so, the prospect perhaps daunted Lady Maundevyle, for she was not seen all day, choosing instead to recruit her strength for the evening's revelry in her own apartments.

When the hour of the proposed ball arrived, Gussie was startled to observe a pair of carriages lumbering their way up to the house remarkably promptly. And they were followed by another, and then two more — and then a great many more. There was a queue, in fact, to draw up outside the house and discharge an increasing hoard of bedecked, bejewelled and beribboned guests, and Gussie watched for some quarter of an hour, near paralysed with astonishment.

'Just what manner of entertainment is this to be?' she croaked to Miss Frostell, who as ever hovered at her elbow.

'A grand and populous one, it seems,' said Miss Frostell, observing the building crush with a more detached interest. 'I wonder what it is her ladyship is intending to show off?'

Such events were always a matter of display; that Gussie knew, despite having never attended a large gathering in her life. The Werths were not much given to these excesses, perhaps on account of the fact that many of their neighbours viewed them with a settled suspicion. And nobody could make either Theo or Great-Aunt Honoria presentable for a ball, which was why it was unfortunate that it had been those particular two, among all the Werths, who had come so far to intervene. She had seen nothing of her cousin either, and had not the smallest idea if he had contrived to get hold of any ball-clothes. She did not imagine it would trouble him overmuch if he had not.

'Starminster itself is worthy of display,' Gussie offered, knowing as she spoke that this could not be explanation enough. Starminster had, probably, always been a splendid palace deserving of grand company, and the lords Maundevyle had not chosen to throw it open to guests in some years. Why now, then?

When, some little time later, Gussie and Miss Frostell ventured downstairs, suitably clad in their costumes, they found Lady Maundevyle herself, appeared at last, and holding court at the bottom of the sweeping staircase. She was dressed as some kind of fire-spirit, putting Gussie in mind of one of the family portraits that had made some small impression upon her. Fire-red silk swirled around Lady Maundevyle's feet with every movement; her sleeves were as light flames, licking coyly up and down her arms; sprays of gold erupted from her hair, like showers of sparks. Her mask was a token only, covering very little of her face; her identity was perfectly obvious. She welcomed her guests with the grace of a queen, and a suppressed excitement which convinced Gussie she expected to triumph in some definite way over the course of the evening.

Clarissa stood at her mother's side. Though she was heavily masked in black, Gussie had no difficulty recognising her, for she wore the self-same men's garb in which she had staged Gussie's own abduction, albeit a finer example: this highwayman was dressed for a ball, in knee-breeches and stockings, and he had met with considerable success in his profession, judging from the profusion of gold and diamonds winking at collar, cuffs and cravat. She ought to cause a stir, except that the costume — and the mask — were so good, and so disguising, that she might pass quite easily for a man. Perhaps the assembling ball-goers imagined themselves meeting Mr. Charles Selwyn, and wondered at the apparent absence of Clarissa.

Gussie had to admire her daring, even as she shook her head. Sooner or later, someone would realise her true identity, and *then* there would be a fine stir. Knowing Clarissa, she was greatly looking forward to it.

She did not see Clarissa leave Lady Maundevyle's side, her attention being briefly distracted by the myriad of costumes filtering into the house; truly, every manner of myth and monster imaginable was in attendance, and some of them were excellent.

Her appreciation of a grand peacock with vast, sweeping tail was interrupted by a hiss in her ear: 'You make a splendid dragon, Miss Werth! Mama has chosen perfectly for you.'

'Miss Frostell said the same,' replied Gussie calmly. 'I cannot think what I have done to give her ladyship the impression I might break into roaring flame at any moment.'

'Can you not?' said Clarissa, and Gussie heard the grin in her voice.

'I am surprised she let you dress like that,' Gussie said. 'Surely it is not proper.'

'Mama gave up on the prospect of my ever observing propriety overmuch,' said Clarissa, unconcerned. 'And it is a good costume, is it not?'

'Very convincing. I stand here trembling in all my jewels, expecting at any moment to be divested of every one.'

'But that would not be very entertaining, since they are only Mama's anyway,' said Clarissa, supremely uninterested.

'Who are all these people?' Gussie gestured in wordless awe at the crowded hall. Many had gone into the ballroom already, yet a crush remained, and more were still coming in at the door.

'Every family of any consequence for quite twenty miles around,' said Clarissa. 'Including several of the noble families of the country; and, of course, every Selwyn in existence. Mama insisted upon the family's attendance.'

'But not so far as to grant them house-room?' said Gussie.

'Oh, no. That would not do. They are quite good enough to come to the ball, but far too irksome to encounter over the breakfast-table. Most of them are putting up at inns hereabouts, I suppose.'

'I wonder that they consented to come at all,' Gussie remarked. 'I would not wonder at it if they were a little piqued at being dismissed to common inns.'

'It is far too important an event to admit of a denial. There has never been a ball here in my lifetime. Who could possibly refuse?'

'And why is there a ball now, Miss Selwyn?' Gussie looked hard at Clarissa as she spoke, intending to convey a settled determination to receive a definite answer.

Her efforts were wasted. Clarissa only smiled, and said: 'You will not be left long in suspense, I am persuaded.'

'Because one or another of you will suddenly be overcome with a need to abandon all this mystery, and answer my questions?'

Clarissa thought. 'No. No, I do not think that will be the reason.'

'You astonish me.'

Whether there was some unspoken signal of which Gussie was not aware, or whether their illustrious hostess had a fixed schedule in mind for the evening's entertainments, a change at that moment occurred. Lady Maundevyle left her place at the foot of the stairs, and led a general exodus into the ballroom — contriving in the process to sweep up her daughter and her honoured guest, and carry them along in her train. Upon entering the enormous ball-chamber, with its mouldings and gildings and statuary and every extravagant thing, she encountered her eldest son standing in an out-of-the-way corner, and bore inexorably down upon him. 'Henry, there you are.

Miss Werth?'

Finding herself expected to follow, Gussie chose obedience over useless rebellion and trailed along in her ladyship's wake. Lord Maundevyle had not entered into the spirit of the event with quite his mother's degree of enthusiasm. He was duly costumed and masked, but with no very marked flamboyance; he wore crimson and velvet and otherwise sober colours, with a mask of burgundy-wine and gold. Gussie could not tell what he was supposed to be.

He made her a bow as she approached. His face was too well covered for her to gauge his feelings, but a slight tightening about the mouth proclaimed him displeased by something.

Lady Maundevyle did not say anything else, but stood by, watching as her son made his courtesies to her guest. She was too evidently waiting for something.

Gussie thought she heard a small sigh escape his lordship.

'Miss Werth,' he said. 'I hope you will do me the honour of dancing the two first with me.'

Gussie blinked. Why, to dance the first two with the lord of the house would be to open the ball! A position of high honour indeed, and one to which she had no claim whatsoever. Any number of high-ranking ladies must be here tonight, any one of whom had a greater right than Gussie to expect such a distinction.

Her eyes narrowed, and she regarded Lady Maundevyle with undisguised suspicion.

Her ladyship merely smiled benevolently, the picture of an obliging hostess tending to her special guest's consequence.

Gussie, of course, had no power of refusal, though she had no real wish to. Lord Maundevyle might prove to be an excellent dancer, and if she found herself the object of general resentment for a distinction that must be seen as misplaced, well, she was a Werth. She was used to rumour and distrust. 'I shall be delighted, my lord,' she assured him.

Behind her, Clarissa clapped her hands. 'Excellent, and then after that you shall dance with Charles. I know he means to ask you, and will soon present himself for the purpose.'

'Yes, yes,' said Lady Maundevyle. 'You must certainly favour my second son with a dance, Miss Werth. I know he will be anxious to secure you. And then, I trust you will find no shortage of agreeable partners among the rest of my guests.'

Surveying anew the crush in the ballroom, Gussie did not doubt it either. Not that she possessed either looks or consequence enough to attract a great many partners on her own merits, but in such a squeeze, surely there must be partners enough for everyone.

Upon a high balcony overlooking the dance floor, an orchestra was secreted; Gussie heard them strike up the opening notes of a lively quadrille. Her company was required at once; she went, with her partner's escort, to take up her place in the dance, and determined upon failing to notice the reactions of her fellow guests as she took up the place of honour opposite Lord Maundevyle. If there were murmurs of dissent, the music was too loud, and too beautiful, to permit her to hear them.

Couples formed rapidly, and soon Gussie forgot everything but the pleasure of dancing. Rarely had she enjoyed such a treat, and never in such company. Her partner, moreover, while taciturn as ever, was a capable dancer, and for the duration of two excellent dances, she felt she had nothing to wish for.

When the second drew to a close, Lord Maundevyle returned her to his mother's side, handing her back to her hostess with a courteous bow. 'Thank you, Miss Werth,' he said politely. 'You are an excellent dancer.'

The compliment felt more a matter of form than particularly sincere, but Gussie accepted it anyway. For someone of her limited experience, to hold her own in the quadrille, and without disgracing herself, was no mean achievement, and she was pleased with her own performance.

Her joyous feelings dimmed a little upon perceiving Mr. Selwyn waiting to take his turn, and though he, too, wore so splendid a mask as to cover much of his face, his demeanour made it quite apparent that he took no pleasure in the prospect of partnering her. She wondered why a man of his age and apparent disposition should consent to follow his mother's dictates at all, if he did not like them, and felt that she had not got the measure of these Selwyns.

'Miss Werth,' he said briefly, and held out his hand, omitting every other courtesy.

Gussie suppressed a sigh, and reminded herself that the duty need be gone through only once, and then she and Mr. Selwyn would both be released. Courtesy compelled them both into a pair of dances, and the forms must be observed.

As she accepted his reluctant offer, Gussie's glance happened to take in Lady Maundevyle, who had not chosen to dance, instead taking up a position from which she might observe the goings-on among the dancers. Her attention was fixed upon Lord Maundevyle, straying once to Gussie; her manner was of heightened interest, even excitement, as though — as though, what? What could she possibly imagine might have happened over the duration of two dances? If her ladyship entertained hopes that either Gussie's heart or her eldest son's might have been smitten with love in so short a space of time, she was destined for disappointment. But as an explanation, that seemed insufficient; for if Gussie was no worthy partner for the opening of her grand ball, she was still less worthy as a potential wife for Lord Maundevyle. And here in the room were a great many superior contenders, many of whom doubtless had very definite hopes about the business.

Still, Lady Maundevyle's anticipation was palpable — with, perhaps, a degree of disappointment, when her elder son turned away from Gussie with no apparent reluctance, and sought the hand of another female.

Gussie's sinking heart as Charles led her into the forming set was somewhat arrested by a glimpse of Great-Aunt Honoria's bodiless head, sailing dreamily up, over the balcony railings, and into the midst of the orchestra.

With a strangled note and an audible curse, the music ceased.

'Aunt?' Gussie called. 'Pray come down. It is difficult to dance without music, you know, and the poor fellows had no expectation of encountering monstrosities when they agreed to play this evening.'

'Monstrosities!' Honoria retorted, her head appearing over the balustrade. 'I like that!'

She spoke in a belligerent tone, as though greatly offended. But Gussie was sufficiently well acquainted with her great-aunt to understand that the words were a literal truth. 'I know you do,' she said soothingly. 'Come down and dance, if you like. Having announced yourself to the gathering, I am sure no objection could be made to your joining us, even if you have misplaced your feet. And Great-Uncle Silvester could partner you, you know.'

'I have not seen Silvester,' Honoria sniffed, but she did come down, and soon disappeared into the sea of dancers. Whether or not she danced, Gussie could not see, but at least the interruption was ended; after a pause of a few minutes, while the musicians presumably got over their shock, the music began again, and the dancing resumed.

The hubbub of conversation among the dancers and those watching took longer to dissipate. Gussie had heard more than one woman scream, and having spoken so calmly to the horrible apparition, and acknowledged her as aunt, she knew she had thoroughly placed herself beyond the pale.

The reflection did not much discompose her.

'I hope you have asked Miss Frostell to dance, or that you intend to,' Gussie said to Mr. Selwyn, in what was probably a transparent attempt to turn the subject away from her disgraceful relative.

It failed.

'I wonder what it can be like to live at Werth Towers,' said Charles. 'Such occurrences are commonplace, I collect. Your manner proclaims it.'

'Like me, she knows no one in this company, and I would not like to imagine her left without a partner.' Gussie had lost sight of Miss Frostell halfway through her dances with Lord Maundevyle, and had seen nothing of her since.

'Is she a ghost?' said Charles.

'Miss Frostell? Oh, no. She is as alive as you and I.'

His lip curled. 'I believe you know what I meant, Miss Werth.'

'Perhaps I do not choose to discuss it, Mr. Selwyn.'

He handed her through a few more forms without making any other remark, but she did not think this was out of consideration for her wishes. His attention had strayed from her. His head turned this way and that, out of sync with the requirements of the dance, as though he were looking for something.

Or someone, for she saw Lord Maundevyle dancing several couples away, with a lady she did not recognise. It was *he* who had drawn his brother's regard, but for no reason she could imagine, for nothing could exceed the ordinariness of his present behaviour. Nor did his partner seem to be of such dazzling beauty as to merit such attention.

'Does something interest you about your brother, sir?' she said at last, when he continued to ignore her. Really, she would take silence over impertinent questions, but to be outright passed over by one's partner in favour of a close scrutiny of someone else was not to be borne.

Charles's head whipped back around. 'Nothing whatsoever, Miss Werth, I assure you.'

The response was not merely meant to silence her. He spoke with chagrin. 'Were you expecting something of interest to happen?' she asked. 'And you are disappointed that it has not.'

Charles said nothing.

'So, I think, is Lady Maundevyle.'

His smile was acid. 'You appear to possess a penetrating intellect, Miss Werth. I may as well tell you, I find it dashed inconvenient.'

'Though I have failed to penetrate your secrets, so I am not much to be feared, alas.' Gussie, having recalled Lady Maundevyle's strange behaviour, sought her out among those watching the dance. She was not far away; Gussie caught a glimpse of her every time she turned.

She was watching Gussie and Mr. Selwyn with a fixated attention that could only be termed unnerving.

'*Something* is intended,' said Gussie, with a little asperity. 'Something is expected. I can see that perfectly plainly. Will you not tell me what it is?'

He opened his mouth; but whether he had done so with any intention of satisfying her curiosity, or merely of issuing another denial, Gussie was never to know. For all at once, something *did* happen, a something of such shocking magnitude as to arrest the entire ballroom, and bring the dance to an abrupt halt.

And it centred around Lord Maundevyle.

A commotion began in that part of the ballroom, and a bustle. Gussie heard a gasp, and a faint shriek, followed by another scream; and that was Lord Maundevyle's partner backing away from him — turning — fleeing to the far side of the ballroom. Others around his lordship followed the excitable lady's example, leaving an open space clearing around the lord of the house.

Though he was no longer recognisable as Henry, Lord Maundevyle, save that the crimson velvet of his mask identified him.

Gone were his pale skin and dark hair. In their place, scales sprouted; not green, like those adorning the features of Gussie's costume, but the same brash red as his coat. His jaw lengthened and changed, became a long, elegant snout; the handsome coat split apart at the seams and fell away, revealing a body swelling in size, gaining in muscle, Lord Maundevyle's bones audibly flexing and growing.

A protrusion erupted from his back, and another. They grew and spread and billowed out into enormous, sail-like wings, their tops brushing the distant ceiling.

When the process was complete, Gussie found that she had been upstaged as the most magnificent dragon in the room. Lord Maundevyle crouched upon the floor of the ballroom, resplendent in scarlet and wine, his scales glittering in the light of a hundred beeswax candles.

Smoke curled from his nostrils.

He did not long remain tranquil. Some disorder of the mind afflicted him, for he began to violently shake his head, and backed towards the wall, almost squashing several transfixed dancers in the process.

People fled, some of them screaming.

Gussie cast a brief glance at his lordship's mother. She was not much surprised to see an expression of wild triumph upon the lady's countenance; indeed, she radiated a satisfaction so profound, she could almost have levitated upon it.

Gussie took a steadying breath.

Lord Maundevyle's transformation had been expected by no one, least of all him. His shock and horror were perfectly apparent.

Well, Gussie amended, thinking of Lady Maundevyle. No one had expected this but his mother, in all likelihood, and perhaps his siblings. But his frenzied behaviour led her to believe that no one had troubled to inform *him*.

Gussie stepped forward.

'Miss Werth!' Mr. Selwyn caught at her arm, halting her

advance. 'I cannot think it wise for you to approach my brother.'

'He is in distress, sir, and clearly needs help. Were you planning to provide it?'

'He might hurt you—'

'I am the only person here with any experience of Wyrding,' said Gussie firmly. 'I can tell that much from the feeble behaviour of your mother's honoured guests. You will release me.'

Mr. Selwyn did so, albeit with a sneer. 'I hope you will not come to regret this foolhardiness.'

'I trust that your poor brother shall not, at any rate.' Gussie did not waste any more words upon him, but advanced upon Lord Maundevyle. She did take due care, for he had clearly gone from merely aloof to thoroughly dangerous. She had never beheld a fully grown, adult dragon before, and found the experience not a little intimidating. Despite her scornful words, she did not altogether blame those who had hastily departed the scene, nor those who stood transfixed with such fear — or fascination — as to have, apparently, no power of removal.

'Lord Maundevyle?' she said, coming to a stop a few feet before him.

His lordship continued to thrash, his great head swinging from side to side. His silver-gilt claws were making a terrible mess of the tiled floor.

'You will not get it off that way,' she observed prosaically. 'It is not an ill-fitting coat, to be shaken off in a fit of temper.' She folded her arms and stood her ground, even as he opened his great jaws and uttered a vast roar in her general direction.

Someone came up beside her: Miss Frostell. 'This is reckless, my dear,' she commented softly.

'No one else seemed minded to help the poor man. Not even his scheming family.'

'You imagine this to be the intended result?' Miss

Frostell spoke doubtfully, her scepticism plain. 'Surely no one could *wish* such a Wyrding on their own nearest relatives.'

'That is exactly what I imagine,' said Gussie, stepping back out of the way of a flailing claw. The ground shook beneath her, and an unpromising rumble of stonework met her ear. 'Something was obviously meant to happen tonight, and this cannot be mere happenstance. Though what it has to do with *me* I cannot—' She stopped.

'You were just dancing with him, were you not?' said Miss Frostell.

'I was. Our dances ended half an hour ago, but perhaps that need not...'

'What are you thinking, Gussie?'

'I hardly know.' Gussie shook off the half-formed thoughts. 'Now is not the time, Frosty. We have a dragon to tame.'

'Dragon-taming is not numbered among my talents.'

'Nor mine.' And Gussie was nonplussed, for having expressed a desire to help poor Lord Maundevyle, and feeling more than equal to the dangers of attempting to do so, she found herself at a loss. None of her words, whether soothing or scolding, appeared to be making any impression upon his lordship; she doubted whether he had even heard her, such a ruckus was he making himself.

She did not quite dare to touch him. Bold she could be, but she disputed Miss Frostell's use of the term *reckless*. She was not so reckless as to insert herself between the thrashing claws of an enraged — or frightened? — dragon, as yet unused to the new configuration of his limbs.

If only she could reach the vicinity of his head. Up there, he might hear her. But the wings upon her own back were only paper and cloth, and she had not the means to propel herself so much as an inch higher.

She looked about for Lady Maundevyle, but could not see the useless woman. How abominable, to create such a situation, and then abandon her beleaguered child to his unwanted fate! Gussie had no patience with her.

If any of the guests were Wyrded, none of them had shown it. Certainly none of them appeared to have the power to fly.

'Nothing for it,' said she, and, lifting her head, she screamed: 'Great-Uncle *Silvester!*'

'Your aunt, too, perhaps,' commented Miss Frostell.

Gussie added, 'HONOOOORIA!'

To raise one's voice to such a degree might be supremely improper, and bound to earn Gussie the label of *hoyden* at least. But when Lord Maundevyle had spectacularly transformed into a scaled, fire-breathing demon in the midst of a lively country-dance, Gussie knew her own transgressions would be swiftly forgotten. The neighbourhood for miles around would talk of nothing but Lord Maundevyle, the Dragon for months.

A dusty flap of wings alerted her to Silvester's arrival, and something shot past her ear. 'See if you can talk him down, uncle!' she called after him. 'He is out of his senses with shock, poor man, and I fear he may do himself an injury.'

'Or someone else,' said Miss Frostell.

'Yes, though I am less concerned about that,' answered Gussie. 'Anyone who has not sense enough to maintain a clear distance quite deserves to be disembowelled.'

'Would you consider three or four feet as a clear distance?' Miss Frostell took a step back.

Gussie surveyed the scant space between herself and the dragon's front legs, and judged it prudent to take a step back also. 'Obviously I was not including us in such general opprobrium.'

'No, indeed.'

Minutes passed, and it did appear that Silvester's efforts, whatever they were, might be working. Gussie spied a small, granite-dark shape winging its way madly about in the vicinity of Lord Maundevyle's left ear, and under the influence of that dark little presence, the dragon's thrashings grew, gradually, quieter. At length, Silvester was able to perch himself upon the arch of Lord Maundevyle's eyebrow, and the great head came slowly down.

Gussie heard her uncle's voice in a ceaseless, grinding whisper. 'Coquelicot for summer bonnets,' he was saying. 'Splendid hue for ribbon. Daughters all wore it. Quite mad for it, the lot of them. Ratafia? No, no, thank you, don't care for it above half. Do ask Edwina, however. Always did have a taste for the stuff.'

He rambled on in like style, making little sense as far as Gussie could tell, and his conversational topics bore no relation to one another whatsoever. What mysterious effect such nonsense could be having on Lord Maundevyle, Gussie did not pretend to understand; perhaps it was simply that his rasping, near-monotone voice offered a soothing counterpoint to the raging tumult of his lordship's disordered wits. Whatever the truth of it, Great-Uncle Silvester talked on until the great head had sunk upon his forelegs, and he lay crouched and quiet.

'Bravo, Uncle,' said Gussie. 'You always were a fair hand in a crisis.'

Silvester shuffled his granite wings, possibly in satisfaction.

'He looks miserable,' said Miss Frostell.

'Great-Uncle Silvester?'

'No. His lordship.'

He did, at that. Gone was the raging terror of Starminster, like at any moment to break into gouts of devastating flame. In his place skulked a creature overcome with dejection, and without hope of reprieve.

Gussie chanced it. She stepped up, and laid a hand upon the nearest of the great, downed feet before her. Her hand looked small and ineffectual against such overblown size and majesty, and she was not surprised when Lord Maundevyle made no reaction whatsoever.

'*Henry*?' came a shriek at her elbow, and Gussie looked

round to see Clarissa returned from wherever it was she had been. 'Half an hour!' she said next, incomprehensibly. 'I go up to the roof for *half an hour* and this happens? What has become of you!'

Either the familiarity of his sister's voice or its penetrating volume pierced the fog of dejected self-pity surrounding Lord Maundevyle, and he opened one eye. It was a clear, golden eye, most attractive, except for its inordinate size.

'He has discovered his Wyrde,' said Lady Maundevyle out of nowhere, and Gussie rounded on her.

'His Wyrde!' she said. 'Yes! That has been the intention all along, has it not?'

'Long have we lamented the loss of our Wyrde!' proclaimed Lady Maundevyle dramatically. 'The noble Selwyn family, so sadly diminished! Our eldritch powers faded, our arcane might vanished into nothing. Long have I sought the means of reviving our flagging fortunes! Long have I hidden in shame in my own manor, unable to face the world, for who could do otherwise than pity and disdain us in our diminished state?' She stood, arms raised, caught in the grip of some feverish elation, and Gussie could only stare. What was this, a stage? And did she have *no* idea how the world in general perceived those touched by the Wyrde?'

'You should really ask Theo about all this,' she said, folding her arms. 'If he ever returns from the dark hole into which he appears to have crawled.'

Lady Maundevyle ignored this, too. 'Happy day!' she said in a ringing voice. 'Happy hour! The dragons of Maundevyle have returned!'

And to Gussie's immense surprise and horror, Lady Maundevyle made her — *Gussie* — the low obeisance that might ordinarily be offered a queen.

'No,' said Gussie, backing away. '*I* had nothing to do with this! This is an abomination! If you cannot see that Lord Maundevyle wanted nothing to do with the Wyrde, it is plain enough to everyone else!'

'But you had everything to do with it,' said her ladyship, smiling blissfully. 'Sweet scion of Werth, have you still no suspicion?'

Footsteps sounded. Strolling up to his mother's side came Charles Selwyn, looking… altered. Not so profoundly so as his brother, for he was still human, still himself. But there was a suspicion of ferality about his suddenly hawkish gaze, and when he smiled — not a nice smile, he had been taking his cues from Theo — Gussie rather thought that his teeth were longer. Sharper.

Gussie looked from Lord Maundevyle to his brother and back, an unpleasant sensation unfolding in her gut. 'No,' she said. 'I — I danced with them both, and only they, but surely—'

Lady Maundevyle, still smiling — really, by now the expression was making her appear quite mad — held out her own hand to Gussie. 'Clarissa's Wyrde sleeps too deeply to wake,' she said. 'Even with such encouragement as *you* can provide, Miss Werth. But, I beg you. Give but one chance to *me*.'

'You want me to take your hand?' Gussie demanded. 'Is that supposed to be effective of something?'

Lady Maundevyle, a vision of patience, waited.

Miss Frostell stirred at Gussie's side. 'I have often wondered why Lady Werth seemed intent on keeping you at the Towers,' she offered. 'Have not you?'

Gussie had, in fact. Not that her aunt had ever gone so far as to forbid Gussie to leave the grounds, or anything so gothic. But by dint of steady, mild discouragement, and on one or two occasions whisking her away to one or another of the Werths' alternate properties, she had contrived to keep Gussie away from large gatherings such as this. When Gussie had danced before, she had danced with her own cousins, together with one or two scant others chosen from the surrounding families by some logic Gussie had never been privy to. It now dawned on her that her few erstwhile partners had all been plain and unWyrded, and Lady Werth had probably had reason to imagine they would remain so. Like Clarissa.

Gussie stared at her own hands as though they might, at any moment, sprout wings and fly away. Or set fire to her own face. 'You mean,' she said slowly, 'that *I* can call forth the Wyrde?'

'It is a source of constant surprise to me that you should never have known it,' said Lady Maundevyle. 'I cannot think what Georgiana was thinking in keeping it from you. *She* has known it these many years, I assure you.'

'As have you?' Gussie left off examining her own, traitorous hands, and directed a challenging stare at her stark-mad hostess.

'We used to correspond. I heard much of your early escapades, Miss Werth, including your aunt's suspicions upon just this point. You caused a commotion at more than one party, before she realised the nature of your powers.'

Gussie blanched, picturing herself at three or four years old, heedlessly sprinkling Wyrde-curses about like an abominable wish-fairy.

'It is a great gift,' said her ladyship, detecting, perhaps, a distinct lack of joy in Gussie's features. 'I beg you to share it now with me.'

'Lord Maundevyle does not find it so,' she said. 'And look at Mr. Selwyn! The gift was *yours*, my lady, in being free of such a mixed blessing. You were ordinary — respectable — and so was I—' Gussie, choked with shameful emotion, was obliged to leave off speaking.

She felt a touch at her elbow, and turned her head, expecting to see Miss Frostell there. Instead, to her surprise, she found Theo. 'Daresay all will be well, Gus,' he said.

Gussie's composure vanished. 'It will *not!* Lord Maundevyle has turned into a dragon and will die of despair, and it is *my fault!*' She stood, trembling and taking in great gulping breaths, unsure just what had so totally undone her customary self-command.

Theo subjected Lord Maundevyle to an unimpressed scrutiny. 'If he's minded to die, let him get on with it,' he said. 'Feeble of him, but each to their own.'

'*I* certainly shall live,' said Mr. Selwyn acidly. 'But mother will pine away if you do not satisfy her life's wish, Miss Werth. I beg you will not subject us to the agonies of watching her waste away with disappointment.'

'Something must be done about Lord Maundevyle,' said Gussie stubbornly.

'Nothing to be done,' said his brother, utterly without sympathy. 'He is changed, and it cannot be taken back.'

Miss Frostell said, 'I hope he shall not forever be a dragon. It would be inconvenient never again to be a man, and he could hardly take his seat in the House of Lords in that state. Why, the chairs could never be big enough.'

Gussie was surprised into a damp laugh. 'Chairs may be more easily altered than his lordship, I fear.'

'*Miss Werth.*' Lady Maundevyle's show of patience was over. She shook her outstretched hand, a sternly beckoning gesture, and her smile had vanished.

Gussie deliberated. She had not yet had time to accustom herself to her changed identity, nor to consider what this Wyrde of hers truly meant. The transformation she had helped to effect in Lord Maundevyle had deeply shaken her, not to mention that of Mr. Selwyn. Was she prepared to do it again, even if it was at her ladyship's own request?

She reflected, with little satisfaction, on the nature of fate. She had demanded an answer to the mystery of Lady Maundevyle's interest in her; an answer she had received. And now? Much as she might deplore her aunt's apparent decision to keep her ignorant as to her own nature, some part of her also wished futilely for the simplicity of those days. Half an hour as a Wyrded Werth, and already she wished to go back to mundane ordinariness.

Feeble, she told herself.

Right, if Lady Maundevyle wanted to gamble with her own fate, let her bear what consequences might come; Gussie would take no responsibility for it.

'Very well, ma'am,' she said. 'But I must be permitted immediately to go home.'

'I have never sought to keep you here against your will,' said her ladyship.

'Only to *bring* me here against my will. And now I understand the reason why.'

'Couldn't have just paid a visit?' said Lord Bedgberry. 'Mauled Miss Werth about a bit on her own ground, and then cleared off? Would have been simpler.'

'That could never have been proper,' said Lady Maundevyle, rather severely, and Gussie was bereft of any possible response to such a distinction of etiquette.

'Right,' said Theo. 'Naturally not.'

Abruptly wearied of the Selwyns' games, and exhausted in general, Gussie stretched out her hand to her hostess. Whether it was her touch alone that could awaken a sleeping Wyrde, or whether a combination of that and her general proximity, she did not imagine the procedure would take longer than a moment or two. If Lady Maundevyle had it in her to turn Wyrded, she would be forever transformed before the evening was out.

Leaving Gussie free to travel all night if she would, just so long as she was restored to all the familiarity and comfort of her own home before many more days had passed.

And could then confront Lady Werth.

Before her hand met Lady Maundevyle's, however, a sudden surge of motion caught her attention, behind and to the left of her. Scarlet scales flashed and shone; something vast loomed over her; an impact knocked her prone, and left her winded, with a smarting pain in her left side.

She glowered up at Lord Maundevyle, whose claws

proposed to keep her in so humiliating a predicament. 'This is a rudeness beyond anything, sir! I demand that you release me.'

He did not, however. His head tossed, in the grip of some heightened emotion once again (truly, she had not imagined that a mere transformation into dragonkin could effect so profound an alteration upon the taciturn lord's character. Who could have suspected that he possessed such fervent feelings?).

'*Henry!*' shrieked Lady Maundevyle. 'How dare you interfere! Release Miss Werth at once!'

His lordship ignored this as well, and remained unmoved.

Gussie felt his talons tighten around her waist.

'Oh, no,' she whispered, seized by a sudden deep foreboding. 'I *do* hope you are not entertaining any thoughts of—'

Lord Maundevyle reared up, his wings spreading wide, and flapped great gusts of wind over the few remaining guests. Gussie's words ended in a choked scream as she was abruptly borne into the air, his lordship displaying none of his siblings' aptitude for abduction, for she was dangled upside-down, a position of neither comfort nor dignity, and he did not even appear to *notice*.

'*Henry!*' shrieked his mother again, as Lord Maundevyle rose into the air. '*I will have my Wyrde!*'

She was not answered. Amid a resounding splintering and crashing and rumbling of ruined stonework, Lord Maundevyle signalled his opinion of his mother's scheming by destroying the ballroom of Starminster Hall, his enormous bulk tearing down half the wall as he forced his way into the skies. A rush of cool night air upon Gussie's face came as a shock, but not half so much as the experience of being carried aloft, still the wrong way up, her posture affording her an excellent view of the ground as it receded to a distance of twenty feet — thirty — one hundred—

Gussie shut her eyes, and tried to pretend that the thin scream splitting the soft and dulcet evening belonged to somebody else.

ELEVEN

'Augusta will be hopping mad,' commented Miss Frostell into the ensuing silence. 'To be carried off twice in one week! What a heroine of romance! Not even Mrs. Radcliffe could be equal to it.'

'Awfully bad luck,' Theo agreed. 'Think she will want to remain with Lord Maundevyle, too?'

'I can hardly imagine it likely,' said Miss Frostell. 'His lordship could not offer her half the comforts she had enjoyed at Starminster, and there is the matter of propriety to be considered.'

Theo duly considered it. '*Is* it improper, for an unmarried female to be alone with an unmarried dragon?'

Miss Frostell seemed arrested by the question. 'I cannot think how it comes about, but somehow I have never before considered the matter.'

'Unaccountable,' Theo agreed. 'For my part, I think—'

'*Will* you be silent!' said Lady Maundevyle, in a tone of such venom as to shock Theo. Really, she seemed an altogether different person. 'Of course Miss Werth must be recovered, and my son also. They must all be brought back to me, and then we may straighten out this deplorable— mess—' Her words faltered as her eye fell on

106

the ruin of her ballroom, and she swayed on her feet. Her remaining son was obliged to support her, lest she disgrace herself with just such a recumbent posture as Gussie had lately occupied.

'Do not trouble yourself overmuch, Mama,' said the highwayman at her elbow. Heavens, but that was Miss Selwyn's voice. Theo stared.

'It's my belief this whole family is mad,' he declared.

'Charles and I will go after Miss Werth,' Miss Selwyn continued, but she directed at him *such* a smile—! Saucy and knowing and not at all ashamed of herself.

Theo felt a stirring of interest.

'In point of fact,' said Miss Frostell, 'Lord Bedgberry, Lady Honoria and I will go after Miss Werth.'

Miss Selwyn's smile turned into a glower. 'I believe *we* are much more likely to anticipate our brother's movements, Miss Frostell. What, do you mean to trail them all over the countryside?'

'Having spent the last three days of my life doing just that,' said Miss Frostell, 'I had imagined it possible to continue. And, you know, following a scarlet dragon across Somerset must be far easier than tracing a mere coach.'

'It is night,' said Charles Selwyn, baring his teeth at Miss Frostell. 'No one will have seen anything of my brother's flight.'

Miss Frostell folded her arms. 'And where do *you* think he will go?'

'He will go to one of our family's lesser properties, naturally. You cannot be imagined to have any notion what, or where, those are.'

'You might, however, consent to tell me. Our goal is the same; why might not we help one another?'

'Nearly the same,' put in Theo. 'No occasion for bringing Gussie back here. We'll take her home to the Towers.'

Theo did not imagine he had said anything wrong, but

Miss Frostell directed a cold stare at him anyway. 'Thank you, Lord Bedgberry,' she said in tones of ice. 'That is most helpful.'

'Gussie should never have been here at all,' he said coldly. 'Look what's come of it!'

'I do not at all disagree, but to say so just *then*—! You will never make a conspirator, my lord.'

'She has promised Mama a service,' said Charles Selwyn. 'It must be performed.'

Theo showed the fellow his teeth.

Charles's lip curled, displaying an incisor to rival Theo's own. Not the *same* Wyrde, his; Charles was a wilder, feral thing, very *low*, in Theo's opinion. But that he had the might to match Theo tooth-for-tooth could no longer admit of a doubt.

Briefly, Theo heaped curses upon Gussie's head, whose very wilfulness and curiosity had enabled the mad Maundevyle family to achieve these lamentable changes. Then, cursing himself for disloyalty, he said: 'Do as you please, Charles. I shall find my cousin, and take her home, with or without your interference.'

'*We*,' said Miss Frostell.

'Yes, *quite*,' said Great-Aunt Honoria, appearing from somewhere in a flurry of cold wind and fresh blood. 'Your uncle and I have been on the watch, Theo dear, and can tell you in which direction to go.'

Theo bowed to the floating severed head. 'Much obliged, Aunt.'

***

'No.'

Sometime later, when the nightmarish flight had at last drawn to a close, thus spake Gussie. 'This is wholly unsuitable. In fact, it is the worst accommodation with which I have ever been presented.'

Lord Maundevyle had not covered himself with glory, in his first outing as an airborne coachman. Unused to the functions of his wings, and also their unwieldy size, he had achieved a drunken progress from Starminster out into the surrounding countryside, more than once dipping so low in his flight as almost to dash Gussie's brains out on the unforgiving ground below. She had quickly lost track of their direction, or ceased to wonder where they might be going. To endure, with her eyes tightly shut and her breath held against any further screaming, was all that she could venture to attempt.

And now she stood in a cave.

'I do not know where you even contrived to find such an unprepossessing place!' she continued, for railing against the privations of cavernly accommodation suited her better than shrieking at his lordship about his crimes as an abductor (apparently it ran in the family); his failings as a driver; and his total inability to communicate anything whatsoever of his intentions.

'I should count myself lucky to have been set on my feet,' she said, attempting, mostly unsuccessfully, to survey whatever the cave might consider to be its stock of comforts. The moon shed a strong enough light over the woods and fields of Somerset tonight, but little of it filtered in through the cave-mouth, and Gussie could discern scarcely anything at all. Even Lord Maundevyle had faded into shadow, and he was the size of a house.

He had, in fact, come close to dropping her on her head as he had landed before the cave's yawning mouth, saving her only at the last instant, with a lucky catch of his claws. Gussie's gown would never forgive his lordship, but her head had an altogether different perspective.

She heard a grunt, and a sigh, and a shuffling.

'You could not manage a word or two?' she pleaded. 'I can imagine it would be no easy matter, with that mouth, but it would really add immeasurably to my comfort.'

Another shuffling sound.

'I should like very much to know why we are here,' said Gussie. 'If you felt the need to escape your family I could in no way blame you, for it's my belief they are all of them mad. But need I be dragged along with you? If your mother wishes to follow your reluctant example and make a dragoness of herself, or some such thing, that must be her own business.'

A snort.

'Your family loyalty is commendable,' said Gussie mendaciously. 'But I do not think your mother will appreciate this masterful attempt at promoting her welfare. Few ladies would thank you for overriding our decisions, though you are always surprised when we are annoyed by it.'

She did not understand what, of all the things she had lately said, summoned his lordship out of the shadows, but his head erupted out of the depths of the cave, so suddenly as to send her scuttling backwards with a small shriek. He glared at her, his golden eyes hard and unamused, and then — then! — shoved her with his snout.

'Shocking reply!' said Gussie, smoothly correcting her balance. 'But I am right, you know. Your mother will be extremely angry with you.'

He snorted, so forcefully as to send streams of smoke billowing from his nostrils.

Gussie took another prudent step back.

Then, his anger dissipating, he laid his head at her feet and looked up at her with big, doleful golden eyes.

'Oh,' said Gussie, recognising this as an appeal. 'I see. It was not so much your mother you wished to help, but yourself? Is that why you made off with me?'

The enormous eyes blinked once, slowly.

'But what do you imagine I can do for you? I did not precisely turn you into a dragon, and I cannot turn you back again.'

A wistful sigh, expressed in twin puffs of steam.

'Until tonight I had no notion I had any Wyrde at all, and I am still only imperfectly acquainted with what it might be. But it appears I am effective only in encouraging your own Wyrde to rise to the fore, and do with you whatever it will. If you would like it to go away again, well, I believe you are out of luck, my lord.'

The eyes narrowed.

'It may be possible to return to your lordly form, but I have no idea by what means. You will have to manage that yourself.'

Silence.

'Perhaps there are other dragons about, one or other of whom you may ask. The Werths are not the only heavily Wyrded family in England. I am sure there must be another dragon or two, somewhere.'

Silence, but a look of such soulful entreaty that Gussie relented. 'Very well. If it is dancing with me that has done the mischief, I can see if another period of minor contact may reverse it.' After all, until today she had been definitely, certainly unWyrded, with no powers at all. What did she know, about what she now may do?

And it was not as though it was very shocking to touch an unmarried man, if he happened to be wearing the shape of a dragon at the time. She did not think even the highest stickler for etiquette and propriety could fairly fault her for it.

Steeling herself — for the results of her last such experiments, however unwittingly performed, had been undesirably spectacular — Gussie laid a finger upon Lord Maundevyle's long, red-scaled ear. One finger, and just upon the tip.

She was rewarded with another impatient snort.

'Oh, do not be so critical,' she snapped. 'This evening has been rather trying for me as well, you know.' She punctuated her statement by wrapping her hand all the way about the ear and giving it a sharp tug.

He gave a growl, curiously like a dog.

'No complaints,' she said severely. 'You are owed for a great many bruises I need not have suffered, and I might add that this has been by far the least favourite of all the journeys I have ever taken in my life. And that is including the one I recently took under the aegis of your esteemed siblings, so you may imagine how strongly I feel upon the subject.'

Nothing much was happening, however she might maul his ear. She laid both hands on his head for good measure, hardly caring that she poked him in one eye and half covered the other.

A dragon he remained.

'Well, perhaps it will take a little time to come into effect,' she offered. 'After all, you did not become a dragon until some half an hour after our dances. In the meantime, I do not suppose you are hiding any blankets hereabouts, or better yet, a bed? I am shockingly tired, and I collect we are not to be going on to any respectable inn this evening.' She amused herself with a brief reflection as to the likely reaction of the innkeeper, were she to arrive there in company with a dragon.

Or, alone and unattended, which would be far worse.

To her dismay, but not to her surprise, Lord Maundevyle gave a shake of his head.

'It did not even occur to you to consider it, did it?' Gussie scolded, but she was too tired to remain angry now. Her vituperation dissolved into a weary sigh, and she sank down where she stood. 'They say the secret to enduring adversity is to remain cheerful, and hold to an optimistic interpretation of events,' she said. 'So if I can contrive to convince myself that this cold stone floor is in fact the softest of beds, and that the disreputable remains of my poor gown are as good as a warm blanket, I imagine I shall be very comfortable.'

Then, because holding conversations with herself was growing wearisome too, she fell silent. His lordship did not appear minded to do anything about her predicament —

not that she could imagine what he might find to do, under these conditions — and since he had ceased to make any attempts at communication either, she concluded him to be too sunk in either guilt or self-pity to be of further use to her.

All thoughts of leaving the cave she soon dismissed, for where would she go? Lord Maundevyle had flown much too far for her to expect to reach Starminster again tonight, even if she did have some idea of how to get there. And even if there were some village or inn hereabouts, she knew what a welcome she would be likely to receive if she were to try their charity. A lone female, attended by neither husband nor maid, her garments torn and her hair (doubtless) in wild disorder. She would be instantly turned out. Gussie resolved to spare herself the humiliation. A night in a bare cave was as nothing to *that*.

So, she made herself as comfortable as she could against the wall of the cave — which was not very, at all — and ordered herself to see it in the light of a fresh adventure. 'You did, after all, want very much to see something of the world,' she reminded herself. 'Well, here you are, well beyond the borders of Werth Towers, and swept up in an escapade many a young lady would sell her mother to participate in. You might *try* to appreciate it.'

Such reflections could brace her up only so far. They could do nothing to alter the chill of the stone beneath her, nor the absolute impossibility of arranging herself upon it so as to achieve a tolerable repose.

Some hours passed before Gussie fell, at long last, into an uneasy slumber. The snores of Lord Maundevyle had been shaking the walls of the cave long before.

Twelve

'Right,' said Theo, at ten past eleven o'clock the following morning. 'This is hopeless.'

After an uneasy night's sleep and a hasty breakfast, he and Miss Frostell had set out, attended by a severed head and a possessed gargoyle, to find the troublesome Gussie.

To his chagrin, the pessimistic predictions of the abominable Selwyn siblings soon proved correct.

'A dragon?' echoed the owner of a smithy some three miles northwest of Starminster. 'A dragon! I like that! Next he'll be asking me if I've seen horses with wings.'

The man had laughed heartily, and gestured with his hammer for Theo to be gone, taking his foolish questions with him.

Miss Frostell had met with similar treatment in the village of Selington, though to her the proprietor of a haberdasher's shop had been still less polite. Even the appearance of Great-Aunt Honoria's head had been of no use, for while the haberdasher's disbelief in so unlikely a story had, in the face of this vision of undeath, soon dissolved, she had not ceased to scream until Miss Frostell and Honoria both were safely out on the street again.

'You would not think,' said Miss Frostell, looking up at

114

an unforgivingly blue sky, 'that the passage of a dragon would excite so little notice, even if it did occur rather late in the evening.'

'Small wonder,' said Great-Aunt Honoria tartly. 'Ignorance flourishes out in the countryside. Now, if this had happened in town—'

'Aunt,' said Theo. 'You are certain Maundevyle came this way?'

'As much as I can be,' floating farther up and turning in circles, as though she might glimpse a scarlet dragon marauding the countryside at any moment. 'He was heading northwest, but I cannot be certain that he did not change his direction sometime afterwards.'

'He is unlikely to have gone due northwest without cease,' said Theo. 'And if there are no witnesses to be found who can point us in the right direction, then we are at a stand.'

Miss Frostell stared at him, nonplussed. 'At a stand? But you cannot be suggesting that we abandon the pursuit, surely.'

'What else might you suggest, Miss Frostell?' Theo, deprived of a satisfying dinner *or* breakfast and feeling the pinch of his insides, endeavoured not to notice the flush of Miss Frostell's cheeks under the influence of a hot morning and an unaccustomed degree of exertion. The flow of blood beneath that pale flesh was of no relevance to the matter at hand, and not at all tempting—

He looked away, scowling.

'Perhaps a bite of luncheon, my lord?' said Miss Frostell, observing these signs of incipient predation with a tolerant eye. 'It is so difficult to think clearly while suffering from hunger-pangs, is it not?'

Theo took her suggestion, and walked out at once into the fields surrounding Selington.

When he returned, happily replete and only a little bloodied, he did not discover himself to have undergone any significant change of heart.

'Now what have you to say, my lord?' said Miss Frostell, evidently full of hope.

'That we are going home.' Theo had enjoyed a half hour's quiet reflection as he stalked his unsuspecting prey, and had arrived at the only course of action that could make any sense.

'Home! We are to abandon Miss Werth!'

'Yes.' Theo licked a stray drop of blood from his thumb, glowering at Miss Frostell, who only smiled indulgently. 'If she did not wish to be carried off by a dragon, why, she ought to have behaved with greater sense.'

Miss Frostell set both hands upon her hips, a sign even Theo recognised as unpromising.

But it was his great-aunt who said: 'A consequence any woman of the smallest sense ought to have seen coming, we quite agree with you.'

'Now you sound like my cousin,' said Theo.

'Since Gussie herself is not here to flay you with her wit as you deserve, I undertake to perform this duty for her.'

'And you are doing a wonderful job of it.'

'Thank you. You, however, are a blackguard.'

'If Gussie don't wish to remain with Maundevyle, it's my belief she will get herself out of it,' said Theo stubbornly. 'In the meantime, I wish to consult my mother.'

'Lady Werth?' said Honoria, evidently startled. 'What can she have to say to the matter?'

'She is the only one among us who seems to have any understanding of the nature of Gussie's Wyrde,' said Theo. 'And if anyone can outwit the Selwyns, it must be she.'

'If we do not find her, the Selwyn siblings will,' said Miss Frostell. 'And then what? Is she to be dragged back to Starminster yet again?'

'She didn't seem to mind it the first time.'

'That was different. She had not then understood the reason for her abduction, nor the extent of the Selwyn madness. I am persuaded they are all out of their wits.'

Theo, watching as Great-Aunt Honoria turned herself upside-down and sprayed a delicate plume of blood into the air, had no response to offer.

'Lady Honoria?' said Miss Frostell. 'Lord Silvester? Surely you will support me.'

No answer came from Great-Uncle Silvester, not that any sensible answer ought ever to be expected.

Honoria only said, 'I perfectly agree with you, but how do you propose to proceed?'

Miss Frostell opened her mouth, paused, shut it again, and returned her hands to her hips. 'Well!' she said.

Theo waited.

'Perhaps — perhaps there may yet be someone hereabouts who has seen or heard of Lord Maundevyle's passage?'

'I shall wait here while you investigate,' said Theo. 'You will not be much above two or three days about the business, I am sure?'

'Miss Werth has always said that you were abominable,' said the governess.

'No, has she said that?' said Theo.

'I have always sternly disagreed.'

'She was quite right, ma'am: I haven't a single virtue to my name. And now that the point has been established, I invite you to step into the carriage, whereupon we shall return to Werth Towers with all possible haste. See, Jem is quite ready to drive us. My mother ought to be recovered from her indisposition before very much longer, I am sure.'

'And what is Georgiana like to do about any of this?' demanded Lady Honoria.

'That's rather up to my mother, isn't it? But she—'

Theo stopped, for a glimmer of something out of place against the clear blue sky had caught his keen eye. A fire-red something, rapidly drawing nearer.

'What?' said Miss Frostell. 'What is it?' This fatuous

query Theo was not obliged to answer, for she turned herself about to follow the direction of his gaze, and promptly gave a scream (Theo could classify it as nothing else) of satisfaction. 'There! Lord Maundevyle! He must have dear Miss Werth with him.'

But he did not have Gussie with him. His claws, once he drew near enough to tell, were empty. The village of Selington did appear to be his destination, however, for he landed with an inelegant *thud* only some twenty feet away, his wings casting up such a wind as almost knocked Theo off his feet, and stomped away in the direction of a baker's premises some two or three doors off the haberdasher's. Only his head would fit inside the door, but this did not appear to trouble him overmuch. He withdrew it presently, a selection of rolls and pastries held carefully in his jaws, and took to the skies again, oblivious to the tumult he left behind him.

This tumult consisted of yet another round of screams (bakers were no more used to dragons than haberdashers were to talkative severed heads); Miss Frostell's futile attempts to get his attention (though she so far forgot her dignity as to jump up and down in the street, shouting his name); and Great-Aunt Honoria's equally useless endeavour to catch hold of his spine-ridges, and sail along with him back to wherever he had left Gussie.

'I did not imagine dragons to be fond of pastry,' said Lady Honoria, once Lord Maundevyle's stupendous form had once again dwindled away into nothing.

'But perhaps he is in want of familiar food,' said Miss Frostell. 'I imagine *I* should be, in such a state.'

'It will be for Gussie,' said Theo. 'Or is she meant to sup upon fresh-killed venison, like his lordship?'

'Is that what he is eating?' said Lady Honoria, in tones of great interest.

'Smelt it on him,' said Theo shortly.

'I should think the Starminster estate well provided with deer,' Lady Honoria said.

'Slightly less so, soon.'

Miss Frostell had ignored this exchange, standing with her face turned to the winds of Lord Maundevyle's passage. When she began walking, Theo trotted to catch up. 'The carriage, Miss Frostell? It is this way.' He gestured in a quite different direction to the one Miss Frostell had chosen.

'Surely there can be no more talk of returning home?' said she. 'We now know exactly which way the dragon went.' She pointed, and strode on, undeterred by Theo's snort of frustration, nor by his acid comments upon the likelihood of their being at all able to follow in the path of an airborne creature, who need not be at all inconvenienced by such trifles as hills, rivers, or buildings.

'You propose to *walk* all the way?' Theo finished. 'It is like to be a great many miles!'

'Come, Lord Bedgberry, this is spiritless stuff,' said Miss Frostell, calm now that she was sure of her course. 'It is *not* like to be many miles, or why would his lordship choose so poor a place as Selington to make his purchases? I am persuaded we will soon come upon them.'

Since his aunt and uncle seemed to be much of Miss Frostell's mind in the business, Theo yielded, though not with any very good grace.

***

'I must warn you,' Gussie had said earlier in the morning. 'I am like to keel over of hunger before very much longer, and you will have a corpse on your hands. Most embarrassing for you.'

Lord Maundevyle, recumbent still upon the floor of the cave, having scarcely moved since the night before, made no answer.

'Though I am not at all sure that my aunt and uncle might not be better pleased to be rid of me,' she reflected. 'I am an inconveniently Wyrded Werth, as it turns out, and my aunt was perhaps justified in keeping me tucked away at the Towers.'

In the strong light of a sunny morning, she had been able to explore her new quarters more thoroughly, though not much to her satisfaction. The cave was large enough to accommodate so monstrously-sized a creature as a dragon, but had little to recommend it beyond this spaciousness. No hidden depths, no trickling stream, no twisting passageways leading into an unknown network of caverns laced through the Somerset hills. It was just a cave, grey and hard and stony and utterly without interest.

Or sustenance.

'Well,' said Gussie, when his lordship evinced no desire whatsoever to move, 'then I shall have to procure my own breakfast, though I hardly know how I am to do so. Still, obstacles exist in order to spur us into useful activity, and activity leads to growth, does it not? I shall be equal to anything, after this.' So saying, she made her disreputable garments as respectable as she could, acutely aware that she proposed to face her fellow man not only clad in the outlandish costume gown of last night's ball, but a shockingly torn specimen of evening attire at that. She might be taken for a beggar, save that the silks of her gown, however tattered or oddly styled, were too obviously costly.

'I shall doubtless be taken up as a thief,' she remarked. 'And I can in no way assist you from the inside of a gaol. That need not trouble you, however.'

This appeared at last to motivate his lordship, or perhaps her commentary had finally filtered through to his sleep-fogged brain. There came a great rustling and scraping behind her as the enormous creature stirred, and rose; and then, just as Gussie was on the point of exiting the cave herself, Lord Maundevyle stormed past her, and

120

with an athletic leap hurled himself into the sky. He was even too generous to swipe her with his tail on his way past, or to contrive, "accidentally", to jostle her into the dirt.

'Excellent,' said Gussie, satisfied, and sat down again to wait.

When Lord Maundevyle returned, some half an hour later, Gussie had migrated to the thready grasses immediately before the cave, and sat sunning herself. The hour was some way advanced, which suggested she had slept longer and deeper than might have been imagined possible, under the circumstances. Weariness must be the cause, and the shock she had sustained the night before. She felt very well now, or she would as soon as her gnawing hunger pangs were satisfied.

'Welcome back, my lord,' she greeted him as he swooped in to land, setting up a thunderous shaking of the earth beneath the impact of his enormous feet. He needed a little practice, though he might never prove a graceful flyer. 'I half thought you might be disposed to leave me here forever.'

Lord Maundevyle snorted, and dropped several somethings at Gussie's feet.

'Nor would I have been altogether inclined to blame you,' said she, browsing through his lordship's offerings. 'I have, after all, been as troublesome as I possibly could.' He had brought her a selection of fare from some local pastry-cook's shop, she observed, and though it was in no way refined stuff — simplicity itself — it was fresh and smelled like heaven. Surreptitiously discarding those one or two things most liberally bedewed after a sojourn in the dragon's mouth, Gussie disposed of the rest at top speed.

She caught Lord Maundevyle watching her as she ate.

'I know,' she said in between mouthfuls. 'I am not at all a ladylike diner. But then, you know, I am ravenously hungry.'

The great golden eyes blinked, unimpressed.

'I see your table manners have left a lot to be desired, yourself,' Gussie added, for the dragon's jaws bore traces of some fresh kill, messily consumed.

Lord Maundevyle abruptly turned away his head, and pawed at his face, without much effect.

'Do not trouble yourself,' said Gussie. 'I have spent too long living in close proximity to Lord Bedgberry, to feel at all disconcerted by a little blood.'

The dragon ceased his ineffectual ablutions, and curled up. He soon fell into a half-doze in the golden sun, and Gussie was tempted to join him. After all, what more was there to do at this moment? To return to Starminster must be the only sensible goal she could have, but the problem of finding it did not strike her as any more soluble this morning than it had last night. Werth Towers, of course, was utterly out of reach.

'Will you take me back to Starminster?' she tried. 'I should be very grateful to you. Young ladies were not made for impromptu adventures in the wilderness, without maid or chaperon, or a cook either. And it is *too* absurd for us to go on this way much longer, both of us dressed in dragon-suits, and only one of us making a convincing display of it.'

The dragon snorted. He had done so before, but on none of those occasions had it sounded nearly so much like laughter.

'I do assure you that I cannot change you back,' Gussie said. 'And since being near me appears to have done the mischief in the first place, I can only assume that a prolonged sojourn in my company could only make it worse. Five more minutes and you shall be a dragon for the next five hundred years.'

Lord Maundevyle was trying to communicate. Gussie was almost sure of it. His jaw worked in the oddest way; he spat; he *appeared* to be chewing his own tongue; and at last he emitted a hoarse croak, like a whole pond-full of frogs in full voice.

'No,' she sighed. 'It's no use. None of those things in any way resembled words.'

His lordship stamped a foot.

'Yes, it is terribly frustrating,' Gussie agreed. 'Let me see if I can guess at what you are trying to say. You remain convinced that, since I have been the instrument of your doom, I must also be the instrument of your salvation?'

The dragon nodded his head, but hesitantly.

'Partially correct? Hm. You cannot think your family holds the solution, or we would be back at Starminster, not picnicking in this charming glade.'

A furious nod.

'Ah! I have it. You mean to hold me captive until my family arrives to extract me, and the price of my freedom shall be your return into manly form.'

Another enthusiastic nod, taking Gussie aback. 'I spoke in jest,' she said. 'You cannot be serious?'

Lord Maundevyle was completely serious.

'There must have been some grave mismanagement in the upbringing of the Selwyn siblings,' she mused. 'And while I have not the smallest doubt that your mother has not a sensible idea left in her head, I cannot imagine what she did with the three of you that has given you so collective a freak for kidnappings. And while,' she added, cutting off his lordship's latest attempt at enunciation, 'I can be fairly said to have colluded in my own carrying-off, at least your brother and sister had the courtesy to abduct me to a place of comfort! I refuse to remain here!'

So saying, she got up from the grass, gathered her shredded skirts around her, and marched away in the approximate direction from which she had seen Lord Maundevyle returning. Yes, she would inevitably meet with difficulties and condemnation in her present state, if she should happen to find the village he had robbed of bread and pastry; but to continue blithely sunning herself while Lord Maundevyle hatched such absurd schemes was in no way tolerable.

'My family,' she called back, 'may know of some way to assist you. Goodness knows but what we have more experience with the Wyrde than anyone. But *this*, sir, is not the way to solicit their goodwill.'

She more than half expected to be stopped, and hauled back, but she proceeded some little distance without encountering any resistance at all. Surprised, she paused, and looked once over her shoulder.

Lord-Maundevyle-as-dragon lay in his cave, his chin on his front feet, watching her leave with great, sad eyes.

'Absolutely not,' she said. 'I will not permit you to manipulate my sympathies! Not that it would avail you anything at all if I did. I undertake, sir, to apprise my uncle and aunt as to the nature of your plight, and if any aid is available to be sent to you, I daresay they will be happy to oblige.'

Lord Maundevyle still remaining motionless, Gussie proceeded on her way.

'Oh, Theo,' she said two minutes later, having almost collided with a tall and ominous cousin angrily on the march.

'Oh, there you are, are you?' said he. 'Quite free, as I told you!'

This last he directed over his shoulder at Miss Frostell, whose dear and sympathetic countenance broke into a smile of such relief upon seeing her that Gussie could almost have collapsed, weeping, all over her.

Which, naturally, would never do.

'I hope you have the carriage with you?' she said. 'The day has been unusually trying.'

'We have not,' bit out Theo. 'Miss Frostell having insisted upon pursuing you on foot.'

'Well,' said Gussie stoutly. 'She was perfectly right, I daresay, for you could hardly have brought the carriage over all this uneven ground. Still, I hope it is waiting at no great distance? I should like very much to be at home, and without further delay.'

'*There* we agree,' said Theo savagely.

'Lord Bedgberry has not much enjoyed his morning,' said Miss Frostell. 'I am sure he is overcome with delight at seeing you safe and sound, my dear.'

'He will properly express his feelings as soon as he has got over his tantrum,' came the voice of Great-Aunt Honoria from somewhere.

'*Tantrum?*' bellowed Theo.

'He never did like being away from the Towers,' Gussie said, by way of apology for her cousin's behaviour. 'He always comes back in a rage, but he will soon calm himself once he is at home.'

'You have left the dragon to fend for himself, I see?' said Great-Aunt Honoria, choosing that moment to rise, ghoul-like, from the grass. 'Very wise, I am sure.'

'He had some idea of holding me hostage,' said Gussie. 'I took exception to the notion. Twice in one week is the outside of enough.'

'But you are not captive now?'

'Oh, no.'

'You fought your way free,' said Theo, 'by some means I cannot guess at, but which was no doubt heroic.'

'Well,' Gussie hesitated. 'I walked away.'

'Ah?'

'And his lordship did not seek to prevent me.'

'An unusually obliging kidnapper.'

Gussie could only agree, for in comparing his behaviour with that of his brother and sister, he featured as a remarkably inept abductor. Or perhaps only a half-hearted one.

Thinking back over their one-sided conversation, a terrible thought struck Gussie.

'He was not serious!' she said. 'He had no thought at all of detaining me.'

'Lord Maundevyle?'

'He was joking me! And looked grave as a judge while he did it. Why, I had not thought him capable of it.'

'He *did* carry you off, however,' Miss Frostell pointed out.

'Yes, and that was rude. I believe he imagined that *I* had turned him into his present draconic shape, and thought that, were he to extract us both from the chaos of the ballroom, perhaps I would be able to reverse the procedure. Naturally I was devastated to disappoint him.'

'Naturally,' murmured Great-Aunt Honoria. 'And what does he now mean to do?'

'I have not the first idea,' said Gussie, smoothing the shreds of her scaled gown. 'I left him in his cave, drowning, I believe, in self-pity.'

'He must come with us,' said Great-Aunt Honoria, and without waiting for a reply, she drifted off in the general direction of Lord Maundevyle's cave.

'He will never fit in the carriage!' Gussie called after her aunt. 'And he will terrify the horses!'

Honoria did not respond.

'She is right, of course?' said Miss Frostell. 'He cannot be left as he is. It would be inhumane to abandon him.'

'For my part, I am tired of every one of the Selwyns,' retorted Gussie. 'A dragon for an heir is what Lady Maundevyle wanted, and it is what she has got. Let *her* manage the business.'

'That is precisely why his lordship ought not to be left at her mercy,' said Miss Frostell. 'It is not what *he* wanted, that much seems clear. And her ladyship has not the resources to manage the matter sensibly.'

'You mean because her ladyship is ignorant, and incidentally, off her head?'

'I could never express myself with such a want of tact.' Miss Frostell was severe.

'My aunt will not be pleased,' Gussie warned.

'I believe she will be thankful to have you back,' said Theo, 'even bringing a miserable dragon in your train.'

And so the whole party departed almost immediately for Werth Towers, coaxing the dejected Lord Maundevyle

126

along in their wake, and heartlessly abandoning his hapless siblings to wander the countryside in a futile search for their brother.

Thirteen

'I will take a gun out later,' announced Great-Uncle Silvester, as the Werth carriage drew up outside the doors of the Towers.

'Oh, hush,' said Great-Aunt Honoria, wafting out of the window.

Gussie stepped down as soon as a footman opened the door for her, and sought at once for a glimpse of Lord Maundevyle. The journey had been rather slow, and fraught with difficulties, not the least of them being the problem of transporting the dragon. He was far too large to travel via carriage, not even to balance atop the roof, so he had been obliged to use his own wings. But keeping him within sight of the carriage, or vice versa, was no easy task when the horses were unused to such company, and showed themselves inclined to take violent exception to it. His lordship, not knowing the way, had trailed along at some distance behind — which worked splendidly, except that halfway through the second day they had lost him altogether for a period of three and a half hours, and had found him at last engaged in entertaining a small flock of sheep, with demonstrations of the efficiency of his talons and his teeth. Harried, Gussie had scolded him into a cessation of his predations, consoling herself with the notion that she might, once arrived at the Towers, send compensation to the farmer.

Fixing upon some convenient inn each night had been no easy matter either, for Gussie herself had no luggage with her, and was forced to borrow from Miss Frostell; and since neither of them possessed a maid, or any other attendant, and were seen to be travelling with a single gentleman, a stone grotesque, and a severed head, their welcome at such establishments had been scant. Poor Theo had resolved the matter by quietly terrorising the landlords into offering rooms, which she knew he hated to do, and his mood had soured on each subsequent occasion he was forced to do it.

Gussie, therefore, beheld the familiar stone-and-brick walls of the Towers with a sense of such relief, she did not think she would even be *too* incensed with her aunt Werth. Here was safety and acceptance, even if she might deplore the secrecy that had, in part, made it so.

Lady Honoria wasted no time in spreading the news, for the family soon came running. Gussie's heart sank a little on perceiving Aunt Wheldrake coming first out into the courtyard, in full, thunderous flow, but her interest settled not on Gussie but Lord Maundevyle, who had claws enough to defend himself; she felt no uneasiness on that score. Uncle Wheldrake followed in his wife's wake, and then Lady Werth appeared.

Theo promptly vanished into the depths of the Towers, and was not seen again for some hours.

'Gussie!' said Lady Werth. 'I have but just received your letter yesterday, and had not the smallest notion of how to proceed — good heavens, what is that you are wearing? Miss Frostell is with you, I perceive, and what of Theo…?'

'Probably disappearing into his own rooms as we speak,' said Gussie. 'And barricading the doors.'

Lady Werth dismissed Theo with a wave of her hand. 'He will be well enough, there,' she decided, and directed at Gussie a searching look, and a close scrutiny, as though she expected to see some profound change come upon her niece, reflected somehow in her personal appearance. 'And you, Gussie? Are you— well?'

'If by that you mean, have I emerged from Somerset leaving a trail of disaster behind me, then yes, Aunt. You see the results approaching through the south gate.'

Lady Werth transferred her gaze to the end of the driveway, but her blank expression informed Gussie that their attendant dragon was not there.

Since a shadow at that moment darkened the sun, Gussie glanced up. 'Or, indeed, from above.'

Lord Maundevyle landed in a spray of earth and loose stones, and the ground shook.

'Oh,' said Lady Werth faintly. 'Oh, dear.'

'His lordship is not desirous of maintaining his Wyrded state,' Gussie said later, restored once more to one of her favourite muslins, and engaged in dispatching a quantity of cakes and wine in her aunt's personal parlour. Tea might more ordinarily be served at such an hour of the afternoon, but Lady Werth, perceiving a degree of strain in her niece not at all usual, had decreed that the occasion called for the "special provisions". The cook, it seemed, had known exactly what she meant.

'For that matter,' Gussie continued, feeling strengthened with every sip and bite, 'I am not altogether satisfied with the nature of my own Wyrde. Some day or another I will have to ask you why you did not tell *me*, at least, but I can quite see why you did not especially want to announce it to the world at large. It is highly inconvenient, and can only make me splendidly unpopular.'

'Except, it seems, with Lady Maundevyle,' said Lady Werth, gliding past Gussie's implied question.

'Yes, but she is quite mad. We were all agreed upon it.'

'Is she, indeed? Why do you think so?'

'Why, to solicit a return of the Wyrde, and across her

whole family! She was not even cast down when her eldest son grew talons two inches long, and teeth to give any reasonable person nightmares. I ask you, who but a madwoman would sacrifice the respectability of their family in exchange for the Wyrde? And such a Wyrde, at that! Mr. Charles Selwyn is at least half animal as well, I am sure of it, though I he is not of the draconic type, like his brother.'

Lady Werth spent a few moments in silent reflection. 'She was always fascinated by our family's history,' she said at length. 'I regret imparting my suspicions as to *your* Wyrde to her, many years ago, but I trusted her at the time. Indeed, she was one of few who not only treated me with unreserved warmth, but who actively sought my acquaintance. I was newly married to your uncle, then.'

'But you stopped corresponding with her?'

'Yes.' Lady Werth hesitated. 'I realised at last that it was not precisely me she sought, but a connection with the family into which I had so lately married. That the extent of her fascination with all things Werth, and indeed all things Wyrde, went rather beyond the reasonable. It made me uneasy.'

'Were you very angry, aunt, when you imagined me to have disobeyed your prohibition, and gone into Somerset anyway?'

To Gussie's surprise — so confidently was she expecting an affirmative — her aunt smiled, an expression of high mischief. 'On that point I was never deceived,' she said. 'Miss Selwyn's letter being a paltry device, and besides, Honoria was on the watch, and saw what had happened. At first I was very frightened for you; not because I imagined you to be in any danger from the Selwyns, but because I foresaw some small part of what has ultimately happened. But upon returning to myself, I began to think differently.' She took a sip of wine. 'If Lady Maundevyle was so anxious to engage with the Wyrde, well, let her do so. I did not imagine her much of a match for you and Theo.'

'No one is a match for Theo, poor boy,' Gussie sighed. 'I left her esteemed ladyship rather angry, though. She wanted me to awaken her own Wyrde, as well as those of her sons, and I was — prevented.'

Lady Werth raised an enquiring brow.

'Lord Maundevyle set himself against it. As you can imagine, he can be persuasive.'

Lady Werth's eyes twinkled. 'But why have you brought him *here*? Not that he is not entitled to claim our hospitality, since his state is *somewhat* of our doing. But I hardly know what it is we will do with a twenty foot dragon.'

'Turn him back into his human state,' said Gussie. 'That is what he wants, I believe. We had both hoped that you, or my uncle, might have some idea as to how the Wyrde might be— discouraged, again.'

'We do not,' said Lady Werth, setting down her emptied glass. 'No one but you, Gussie dear, could ever imagine we might wish to.'

'Not— not even Theo?'

'There are drawbacks to Theo's condition, certainly. But he would not be Theo without it, would he?'

A reflection which rendered Gussie speechless, for a short time. She had always felt that Theo detested his Wyrde, and would cheerfully give it up if he could. But when had he ever said so himself? She had only felt that *she* would be glad to be rid of such a Wyrde, were it hers. But Lady Werth was right. Theo was Theo.

Gussie sighed. 'Still, I cannot but be disappointed.' She spoke with regret for herself, as well as Lord Maundevyle. The general prohibition against the world imposed by her aunt, she would now have to impose upon herself. She could not wander about the country, attending dances and balls hither and thither and leaving a trail of Wyrded destruction behind her. Few people would see the matter as Lady Maundevyle did; she would become a pariah. 'Shall he always remain a dragon, then?'

'I cannot say. I believe there have been one or two dragons among the Werths, but not for a great many years.'

'What of Margery?' said Great-Aunt Honoria, causing Gussie to startle, for she had not known her to be in the room.

Lady Werth looked up, frowning. 'Honoria, I believe we have spoken about eavesdropping?'

'I believe we have,' said Lady Honoria placidly.

Lady Werth sighed. 'Who is Margery?'

'A dried old stick of a thing even when I was a girl,' said Honoria. 'But dragons do live a tiresomely long time.'

Gussie sat up. 'Margery Werth?'

'She would be your grandmother,' said Great-Aunt Honoria. 'Some seven or eight times removed.'

'But that is perfect!' said Gussie. 'I am sure she could help Lord Maundevyle. At the very least, she may be able to communicate with him, which is more than any of the rest of us have managed to do.'

'And where is she to be found?' said Lady Werth.

'You cannot imagine that *I* have any notion.'

Aunt Werth was observed to direct an exasperated look up at the ceiling, and may have gone so far as to mutter something unflattering under her breath.

'I am dead, not deaf,' snapped Great-Aunt Honoria.

Lady Werth rose gracefully from her seat, with an air of purpose about her that instantly arrested Gussie's attention. 'I am going,' said she, 'to consult the Book.'

'Is that safe?' Gussie said doubtfully. 'Uncle has but just recovered the use of his left hand.'

'We will not involve your uncle.' Lady Werth swept out without another word, trailed by Great-Aunt Honoria's head. Gussie set aside her misgivings, repressed likewise a thrill of excitement, and followed in her train.

FOURTEEN

Some said that the Book was haunted by the spectres of past Werths. Some said a former Werth had *become* the Book; that it was, itself, the product of the self-same Wyrdings that were recorded within.

If the latter was true, Gussie reflected, whoever it had been was not best pleased about it.

Beneath the great, massed pile known as Werth Towers was a set of cellars. The upper cellars were devoted to the storage of wines, as is usual, and liberally haunted with the spectres of past relations, which is not. These did not trouble Lady Werth or Gussie overmuch; most of them were thin, faded things whom only Nell could reach. Great-Aunt Honoria, though, was a different matter.

'Watch where you are going,' she snapped, as the exploratory party reached the bottom of the cellar stairs. And, 'I heard that, Archibald!'

That would be Gussie's great-great-grandfather's youngest brother, if she did not misremember her family tree.

'Yes! Well!' barked Honoria. 'Your wife had two heads, but you don't catch me mentioning it!'

'Honoria,' murmured Lady Werth. '*Do* try to act with a

little decorum.'

Great-Aunt Honoria sniffed, and sailed past her ladyship down into the second level of the cellar. 'Provoking creatures,' she snarled. 'And Archie was never even handsome.'

She whisked ahead down a wide passage lit with bright, new gas lamps, unaffected by the chill — or perhaps the atmosphere — which raised the hairs on Gussie's skin. Pausing before the forbidding aspect of a huge, heavy door of solid oak, bound with black iron hinges, she bobbed up and down with impatience. 'Quickly, quickly!' she said. 'The Book!'

Lady Werth appeared serene as she approached the door, drew back the bolts, and unlocked it with an enormous iron key. But Gussie, who knew her aunt well, detected tension in the line of her jaw, and the rigidity of her posture.

Gussie was not perfectly composed herself, and suffered a racing heart and a thrill of horror as she entered the room at her aunt's side.

The Book of Werth lay on a pedestal in the centre of a stone-walled room otherwise bare, save only for the lamps set into the walls. It did not move, nor did it offer any reaction to the entrance of three visitors at all, and Gussie permitted herself the hope that it might be in one of its better moods.

'Shut the door, Gussie,' murmured her aunt, passing her the key.

'Naturally,' Gussie returned. 'What could be more sensible than to lock the three of us in with the Book?' But she obeyed, for she knew that letting the Book *out* could be more disastrous than locking anyone *in*.

Only once the door had clanged shut behind them, and the key scraped in the lock, did Lady Werth approach the pedestal. Honoria soared up into the air, affecting unconcern, but a thin trail of blood leaked from the ragged edges of her severed neck.

A droplet of it fell onto the covers of the Book.

A low snarl rolled through the room.

Undeterred, Lady Werth seized the Book, and swiftly opened it.

Gussie had seen the thing before, some once or twice, and felt no need to examine it closely now. It was a manuscript of advanced age, its pages bound some centuries before. Being as thick through as the span of Gussie's hand, it possessed plentiful space for the family records it contained: one page for every Werth who survived past their third birthday.

Lady Werth had brought a pen with her, Gussie now saw: a majestic object, made from the feather of some exotic bird in hues of crimson and gold. She dipped the tip in a pot of red ink, and began writing on a fresh page. Lizzie's entry, Gussie saw: a new gorgon among the ranks, her powers recorded for posterity.

Aunt Werth had not written more than five or six lines when the Book snarled again, and bucked, causing a red blot of ink to blossom over the page.

'Gussie,' said she, and there was winter in the word. 'Pray assist me.'

Gussie took one side of the Book and her aunt the other. Between them, they contrived to wrestle the enraged Book into submission, and Gussie held her half of the tome in place as her aunt continued, calmly, to write.

But waves of icy-cold were emanating from Lady Werth, and Gussie shivered.

'Good,' said her ladyship in due course, and turned a few pages back. Gussie tried not to notice as a slim, scaled tentacle slithered from between the pages, and coiled itself lazily around her own wrist.

She was startled to observe that her aunt had opened up Gussie's own page in the Book; and also to note that there was not, as yet, much written there.

'What about Margery?' barked Great-Aunt Honoria. 'You had better hurry, Georgie, if you don't want to lose a finger.'

'In a moment,' murmured Lady Werth, writing more quickly now.

'It is empty,' said Gussie. 'My page.'

'When you turned three,' said her aunt, her pen scratching away, 'we imagined you unWyrded. It was only later I began to suspect the truth, and I was never certain enough to record it in the Book. You see, Gussie, you are unique among the family; possibly in the whole of England. I have never heard of such a Wyrde as yours.'

Gussie blinked, silenced.

'In a way, then, I am grateful to Lady Maundevyle. It is a pity for you, perhaps, but it is well to be certain of the facts of the matter. Now we may determine how best to proceed.'

'You could not have mentioned it to me somewhere these past twenty years?' Gussie said.

'Had I been certain, I might have.'

'Had you let me out more often, you might have had this certainty sooner.'

'At whose expense, if I was right?' Lady Werth directed a swift, cool look at her niece. 'Yours, undoubtedly; and that of some hapless soul who might rather have gone on unWyrded.'

'Like Lord Maundevyle.'

Lady Werth sighed. 'It is a pity he and his mother could not agree. The younger Selwyn seems unperturbed.'

'The younger Selwyn is not precisely a model of good judgement.'

'Good judgement consists of accepting the truth about oneself, however much one might sometimes deplore it.'

'I cannot altogether blame his lordship for regretting the loss of his hands. Or his coats. Or his capacity to enjoy toast and tea without destroying the dining-room.'

Gussie's entry completed, Lady Werth put away her pen and began briskly to turn pages, ignoring the Book's growling with admirable serenity.

'I do think we ought to hurry, Aunt,' said Gussie uneasily, feeling a tremor shoot through the pages under her hands. The tentacle coiled about her arm tightened, and declined to be scraped off.

'We have almost finished,' said Lady Werth. 'I want only to find Margery's pages — yes, here they are.' She had turned a long way back through the Book, not far from the beginning, and the vellum under her fingers was crisp and yellowed with age. 'A dragon! You were right, Honoria. Turned upon her third birthday…' She read on.

But Gussie pointed at the sentence her aunt had just read. 'It says *first* turned, Aunt. Does that not suggest that she had occasion to turn draconic a second time, and perhaps more? In which case, she must have had the capacity to change *out* of it again.'

'Nothing is explicitly said to that effect, but you are quite right. It is implied.' She finished skimming through Margery's entry, at a speed Gussie wondered at, for the writing was tiny and crabbed and faded. She herself could scarcely make out two words in every three.

'She lived in the cellar,' said Lady Werth, her brows rising in surprise. 'Perhaps in these very rooms, and a hoard was kept here for her amusement. Is that not nice?'

'Delightful,' Gussie murmured. 'If we contrive to strip the Towers of all of its valuables, I am sure we could get up just such another for Lord Maundevyle's entertainment.' As she spoke, her glance strayed back towards the unreasonably large door, whose unwieldy proportions now made rather more sense.

Lady Werth shut the Book and backed quickly away from it. A sheen of ice glimmered upon her cheek. 'Now, I think we had better return above. The key, Gussie?'

'I appear to be attached,' said Gussie, for both her arms were now wound about with tentacles, and she was being drawn, slowly but inexorably, nearer to the Book.

'Oh, dear,' said Lady Werth, and advanced upon Gussie. 'This is *just* what happened to Aunt Beatrice.' She set herself to unwinding the tentacles around Gussie's left arm, though they furiously resisted her efforts.

'She's been seen since, I suppose?' said Gussie, striving to keep her voice even.

'Oh, yes,' said Lady Werth. 'That is, I am almost sure of it... ah, there.' The grip on Gussie's arm fell away, and she began at once to work on those still pinning her right arm to the pedestal. But even as she worked, something chilly slithered around her leg, and her aunt's wrist.

'Very well,' said Lady Werth, and a puff of frost erupted from between her lips as she spoke. 'Nothing else for it. Honoria?'

Something of bright metal, sharply agleam, fell from above: a small axe with a wicked blade. Lady Werth caught it in her free hand, and swung it without hesitation at the tentacles still woven around Gussie's arm. The axe missed her skin by a hair's breadth and sliced mercilessly through the Book's appendages.

A terrible, hair-raising shriek split the air.

Unfazed, Lady Werth performed the same operation twice more, freeing her own arm and Gussie's leg. Gussie at once backed away from the pedestal, and barely caught the axe as her aunt hurled it towards her. She hefted it as she threw back the key, and stood guard over the Book while her aunt grappled with the door.

'I really must send somebody down to oil this lock,' said Lady Werth coolly, as the door swung open.

Something slithery made a grab for Gussie. She hacked about with the axe, slicing through flesh, and as the Book keened and roared with rage she fled the grasp of its reaching tentacles and made for the door with all speed.

Once safely restored to the other side, its comforting wooden weight firmly closed and bolted, Gussie hung the axe upon a small hook by the door, resettled her rose shawl about her shoulders, and smoothed her gown. Livid red welts were fast appearing upon the bare skin of her arms, everywhere the Book's appendages had grasped at her. 'I should think *I* would not much like to be a book, either.'

'That is no excuse for bad manners,' Lady Werth said, taking a deep breath. 'I believe tea is in order.'

'Something warming, certainly,' Gussie agreed, watching as frost crept over her aunt's hair, and crusted upon her eyelashes.

'I shall be well in a moment,' said Lady Werth, and swept up the stairs.

Gussie followed, leaving Honoria camped outside the Book's prison, crooning endearments through the door.

***

Nothing but a vast hunger could have forced Theo out of his tower, having been deprived of it for so many days. But such a hunger came upon him eventually. Late in the afternoon, when the sun slanted golden across the clear lawns of the Towers and the thunder of Aunt Wheldrake rolled sulkily away, Theo ventured down the many stairs, and out. He went with rolled-up sleeves and no coat, the temperature being high; and *now* he need not trouble himself about propriety of dress. No one to see him out here, and the rabbits wouldn't care.

He stalked across the pristine lawns and into the taller grasses behind, running his hands through their feathery tops as he passed. Odd, for his senses discerned little that was alive, and there ought to be plenty for dinner at that hour—

A flash of crimson scales materialised between the grassy stems, and a bulky, ungainly dragon-shape appeared.

Theo growled.

'When you have been here a little longer,' said he, 'you will come to understand what everybody else here knows, and that is that this is my — promenading ground.'

Lord Maundevyle sat with a stalk of grass sticking out of his mouth, doing his best to chew it with teeth made rather for ripping and tearing. He did not appear chastened.

'Not that I am so overpoweringly fond of rabbit,' Theo said, glowering. 'Only it wouldn't be the done thing to snack upon one's relatives, now would it? Not even in *this* family. And that, my lord, is exactly what I shall be obliged to do if you go on scaring off my dinner.'

Lord Maundevyle spat out the grass, and heaved a sigh.

'Not that anyone would object were I to inconvenience Aunt Wheldrake, only it isn't *done*. You understand?'

Lord Maundevyle gave no sign of doing so.

'What are you doing here, anyway?' said Theo, walking a suspicious circle around the dragon. 'Dragons don't eat grass, and I hope you are not expecting to survive upon rabbit. There aren't nearly enough to feed both of us.'

The dragon's head drooped, and he snapped irritably at Theo as he walked past.

'Ohh,' said Theo. 'Couldn't catch one? Dear me. And too polite to begin on my uncle's sheep?' He stopped again before Lord Maundevyle, and considered the sorry sight. 'You had better come with me,' he decided. 'We'll see what the kitchen can scrounge up for you.'

Another two minutes saw him halfway back across the lawns, the dragon lumbering along next to him. 'Leave my promenading spot alone,' Theo said severely. 'Or we shall both starve to death. Not but what they would oblige me in the kitchens, for there's always something going. But it isn't fresh, and the one time I ventured upon a kitchen-maid, mother kicked up such a fuss! Unjustly, too, for the girl volunteered. Wouldn't take no for an answer, in fact.'

Lord Maundevyle snorted, which Theo decided to take as sympathetic commiseration.

'Doubtless my ancestors had an easier time of it,' Theo glowered. 'Nobody objected to Lord Anthony swanning

141

about the countryside, feasting upon the peasantry. I was born in the wrong time, Maundevyle.'

The dragon snorted again, and to Theo's indignation, this time he could take it for nothing other than laughter.

He encountered his mother so immediately afterwards as to cause him a moment's discomfort. 'Hallo, Mother,' he said, with a sideways glance at Lord Maundevyle. 'Er — been there long?'

'No,' said she, blandly.

Lady Werth was in the shrubbery, taking the sun. Gussie wandered along at her side, all solicitous attention. Small wonder, either, for Mother appeared halfway to an icicle already.

'What's happened to upset you?' said Theo.

'You would not have enjoyed the sixteenth century, Theo,' said his mother without answering.

'I think he would have enjoyed it far too much,' said Gussie. 'And been burned at the stake as a consequence.'

Theo's gaze sharpened upon the thin arms tucked under the fine fabric of his cousin's rosy shawl. Red marks. 'Good God!' he cried. 'You have not consulted the Book?'

'It was necessary,' said Lady Werth.

'Not that it has availed us much,' said Gussie. 'Margery Werth was indeed Dragon-Wyrded, and while it is implied that she may have been able to change herself out of it again, we are no nearer to discovering where she might be, or how she might have contrived to do it.'

'I should be surprised if she is still alive,' said Theo. 'Surely she would be here, if she was.'

'Why?' said Gussie.

'Well—' Theo groped for an answer.

Gussie waited, but Theo had nothing to add. 'If you are taking his lordship to the kitchens,' said Gussie, 'which from all your talk of starving to death I collect you are, I should get on with it. Especially if you want anything raw.'

'Why did not you take me along?' Theo demanded, reverting to the subject of the Book.

'Of what use would you have been?' Gussie folded her arms, in no way attempting to cover up the crimson evidence of her foolishness.

'Wouldn't have those welts, if you had,' Theo said. 'Nor would you be icing over, Mother.'

'You are bosom buddies with the Book, of course; with you, it is docile as a lamb,' said Gussie.

'No,' said Theo, and that was all he said, but he smiled, and was gratified to see Gussie shudder a little.

'Very well,' she said. 'Next time, you may have the axe. But if I emerge with any of my fingers missing, I shall be taking some of yours in recompense.'

Theo flexed the fingers in question. 'No fear of that. Come along, Maundevyle. If the Book misbehaves too badly, we will simply feed it to you, eh? I should imagine it to be digestible enough. Probably not pleasant-tasting, but then one cannot have everything.'

As he walked away, he heard his mother sigh, and say: 'I cannot think how we are ever to find him a wife.'

'Perhaps,' said Gussie, her voice fading behind him, 'he does not want one.'

FIFTEEN

The next morning, the breakfast table was notable for Lord Werth's absence. Ordinarily, he liked to linger over the meal, and generally remained there until most other members of the family had taken their repast. The latest books and papers were typically left for his perusal, by servants who were accustomed to his lordship's habits.

This morning, his seat was empty, and the day's papers evidently untouched.

Delicacy not being Theo's strong suit, as he helped himself to a cup of chocolate and steadfastly avoided the food, he said: 'Papa's out raising the dead again, is he?'

'Yes,' sighed Lady Werth. 'There was something he rather wished to consult Felix about, and it could not wait until moon-wane. I do not precisely understand why.' Not before she had got all of this out did it occur to her that her son's voluntary presence in the dining-room at any hour was worthy of note, and especially in the morning. She looked hard at him. 'What are you doing out of the tower so early, Theo?'

'Thought I ought to take something out to Maundevyle,' said Theo. 'The fellow's diffident. Would not have thought it of a twenty-foot viscount with teeth as

144

long as my forearm, but there you go.'

'His lordship finds himself in unusual circumstances,' Lady Werth said. 'There has not been an abundance of rules laid down for the proper conduct of a dragon, I believe.'

'That will have to change, what with Gussie making dragons of people left and right.'

'Gussie will be doing no such thing.'

'Won't she?' Theo raised his brows. 'She cannot be kept in a cage all her life.'

'What do you propose we do with her?' Lady Werth sipped chocolate. Theo pretended not to notice the film of ice forming around her silver cup.

'Gussie can decide what to do with herself, no? She is not a child now.' Theo downed the remainder of his own chocolate in two gulps, and set down his cup. He ought not to drink it, really; it rarely agreed with him. But the taste made a pleasant change. 'I think I would like to consult Lord Felix on one or two points myself, regarding Maundevyle.' Theo turned to leave, but was halted by his mother's voice.

'No, do you think Felix might know something of relevance? I had not thought it.'

'He was a contemporary of Margery's, no? Or something thereabouts.'

Lady Werth rose from her chair, abandoning her breakfast. 'That had not entered my head, but you are perfectly right. I shall go with you.'

Secretly Theo was glad of his mother's escort, for while Lord Werth sometimes preferred not to be interrupted when he was working, he was never sorry to receive a visit from his wife. Together they passed out of the dining room, and then out of the house altogether. A narrow lane led down to a little church, which served both the Towers and their tenants; Theo was not surprised, upon arriving there, to find no sign of the reverend Mr. Scrivens, for he was wont to keep out of the way whenever Lord Werth appeared.

Father was to be found at the rear of the church, in sole possession of the ancient, moss-grown graveyard. He sat perched upon the tomb of Lord Ambrose Werth, whose vanity had caused an unusually large sarcophagus to be placed for him, with a recumbent statue of himself laid along the lid. The present Lord Werth sat comfortably upon Lord Ambrose's right arm, oblivious to any indignity. The night winds had played havoc with his iron-grey hair; a night without repose had etched craggy shadows beneath his eyes; and his hands and forearms were crusted with dirt, and other substances Theo did not like to think about too closely. Nonetheless, he looked very much at his ease; quite in his element, engaged as he was in conversation with a cadaver.

Lord Felix had no right to have retained any flesh at all, at such a distance of time. He ought by now to be reduced to nothing but bones, Theo thought, eyeing his unearthed ancestor with some misgiving. He retained the use of his decaying parts out of pure wilfulness; it was vanity that did it, for what need had he for eyes or hair or skin? Still, it made him a trifle less terrible to look upon, and Theo was able to make his bow with tolerable composure.

'Morning, Father,' he said. 'Lord Felix. I hope we are not interrupting?'

Lord Felix had been engaged upon some windy tale involving much cackling laughter, and the slapping of one bony, decayed hand upon the mouldering flesh of his thigh; but he paused upon beholding Theo and Lady Werth approaching, and got up from his perch atop his own gravestone. He bowed. 'Lord Bedgberry,' he said. 'You were only half as tall, the last time we met.'

'I have done a spot of growing, come to think of it,' Theo allowed.

'Lady Werth,' said Lord Felix. 'Time has robbed you of not a single personal grace.'

Mother made her curtsey. 'Nor you of your charm,

146

Felix.'

Lord Felix smiled, a ghastly expression, though his teeth might be said to be in better order than the rest of him. 'I was just telling his present lordship about my time with——' He broke off, and appeared to think better of whatever he had been about to say. 'No, it is a tale not at all suitable for ladies.'

'I should think not,' said Lord Werth. 'What brings you out to the graveyard, my love? I hope Theo did not persuade you into it. And I see you are without your shawl.'

'It is a pleasant morning,' said Lady Werth. 'I am not at all cold.'

'We came to hear about Margery,' said Theo. 'We seem to have developed a dragon, and have not the first idea what to do with it.'

'A dragon!' crowed Lord Felix. 'It is past time there was another dragon at Werth.'

'He is no Werth,' said Theo. 'He is the present Lord Maundevyle, and he does not at all appreciate his good fortune. Wants rid of his Dragon-Wyrde, if you please! We thought Margery might know something of benefit, but no one has seen her in ages.'

'Is she not dead?' said Felix, interested. 'I always said she would outlive the rest of us.'

'In point of fact, no one has any certain information upon that subject.'

Lord Felix shrugged his bony shoulders. 'Cannot say as I can help. Secretive, Margery. Always sneaking off somewhere, and never would say where she was going. It's my belief she had a hoard in some other part of the kingdom, and did not want to share it with the rest of us.'

Theo, conscious of a feeling of disappointment, said nothing. If Lord Felix's account of Margery's habits was true, then it was of no use to ask anyone in the family, however long-dead; no one would be able to give any certain information as to Margery's likely whereabouts, except Margery herself.

'We have not happened to produce any other dragons, I suppose?' he said. 'Anyone more… accessible?'

It was Lord Werth who shook his head, and said with decided information, 'No. Lady Margery Werth was the only one, rather to my mother's regret.'

'See!' said Theo. 'And Maundevyle has no appreciation for it! The rarest of Wyrde-curses, and a handsome one, too.' He sighed.

'Not quite the rarest,' said Lady Werth. 'For there is Gussie's, of course.'

'Good God, yes,' said Theo. 'I was forgetting that.'

Lord Felix looked an enquiry.

Lady Werth exchanged a look with her husband, whose countenance apparently expressed approval, for she said: 'It appears our niece has a talent for drawing forth a dormant Wyrde. It is her doing — unwitting, of course — that Lord Maundevyle is become a dragon.'

To Theo's surprise, Lord Felix burst into laughter. 'But that is priceless!' he gasped. 'How I wish I were alive! I should dearly like to watch that girl's progress about the country.'

'Well, we would not!' said Theo. 'Let her wander about a few watering-places, and every family in England will be after us with pitchforks.'

'And how would that differ from the regular state of affairs?' said Lord Felix, not without justice.

'Well—' began Theo.

Lord Felix interrupted. 'Why do not you hold the Assembly?'

'The what?' said Theo bluntly.

'The Assembly.' Lord Felix looked from Theo's blank face to Lord and Lady Werth's equally uncomprehending countenances. 'Do not tell me you have forgotten it?'

'I have not the smallest idea what you mean,' said Theo. 'And it's clear Mama and Papa haven't, either.'

'But— how then do you gather the family, for the

Wyrding ceremonies?'

'By letter,' said Lady Werth. 'Being always the third birthday, it is no difficult matter to plan for.'

'Letter!' Lord Felix looked as though he wanted to laugh again, but was torn between mirth and indignation. 'Letters!' he shouted, and then to some degree calmed himself. 'A family is nothing without its traditions, you know,' he said in a more reasonable way. 'I cannot think how you have contrived to go on without the Assembly, but you must certainly employ it now.'

'And what is it?' said Lady Werth coolly.

'It is a ritual,' said Lord Felix. 'Performed properly, it will compel every Werth who yet lives — and some who do not — to present themselves at Werth. And make no mistake, they will come.'

Lady Werth looked as though she did not know what to make of such an idea. She gazed, speechless, at Lord Felix, her eyes rather wide, and said nothing.

'What, *all* of them?' said Theo.

'All.'

'Mercy! But there must be hundreds of us about the world.'

'I should think it improbable,' said Lord Felix. 'Margery excepted, a typical Werth is unlikely to enjoy a life of any very great span. I myself died at eight-and-forty.'

'I am sorry to hear it,' said Theo politely.

'It was quite my own fault.'

Theo changed the subject. 'Ah— you do not happen to recall how this ritual of the Assembly is to be performed?'

Lord Felix recoiled. 'Do not tell me the Book also is forgotten?'

From his mother, Theo heard a soft sigh.

'No, though it ought to be,' he said grimly. 'Cursed thing grows more difficult with every passing year.'

'It always did have spirit,' said Lord Felix with approval.

'It almost took father's hand off.'

'Ah!' said Lord Felix, faintly regretful. 'Almost!'

'There is nothing of that kind in the Book,' said Lord Werth. 'You may believe me. I have often consulted it.'

'Then it is hiding it from you, no doubt for some mischievous reason of its own. You will have to get yourselves onto its good side.'

'That Book,' said Theo severely, 'has no good side!'

'Perhaps not, anymore.'

'It's my belief it ought to be burned.'

'As I said.' Lord Felix resettled himself atop his gravestone. 'Werths do tend to meet with accidents, more often than not.'

'Is it a Werth, then?' said Mother. 'The Book?'

Lord Felix said nothing for a moment. 'The Book of Werth,' he said slowly. '*One* thing I am almost sure of: it is older than any of us.'

'How can that be?' said Lady Werth.

'And,' continued Felix without answering, 'it is certainly far more than a mere Book. But as to the precise nature of its workings, I cannot say.'

'Thank you, Lord Felix,' said Lady Werth. 'We will give the matter due consideration.' Then, looking at her husband, she said: 'Perhaps it will be well to leave his lordship to his rest? I have asked cook to serve a second breakfast, and it ought to be ready in ten minutes' time.'

Theo's father developed the ravenous look of a wolf about to spring upon fresh prey. 'I am rather hungry,' he admitted.

'Right.' Lord Felix made his bow to the company, and clambered back into his coffin. 'Come back another time, Werth,' he said. 'We will finish that story.' What was left of his eyes, turning towards Lady Werth, went shifty, and he grinned.

'I shall be sure to do so,' Lord Werth promised. As Lord Felix drew the coffin's lid back over himself, Lord Werth hefted his shovel, and began to hurl wet-smelling earth back down upon the grave.

'Leave that for the gardeners,' Lady Werth instructed.

Lord Werth put his hands to his lower back and stretched, producing some sharp cracking sounds. 'It really is a young man's pursuit,' he said by way of agreement, and set down the shovel again.

'Raising the dead?' Theo said. 'Undoubtedly. Not at all respectable in a man of your age, father. When you were ten years younger, now, that was a different matter.'

Lord Werth grimaced. 'I believe you've been spending too much time with Augusta.'

Theo grimaced, too. 'Good God. I really have.'

***

No one knew, later, what Theo had done to the Book.

Gussie arrived at the Towers late in the morning, and upon conducting a search for her aunt, found her at last hovering at the top of the cellar stairs. Her hands were clasped tightly before her, her face was quite white, and she jumped when Gussie spoke to her.

'Oh!' she said. 'It is only you. You frightened me, creeping up like that.'

'I am incapable of creeping,' said Gussie, with perfect truth, for she had a rather heavy tread, considered most unladylike. Lady Werth had never managed to cure her of it. 'You must have been elsewhere in your thoughts.'

She was interrupted by a thin scream of rage, echoing from somewhere below.

Gussie, wide-eyed, took a small step back. 'Who can have been so foolish as to enrage the Book?' she said. 'And so soon after the last time?'

Lady Werth sighed. 'Theo has gone down there. He would accept no escort, no matter how I pleaded.'

'Oh! If it is only Theo, then I am not at all concerned.'

Gussie relaxed.

'That is unkind,' said Lady Werth. 'You would be as cast down as any of us, were something to happen to him.'

Gussie thought about that. 'Not really very much, no,' she said. 'But I meant to say something else; namely that, since Theo is at least twice as horrific as the Book, the two of them are no doubt having a comfortable cose.'

A muffled, slamming sound followed the scream; Gussie rather thought it was the sound of an axe striking down, and probably burying its blade in the table-top. Or the wall.

'See?' she smiled. 'What did I tell you! The best of friends.'

The sounds came again, several times repeated, and Lady Werth winced. 'For some reason, I find that a still more appalling thought.'

'It is, isn't it?' Gussie agreed.

After that, everything went quiet. Gussie expected to see her cousin soon stalking up the stairs again, but there was no sign of him, even after some minutes.

'I suppose it was important, whatever has sent him down there?' she said after a while.

'It is all Lord Felix's doing,' said Lady Werth, with some distaste.

'Has not he been dead for some time— oh. Uncle has been at it again, has he?'

Lady Werth sighed, and nodded. 'It is all about this Assembly notion, you see,' and she told Gussie an extraordinary tale of rituals and far-off Werths and ancient, unsociable dragons.

'Heaven forfend!' said Gussie, when her aunt had finished. 'The Towers swamped in obscure Werths, and all for the pleasure of consulting one dragon? I had not thought Lord Maundevyle's plight of sufficient interest to drive us to such measures.'

'It *is* rather our fault,' said Lady Werth. 'We are bound to help him, if we can.'

'It is not. It is Lady Maundevyle's own doing, and her horrible son and daughter. They have brought it on themselves.'

'But they have not,' said her aunt gently. 'They have brought it on Lord Maundevyle.'

Gussie frowned. 'Still, these seem dire measures, when we do not even know that Margery can help us. Besides, has it occurred to no one that the Book might have had reason to hide this ritual from us?'

Lady Werth's mouth opened. 'It is by nature disobliging…'

'Yes, but that does not necessarily mean that it is always wrong to be so.'

This possible interpretation of the Book's behaviour plainly had not occurred to her aunt. Gussie watched as she thought the idea through. 'But what harm could come of a mere family gathering?' said Lady Werth.

'An enormous family gathering, no doubt including many people whom we have never met, and perhaps could never wish to?'

An echoing *crash* resounded through the cellar, and the stairs shook. The door to Book's prison, Gussie thought, hurled shut by an irate Lord Bedgberry. His tread was soon heard coming up.

'Is that you, Theo?' Gussie called. 'If you have perchance been possessed by the Book, pray let us know *before* we are summarily dismembered.'

'I do not at all see how that would help,' Theo answered.

'It would not, very much. But there is a certain satisfaction in knowing the reason for one's demise, is there not?'

'It is my belief that your wits are wandering,' said Theo, reaching the top of the stairs.

'Aye, but they were always wayward,' said Gussie with a sigh. 'I see that you have prevailed.'

Theo looked rumpled and flushed, to be sure, as

though he had lately exerted himself in some vigorous exercise. But he was not bleeding, he was missing no fingers or limbs, and he was free of the welts which marred Gussie's own skin. 'I have told you,' said he calmly. 'You only have to deal with it firmly.'

Gussie, picturing what that might consist of, shuddered and let the subject drop.

'And have you got it, Theo?' said Lady Werth.

'The ritual? Yes. I rather think you will not want to use it, though.'

'Whyever not?'

'It calls for the sacrifice of a maiden Werth.' Theo looked significantly at Gussie.

Who stepped prudently backwards. 'I had no notion our ancestors were so barbaric!' she said. 'Really, I am impressed.'

'Then you will not mind offering your neck, for the purposes of our reunion with Lady Margery.'

'I hope you will not think less of me if I do mind, just a little,' said Gussie. 'I am not blessed with an overabundance of necks. In point of fact, I only have the one.'

'Theo,' said Lady Werth. 'It says nothing of the kind, does it?'

'Of course not,' said Theo irritably. 'No one but Gussie could imagine it possible. Here.' He thrust his pocket-book into his mother's hands. 'It is all in there.'

'But why did the Book conceal it from us?' she said, opening up the little book, and turning through the pages.

'Was the Book concealing it?' said Theo. 'Or did you simply have no notion to ask?'

Gussie, thinking that through, blinked. 'Why, but that suggests there might be a great deal more written there, that we have never seen either.'

'I should imagine it likely,' said Theo. 'Next time Father is struck with a desire to go grave-digging, Mother, you might encourage him to enquire.'

'Your father will not be going grave-digging again for some time,' said Lady Werth firmly. 'It is injurious to his health.'

SIXTEEN

'It must be performed by the head of the family,' said Gussie, pointing at a nigh-upon illegible section of scrawl in Theo's pocket-book.

'Cannot Theo do it?' said Lady Werth plaintively. 'You would not think it to look at your uncle, but such feats take a terrible toll upon him. He is no longer a young man, after all.'

Privately, Gussie thought her aunt over scrupulous of Lord Werth's health. He was not unlike his son in certain respects, and Lord Bedgberry was the nearest thing to indestructible mankind had to offer.

'He has recovered admirably from his meeting with Lord Felix,' Gussie said, and with justice, for a day had passed since his erstwhile lordship had returned into his grave, and Lord Werth had already fully regained his natural colour. 'And he ate a hearty breakfast. I am persuaded he is equal to it, Aunt.'

'I suppose it does not appear so very taxing,' said Lady Werth dubiously, surveying Gussie's neatened rendition of her cousin's notes once again.

They had adjourned to the shrubbery to discuss the matter, the morning proving fine. Gussie had gone out with only a parasol, eschewing her shawl. She would have dispensed with the parasol, too, had her aunt been willing to countenance the idea.

'For my part, I am relieved to discover that there is no singing,' Gussie said. 'Of all things my uncle would dislike, it's that. Really, there would be no taking oneself seriously, standing in state at the heart of the Towers and warbling away like a lark. One could hardly blame him for objecting.'

Lady Werth smiled at the idea, as Gussie had hoped. The events of the past fortnight had upset her aunt's usual composure; twice she had only narrowly avoided another icing, and this fretfulness over her husband's health was of a piece with the rest. Gussie could not blame her for that, either, not with the spectre of Lady Maundevyle and her deplorable descendants hanging over them all. And Gussie's own plight was not to be dismissed. If Lady Werth had quietly hoped to be proven wrong about her niece, she was suffering all the disappointment of it now — and all the anxiety for Gussie's future that came with it.

In moments of greater self-knowledge, Gussie wondered if she and her aunt had not both seized upon Lord Maundevyle's problems as an appealing distraction from their own. Until they had determined what was to be done with the dragon, neither of them need devote too much attention to the insoluble problem of what was to be done with Gussie.

'It is only a little reading,' said Lady Werth. 'Perhaps he could manage that very well.'

'He has always possessed a splendid reading voice,' Gussie agreed. 'Very sonorous.'

Lady Werth pointed. 'But this part about the letting of blood, Gussie. That concerns me. In your uncle's present state of health—'

'Perhaps Theo could do that part,' Gussie suggested hopefully. 'His is good, Werth blood, and he will bleed creditably.'

'But it does say the *head* of the family?'

'Lord Bedgberry must be considered the next best thing. He *will* be the head of the family in due time, God help us all, and he will make an excellent proxy for my uncle.'

'I am not sure Theo would thank you for volunteering him for bleeding duty. Especially not *quite* so enthusiastically.'

Gussie waved this away. 'There is plenty of blood in him. He can spare a little.'

Both women fell silent as a shadow passed over the sun: the expansive form of Lord Maundevyle on the wing, darkened to black against the glare of the light, and doubtless in pursuit of some hapless prey for his breakfast.

'It does seem barbaric that there should be any blood-letting at all,' Lady Werth resumed.

'The ritual dates from barbaric days,' Gussie agreed. 'One need only listen to one or two of my uncle's tales to realise that. Lord Felix is positively civilised compared to some of his predecessors.'

This reflection did not please Lady Werth. She said nothing for some moments, and then offered: 'Perhaps you are right. Perhaps it is unwise to perform so ancient a ritual. Can we be certain that any Werths presently unknown to us will not hearken back to these uncivilised times?'

'No,' said Gussie. 'We cannot.'

'And there may be another way to reach Lady Margery.'

'Indeed,' said Gussie. 'Or another way to help Lord Maundevyle, come to that. Dragonlore cannot be wholly forgotten across England, can it? There must be books, somewhere — scholars devoted to the subject — experts in Wyrded form-shifting — any number of alternatives. May I propose a trip to town as a preferable scheme?'

'London!' said Lady Werth. 'My goodness, it is a positive age since I was last there.'

'And I,' Gussie thought it worthwhile to point out,

'have never been at all.'

Aunt Werth looked her over. 'No, and I ought not to take you now.'

'For inevitably I shall run amok in the streets, Wyrding every unsuspecting passerby.'

Lady Werth hesitated. 'It is not that I suspect you of any such propensity, only…'

Gussie waited.

'You can have no notion of the extent of the scandal we would cause,' she said, 'were your experiences with Lord Maundevyle to be repeated in the heart of the capital.'

'I shall wear gloves, everywhere.'

'In summer? It is not at all the fashion.'

'Then I shall be set down as an eccentric, which can hardly be avoided anyway, considering that my name is Werth.'

Lady Werth sighed. 'That is a just reflection.'

'I did not mean for you to be cast down by it, Aunt.'

'We will take Theo with us,' continued Lady Werth.

'Then it is settled. We shall be set down as the most complete eccentrics London has ever seen.'

'And Miss Frostell.'

'Her very ordinariness will lend us respectability, and disarm criticism. She will be delighted.'

'And Great-Aunt Honoria.'

Gussie hesitated. 'You did express a wish to *avoid* scandal, Aunt?'

'Lady Honoria presents a ghastly appearance, but she is not in herself dangerous. Not in the way that you are.'

'Oh,' said Gussie, disconcerted.

'And there will be other Wyrded families in town, of course. The Gouldings, I should think will be in residence; and perhaps the Whytes.'

Gussie spared no efforts to encourage this happier flow of reflections, content to see her carefully written page of notes disregarded. If a hint of an unpleasant aroma chanced to assault her nostrils in the midst of her aunt's conversation — something redolent of grave-earth and decayed flesh — Gussie set it down as some leavings of Theo's, or possibly of Lord Maundevyle's, left too long undevoured in the heat of the summer, and rotting slowly away.

***

Came the midnight hour, and Lord Bedgberry, as was his custom, was still awake.

Convention required that a gentleman's waking hours should, in general, coincide with the daylight hours; and while many a gentleman might lie abed until noon, and carouse until the early hours of the morning, to sleep all the day through and prowl the world at night could not be considered behaviour befitting a gentleman of rank. Even at Werth Towers.

Theo resented this. He belonged to the night. The hours from midnight until dawn offered all the peace and silence he could require, not to mention a surplus of unwary prey, and he had for some years made a habit of setting out into the park just as the church clock struck twelve, and taking his solitary perambulations until at least two.

Summer nights being especially agreeable, clear-skied and mild, Theo set out in good spirits, anticipating a pleasant stroll. But he had not got much beyond the shrubbery before his sensitive hearing registered a most unusual sound: a muffled curse.

Theo stopped.

The sound came again, and more followed; a veritable stream of vituperation, in short, directed at who-knew-whom in a voice Theo recognised.

Since a longing look directed at the darkened fields Theo would not, now, be exploring did not obligingly whisk away the disturbance, Theo adjusted his ideas, and directed his steps towards the sounds of the scuffle rapidly becoming an all-out fight.

Before Theo came upon the combatants, however, there came the noises of a deciding blow delivered; the *thud* of a body striking the ground; and the satisfied murmurings of the victor.

Theo's nose had, by this time, given him some inkling as to the victor's identity.

'Lord Felix?' he said, wrinkling said nose in distaste, for the aroma of advanced decay souring the fresh night air threatened to turn his stomach. 'What have you done to my father?'

For it was the unfortunate Lord Werth lying prone among his wife's shrubbery, dressed in his night-gown and cap, and obviously hauled from his bed.

Lord Felix, bending over his victim with some unknowable purpose in mind, straightened. He regarded Theo in silent thought for some moments, and then said: 'In point of fact, that is an excellent idea.'

Theo had no time to enquire as to the direction of his ancestor's thoughts. Lord Felix favoured him with an urbane smile, shot back the sleeves of his disreputable coat, and leapt at Theo.

The unfortunate Lord Bedgberry, unsuspecting of such an attack, took a sharp blow to the temple, and collapsed like a felled tree.

He woke soon afterwards, and lay for a short time, staring up at the distant moon. Trees ringed some sort of a clearing in which he lay, and the said moon, almost full and blazing with silver light, did a creditable job of illuminating the otherwise pitch-dark grove. Theo rather thought he had fetched up in that odd little nook in the park, the bit no one could imagine a purpose for. The grove, well-kept despite its lack of appointed use, was empty save for two articles: a statue of some former scion of Werth, a sorrowing lady with head bowed — and a slab of white stone, plain and unadorned.

His head ached abominably.

More unaccountably, so did his wrists. They stung, and he felt a warm dampness seeping through the sleeves of his shirt.

'Someone,' he mumbled thickly, 'has caused me to bleed.'

This idea ought to have troubled him more; but Theo was not unused to blood, and some little time passed before he hauled himself into a sitting position, and then to his feet.

A succession of unusual and shocking sights met his eyes. His father lay supine upon the slab of stone, while Lord Felix, more composed than a man so covered in blood had any right to be, held a small book in his bony hands, and was engaged in reading from it. Stumbling nearer, Theo was intrigued to recognise his own pocket-book.

But he did not recognise any of the words Lord Felix was in the process of uttering. If it were English at all, it came from so distant a past as to be unintelligible.

Understanding dawned. Had he not copied these unfamiliar phrases into his pocket-book himself, and recently at that? Hearing them uttered aloud in no way enhanced his understanding.

'I say,' said Theo, marching up to Lord Felix. 'Have you *any* idea what it is you're doing?'

Felix broke off, and cast at his great-great-grandson a look of intense annoyance. 'Is this not your foolish little book? You must be perfectly aware of what I am doing.'

'Yes,' said Theo. 'But that is not what I asked.'

Lord Felix gave a shrug, expelling a cloud of foul-smelling dust. 'I am doing what your father ought to have done years ago.'

'Called a gathering? Why?'

'I remember *my* day,' said Lord Felix dreamily. 'The family was strong, Theodore! The mightiest of all the Wyrded families in England! No one trifled with us.'

'How gratifying,' said Theo.

Lord Felix brushed a quantity of dust and earth from his shoulder. 'And look what has now become of you,' said he, as though Theo had not spoken. 'Spread to the four corners of England; all the power and might of the Werths forgotten, abandoned and useless! Why, a Werth was snatched from this very doorstep, and in broad daylight! And it would be of no use to tell me that ruin has been wreaked upon the perpetrators, for I know it to be the most scandalous falsehood!' Lord Felix paused, and glared at Theo.

Theo glanced at his father, who had not stirred. 'He is alive, I suppose?'

Lord Felix sighed and shook his head, causing Theo a moment's alarm, until he perceived that the former Lord Werth continued to pursue his own reflections, and had paid not the least heed to Theo's remark. 'He is a good man, in his way,' he said, apparently referring to Lord Werth. 'But as head of the family — insufficient.'

Somewhat reassured by Felix's use of the present tense, Theo remained where he was. 'What do you mean to achieve by conducting the ritual?' he said. 'Put every living Werth in the same room together, and I am afraid we would only squabble with one another. There is never any shortage of *that*.'

Lord Felix looked appalled. '*Squabble*?'

'Like little children,' Theo assured him.

Lord Felix hesitated, and glanced down at the book in his hand as though he might prefer to destroy it than to continue reading from it. His hand spasmed, and he gave a convulsive swallow.

'But the dragon!' said he, after a moment. 'Lady Margery still lives. Is that not the truth? I have heard it said!'

'She *may* be still living. What can that possibly matter?'

'Oh!' said Lord Felix. 'Why, no one will trifle with Werth if there is a dragon on the premises. The mere chance of it is enough.'

'We *have* a dragon on the—'

'Borrowed,' said Lord Felix, dismissing Lord Maundevyle's existence with a wave of his emaciated fingers. 'And a sorry, lugubrious excuse for a creature at that. Whoever heard of a melancholy dragon? No, no, Margery it must be. A worthy Werth! Nothing ever withstood *her* for very long! And there is no saying who else may appear, you know.'

With which words, Felix appeared to dismiss the subject altogether, and went on with his reading. He had proceeded some way into the ritual already, Theo perceived, for in addition to the quantities of blood smeared upon the stone slab — Theo's as well as his father's — he had uttered enough of the ritualistic words to create no inconsiderable effect. Theo felt some current flowing through the grove, a sense of pressure and potential which caused his skin, faintly, to itch.

He had only a moment to consider. What ought he to do? Had Lord Felix already gone too far to be prevented now? What would Theo achieve by trying?

'Oh, well!' he said, and mentally washed his hands of the subject. 'After all, it is what m'mother wanted. And there is something in what you say, after all.'

Lord Felix cast him a swift look of approval, to which Theo felt perfectly indifferent. He sat himself down by his father's side, having satisfied himself that Lord Werth still breathed, and awaited the results of Lord Felix's endeavours.

These came swiftly. Only some eight or ten more words rolled from Felix's mouth, gaining in volume with every syllable, until the final phrases crackled like lightning. Having finished, Felix shut the book, tossed it to Theo, and said: 'I have high hopes for your time as head of the family, Theodore. There is a ruthlessness in you, and an indifference to public opinion, entirely absent in your father.' With which encouraging words, he rolled his shoulders, producing an appalling crunching and popping sound, and took a deep, and probably futile, breath. 'Now, if you will excuse me, I shall return immediately to bed. Rituals are so very fatiguing.'

Theo watched in silence as the dead man's withered figure disappeared into the night. His wrists had ceased bleeding; thankfully, Lord Felix had not been so carried away by enthusiasm as to make too mangled a mess of his great-grandson's flesh. Lord Werth's wounds were more minor still, suggesting that, for all Felix's judging words and ringing pronouncements, he did not wish his descendants ill. Or not so *very* much.

Lord Werth woke some little time later, and groggily sat up. 'Theo?' he said. 'Where is Lord Felix?'

'Gone back to bed,' said Theo, rising to his feet. 'I would recommend you to follow suit, father.'

Lord Werth sat upon the pale stone slab, his knees drawn up and his clothes bloodied, and looked silently around the grove. 'I perceive we are to be descended upon by relatives,' he said.

Theo gave a gusty sigh. 'Again?' he answered. 'Why, yes. I believe we are.'

Lord Werth rose to his feet, swaying a little, but contrived not to collapse. 'In that case,' he said, 'I had better speak to the cook.'

SEVENTEEN

In fact, it proved to be Gussie's unhappy lot to speak to the cook, Lord Werth recollecting that more important matters awaited his attention than wrangling over provender, and his wife too occupied in scolding her son, her husband, and her ancestors to soon turn her attention to the matter.

Gussie did not ordinarily object to arranging the menu, food being a topic of some interest to her. But the conversation with Mrs. Gosling did nothing to brighten Gussie's morning. And since she had no desire to interrupt Mrs. Gosling's work while she was at the same time adding to it, she refrained from summoning that harassed woman above-stairs, and descended to the kitchen herself.

'*How* many people?' said the cook, only half attending to Gussie, for the kitchen maid at her elbow required a supervisory eye as she whipped egg whites for a cake, and Mrs. Gosling herself was engaged in crimping a pie crust.

'I do not precisely know, Mrs. Gosling, and I am sorry, for I quite realise how difficult it must be for you to cater for an imprecise number of estranged Werths. If I were to tell you that my uncle places no restrictions whatsoever upon his purse, and that for the time being you are free to order whatever you like, and in any quantity—'

'That is gratifying, to be sure, but scarcely to the purpose,' said Mrs. Gosling. 'I can't make an "imprecise" number of pies. And of what order are these estranged Werths, I'd like to know? Have you given any thought to *that*? You won't want me serving all the master's delicacies to his inferiors.'

As it happened, Gussie had not given that particular question any thought, but Mrs. Gosling was of course correct. Any scions so entirely forgotten by the family were, in all likelihood, not in the same rank of life as his lordship. Not that such a consideration was likely to weigh with Gussie, nor, she felt persuaded, with Lord Werth. But that *others* might object to such a jumble, there could be no doubt.

She took a deep breath.

'They must be well fed,' she said firmly. 'I do not imagine his lordship will draw any such distinction when it comes to mealtimes; pray make everything that is best. There will certainly be Mr. and Mrs Wheldrake in attendance, with their daughter, and Mrs. Thannibour, whose tastes you will of course be familiar with. If you require additional staff, please send word to her ladyship and we will arrange to take another girl.'

Mrs. Gosling may have permitted herself a small noise of scepticism, which Gussie thought too justified for reproach. It was not that Lord Werth was likely to begrudge the expense; more that a full complement of servants for the Towers was not so easy to procure or maintain, there being much said in the villages about *ghouls and horrid creatures,* and *thunderstorms at all hours, so loud you'd hardly hear yourself think,* and so on. The second housemaid still refused to go anywhere near Theo, and a scullery-maid had resigned her post upon finding herself obliged to scour a succession of laundry-tubs, which had been used to serve meat to Lord Maundevyle.

The management of the Werth households offered all

manner of unusual challenges, and Gussie foresaw a great many more about to descend upon them all.

She might cheerfully have brained Lord Felix, if she thought it would do any good. His erstwhile lordship had precious few brains left; his abominable conduct was proof enough of that. Upon receiving the news from Theo, she had entertained brief fantasies of filling Lord Felix's grave with beetles, and her cousin's bed as well, before regretfully abandoning the idea. She would be too busy arranging for all these extra Werths to be fed, watered and housed to have time for sweet, brutal revenge.

'Just do the best you can, Mrs. Gosling,' Gussie finally sighed. 'Complaints may be sent to St. Mary's churchyard, the second grave from the end of the third row.'

'The one with the horrid wolf carved into the headstone?' said the cook.

'The very one.'

'I know it.' Mrs. Gosling subjected her pastry to a particularly violent beating.

Gussie spared a hope that she might subject the occupant of the second grave, third row to a similar such beating, and smiled. Not for nothing had the imposing Mrs. Gosling held the position of head cook in Lord Werth's household for nearly twenty years. Even Lord Felix, Gussie fancied, might look a little blank, when obliged to explain himself to *her.*

She left Mrs. Gosling to her pastry and her mutterings, and took herself off to see the housekeeper.

That Gussie's Aunt Wheldrake should be among the first to arrive was of no surprise, for she and her family lived only ten miles away, and were forever popping in on some pretext or another.

That she should prove disconcerted and displeased by the summons was of little surprise either. Her approach being announced, some minutes in advance, by the rumblings of a severe storm, and a lashing of rain against the windows, Gussie steeled herself for another unpleasant interview.

In the event, it was Lord Werth who bore the brunt of his sister's displeasure.

'Werth!' she intoned, upon sweeping through the great doors, trailed by roiling wisps of storm-cloud and an earth-shaking boom. 'What can you *mean* by such a compulsion? It is not seemly!'

Lord Werth, having likewise heard the approach of disaster, had not chosen to shut himself away. To Gussie's relief and respect, he had stationed himself in the main hall, and awaited Aunt Wheldrake's approach with a serene and enviable patience. Now he bowed, rather formally, to his sister and said: 'The manner of it has not been what I would like, but on a matter of such grave importance, Lucretia, we surely could not have left you out?'

'Grave importance?' said she, stopping inside the door. 'Why, what is amiss?'

'There is a dragon,' he said.

'No!' said Aunt Wheldrake. 'Tell me it has not eaten Theo!'

Lord Werth blinked. 'Not to my knowledge. Indeed, they appear to be friends.'

'Friends?' Aunt Wheldrake faltered.

'You will find Lord Maundevyle in the shrubbery,' said Lord Werth. 'Or possibly, *on* the shrubbery.'

Aunt Wheldrake stared.

'The dragon,' Gussie supplied. 'The fourth Viscount Maundevyle. I believe he does prefer to be addressed by his full title.'

Aunt Wheldrake for once finding nothing to say, she looked from her brother to Gussie with an expression of wondering suspicion, as though she imagined some prank were being played upon her.

Quietly, her thunderings receded.

'The shrubbery?' she said.

'The shrubbery,' Lord Werth confirmed.

Away went Aunt Wheldrake, her husband and snake-haired daughter trailing in her wake.

'That was not so very bad?' Gussie ventured, when they had gone.

Lord Werth permitted himself a small smile. 'Lucretia always did hate to be left out of anything. And I never knew a woman more prone to curiosity — except, perhaps, yourself.'

Finding this too accurate a portrait for complaint, Gussie bowed her head. 'Ah — he is not really *on* the shrubbery, I suppose?'

'One might venture so far as to expect precision of movement from a twenty-foot dragon,' said Lord Maundevyle. 'If one is accustomed to disappointment.'

'Oh, dear,' sighed Gussie, and went immediately to the shrubbery.

EIGHTEEN

Some three days passed before the Towers received a visitor unknown to Gussie.

He came up the driveway on foot, his somewhat shabby overcoat proclaiming him a man of no particular means, but his posture that of a man accustomed to command. Gussie, perceiving him from an upstairs window, paused to watch his approach, intrigued, for he had an arresting appearance. He could not be above forty in years, she thought, and perhaps rather less; he had an untidy shock of dark hair, a build that contrived to be bulky, but without running to fat, and a long, stamping stride suggestive of either some great annoyance, or a touch of bravado.

When she ran lightly downstairs, she found herself the only member of the family in the hall as a footman admitted the newcomer.

He came inside with a heavy tread, the footman having received orders to admit anybody who presented themselves at the door, immediately and without question. As the man discreetly withdrew to summon his lordship, Gussie took stock of their visitor.

He returned her stare calmly, with a question in his

rather cold blue eyes.

'It is not my place to welcome you to Werth Towers, sir,' said Gussie, making her curtsey. 'My uncle and aunt will soon do so, I am sure. But in case you are wondering who you have run into, I am Miss Werth.'

His eyes narrowed. 'Should you not have waited upstairs, or some properly missish thing?'

He spoke, to Gussie's startlement, with a mild Scottish burr, which somehow robbed his words of some of their offence. 'I ought to have, of course,' she admitted.

'Then why didn't you?'

Gussie might have been goaded into offence after all, save that he spoke as though he were more curious than judging, and he regarded her with an air of keen interest.

'When you have been here a little longer,' she replied, 'you will learn that there is no degree of adhering-to-propriety, or of engaging-in-expected-behaviours, that will make the Wyrded Werths acceptable to society.'

'Hm,' said he.

'And there being no mutual acquaintance to introduce us, and your presence here having come about by means which no etiquette has yet been contrived to cover, I am persuaded I might be forgiven my curiosity,' Gussie continued. 'Why *should* I exile myself upstairs, when everything that is interesting is going on below?'

He turned in a slow circle in the middle of the hall, his arms spread wide. 'By all means, look your fill at the outlandish novelty,' he said. 'I hope I don't disappoint.'

'Not at all,' said Gussie politely. 'I am poorly supplied with cousins, or at least those of an age to hold a conversation. I have already engaged to be enchanted with every new acquisition of the kind.'

'Cousins?' said the newcomer, with a contraction of the brow. 'If you are my cousin, ma'am, perhaps you would be so kind as to explain what I am doing here?'

'Ah—' said Gussie, but since the footman at that moment returned, with, remarkably, her aunt and uncle in tow, she was not obliged to confuse (or annoy) him further; that honour fell to his lordship.

Her distant new cousin made his bow to Lord and Lady Werth with rather more respect, perhaps due to their age more than to their rank, for he had not seemed to be impressed with Gussie's. In short order, she discovered him to be a Runner of Bow Street, come into the east on some business he had been obliged to leave unconcluded, due to the insistent nature of the summons. And his name was not Werth, but Ballantine.

'As honoured as I am to make my bow to you, sir,' he said to Lord Werth — with, to Gussie's ear, a trace of sarcasm — 'I hope I shan't be staying long? I do have business to attend to.'

'The capture of a daring thief, I hope?' Gussie put in. 'And there will be a great chase, and you will make a heroic arrest. Naturally, we shall not long detain you from such adventures.'

Mr. Ballantine regarded her again with that keen, searching look, and Gussie was unable to tell whether he approved of her or not.

Not that it signified. No one ever did approve of her, quite, and it had not much inconvenienced her before.

She smiled.

'You are not, by chance, much acquainted with dragons?' said Lady Werth, and at the word "dragon" Mr. Ballantine's attention shifted abruptly to her ladyship.

'I beg your pardon?' he said.

'Dragons,' she repeated.

'We have acquired one, you see,' Gussie put in helpfully. 'And since he is both reluctant to retain his draconic state *and* steadily destroying my aunt's shrubbery, we are desirous of a cure.'

'Is *that* why I am brought here?' said Mr. Ballantine.

'In a manner of speaking. We were expecting another dragon,' said Gussie. 'You do not happen to be in the habit of form-shifting, I suppose?'

'I am not,' he said, flatly.

Gussie waited. She longed to enquire whether he was himself Wyrded, and if so, how; but while Society had yet to develop many particular rules governing the conduct of the Wyrded few (and generally resolved any incipient problems by pretending they did not exist), there *was* one unspoken agreement: to enquire directly into the nature of another's Wyrde was the height of rudeness. She had spoken in jest, and could do no more; Mr. Ballantine must begin the subject himself, or his status as cursed (or otherwise) must remain forever a mystery.

Mr. Ballantine did speak, but not on the subject of his own Wyrde. 'Forgive me,' he growled, 'but if you're tired of the dragon you already have, why on earth would you go looking for another one?'

'In the hopes,' said Lord Werth, 'that she may be able to assist Lord Maundevyle.'

'Or at least get him out of our hair,' Gussie put in, ignoring the quelling look her aunt subsequently directed at her.

'Lord *Maundevyle*?' said Mr. Ballantine.

'The fourth viscount,' explained Gussie, and foresaw that she would likely be repeating herself on that subject rather often.

Mr. Ballantine, apparently bereft of words, did not seem disposed to break the ensuing silence. In the end, Lady Werth did so. 'Please accept our apologies for bringing you here unnecessarily,' she said. 'If you would like to rest yourself before returning to your business, a room shall be prepared for you. And if you will join us in the parlour, refreshments shall be provided at once.'

'I would be glad of both,' said Mr. Ballantine. 'And after that, if you've no objection, I would like to see the dragon.'

Whether Mr. Ballantine was impressed by the dragon or

not, Gussie could not tell, for he regarded Lord Maundevyle's noble bulk with so collected a demeanour and so unreadable an expression as to keep his private thoughts wholly hidden.

They found Lord Maundevyle reposing himself at the far end of the shrubbery, half of his scaled body sprawled through a once-handsome profusion of lavender bushes, the other half stretched out upon the lawns beyond. The scent of crushed lavender stalks and shed blossoms was so thick that Gussie sneezed, causing Lord Maundevyle to regard her through one, half-opened eye.

'I beg your pardon,' she said, fancying the expression affronted, 'but you have set up a tremendous stink.'

The eye closed.

Mr. Ballantine, paused at a safe distance of some ten feet from the prone dragon, cast a questioning look at Gussie.

'He is safe enough,' she said, answering whatever she could decipher of the Runner's appeal. 'He has yet to devour a person, that we know of, and contents himself well enough with mutton.'

'I'm fond of a dish of mutton myself,' said Mr. Ballantine.

'Delightful that you have so much in common,' Gussie murmured. 'You will be such friends.'

Mr. Ballantine's only response was a sideways look, a mix of annoyance and bemusement, and Gussie reminded herself to hold her tongue. Her new cousin was not, as yet, accustomed to her ways.

She stood demure and mute while Mr. Ballantine ventured forth, and — to her secret amusement as well as approval — made a respectful bow to Lord Maundevyle. 'My lord,' he said, loudly and clearly. 'It is my duty to arrest you for an unsanctioned shift into a form deemed hazardous to the public, without the possession of the proper license. It is a violation of His Majesty's Law.'

Lady Werth gave a startled exclamation, and started

forward — only to stop, and glare frostily at the Runner.

'What?' said Gussie in disbelief. 'What law?'

Mr. Ballantine stood, tall and firm, in the face of the general outcry. 'Last year,' he said, 'a son of a House previously unknown to suffer any affliction by the Wyrde changed suddenly from his human form into that of a wyvern, and went rampaging across London. He ate four people, injured many others, and destroyed a number of houses and other buildings. He also caused eight carriage-accidents, and rendered a section of public road unusable for three days. It was later decreed that a proper license must be held by all those proposing to shift their form; their identities must be registered with His Majesty's government; and the proper supervision and accountability must thereby be maintained.' He presumed to fix Lord Werth with a disapproving eye, and added: 'I find it remarkable that the most notoriously Wyrded family in the kingdom should not have heard of it.'

'We do not leave the Towers much,' Gussie said. 'On account of that *notoriety*, you know.'

Mr. Ballantine's cold blue eyes swept briefly over her, but he did not reply.

'I stopped taking the London papers,' said Lord Werth, though he did not elaborate as to why. 'You must understand, Lord Maundevyle's transformation was sudden and unexpected.'

'But he ought to have registered himself immediately.'

'He might have,' put in Gussie, 'if he were aware of the law.'

'Ignorance as to the law is rarely accepted as reason enough to break it,' said Mr. Ballantine.

'And if,' she went on, 'he were in possession of hands and fingers enough to do so.'

Mr. Ballantine stared. 'I don't understand you.'

'Have you ever seen a dragon sign papers?'

'What about when he's not a dragon?'

'If you happen to know of a way for him to alter his

present state, I dare say we should all be delighted to hear of it.'

'You mean he is stuck.'

'Precisely.'

Mr. Ballantine regarded Lord Maundevyle's obliviously sleeping form in silence.

'His family—' he began.

'Little that is rational is to be expected from his family,' Gussie said firmly. 'Why else do you imagine he is here, and not at home at Starminster?'

Mr. Ballantine developed the pinched look of a man encountering an insoluble problem.

'He hasn't eaten anybody,' Gussie repeated, trying not to sound too beseeching. 'I am persuaded he has no intention of doing so. Furthermore, he has not destroyed any buildings, or any carriages either, and I do not believe him to be hazardous to the public in his present state.'

'He must still be registered.'

'Then you shall help us to do so, if you please.'

He inclined his head. 'And that other dragon, also.'

'Lady Margery has yet to join us,' said Gussie cheerfully. 'Indeed, she may be long dead, for all that anybody knows of the matter.'

Some of the energy went out of Mr. Ballantine. He developed the slightly sagging look of a beaten man. 'Did you *have* to summon me?' he said, not without a touch of plaintiveness.

'We did,' said Gussie. 'On account of your being family.'

'Family?' came Theo's voice. 'Ah, do they begin to arrive? Tremendous.' He had, at that moment, arrived from one of his perambulations about the park. He now turned about again, and strode away without a backward glance.

'Lord Bedgberry,' said Gussie, into the ensuing silence.

Mr. Ballantine had not spoken. His gaze now moved to Lord Werth, looking innocuous enough in a dark green coat, with no obvious signs of his more unusual pursuits about him. 'Does your lordship not raise the dead, or am I misinformed?' he said.

Lord Werth merely bowed.

'And your ladyship has a talent for ice-sculpture.'

Lady Werth pursed her lips, and looked away.

'Lord Bedgberry's predilections I need hardly mention, and as for you—' Mr. Ballantine looked enquiringly at Gussie.

'Oh!' she said. 'You may think of me as the hand of Fate, if you like. The source of the Wyrding "affliction". A spreader of the disease. A perambulating plague.' She smiled.

Mr. Ballantine's brows rose.

'Welcome to the family,' added Gussie.

NINETEEN

'I am not really a plague,' Gussie said later, once Mr. Ballantine had been persuaded into leaving the slumbering Lord Maundevyle alone. 'I spoke in jest, of course.'

'Then you cannot turn an unWyrded person Wyrded?' said the Runner.

'Well, yes, I can,' she admitted. 'But only if they possess some latent capacity for it already. I could have no effect whatsoever on any ordinary human.'

'You're sure of that, are you?'

Gussie opened her mouth to say, with her customary confidence, that of course she was, but was obliged to close her lips again without speaking. *Was* she certain? She had, until recently, firmly believed herself unWyrded. Since then, her abilities had been tested only on Lady Maundevyle's three children, two of whom had been deeply affected by proximity to her. *Three*, perhaps — for though Clarissa had appeared unchanged, she might, like Gussie, have changed in ways that were not so obvious as her brothers. Had Gussie permitted her knowledge of the Selwyn family's formerly Wyrded ways to influence her conclusions?

What if their Wyrding had nothing to do with the past

history of their family, and was wholly attributable to Gussie's presence?

The thought turned her nauseous, and she turned an appalled look upon Mr. Ballantine.

'Aye,' he said grimly. 'Didn't think of that, did you?'

Collecting herself, Gussie sighed. 'I suppose I shall need a license, too.'

'Whatever *you* are is as yet undocumented,' said Mr. Ballantine. 'There is no such license, Miss Werth.'

'Am I entirely illegal?' said she with a bright smile. 'A law-breaker! There, Aunt. I always told you I would someday come to good.'

'There is no law against whatever it is you do,' said Mr. Ballantine. 'But in my opinion, there probably ought to be.'

'I know,' said Gussie with regret. 'I am a walking disaster.'

Lady Werth here interjected. 'I suppose it likely that this new policy will shortly expand to cover *all* the Wyrded, not merely those capable of dangerous transformations?'

'I imagine it probable, ma'am,' agreed Mr. Ballantine.

She gave a little sigh, and tapped her fingers against the arm of her chair. 'Lord Felix will not like *that*.'

'Who is Lord Felix, ma'am?'

'My husband's great-great-grandfather, I believe, or something of that nature. Perhaps the relationship is rather more distant.'

Mr. Ballantine blinked.

'My uncle does raise the dead, after all,' Gussie explained. 'I do not know where you read of it, or heard of it, but it is quite true.'

'I do not imagine Lord Felix will readily submit to being *licensed*,' said Lord Werth, as though the word tasted foul. 'He is not much in favour of modern methods.'

'What will the penalty be, for failing to acquire the proper license?' Gussie asked. 'You cannot arrest us all, I suppose?'

'Arrest is only a consequence for those deemed

hazardous to public safety,' said Mr. Ballantine. 'For the rest, there's a fine. Further punishments may be introduced, after the next parliament.'

Gussie saw her aunt and uncle exchange an uneasy look. Ill news for their family, and all who were like them.

'How do you come to be so knowledgeable, Mr. Ballantine?' asked Gussie, to cover the chilly silence.

'You may not be aware,' he said, clearly assuming this to be the case, 'that crimes perpetrated by Wyrded citizens, and through Wyrded means, have been steadily rising across the kingdom for some years. I am part of a set of Runners dedicated to the pursuit and punishment of all such criminals, Miss Werth.'

Gussie again wondered whether he were Wyrded himself, and found it impossible to ask. Surely he must be? Who better to chase down Wyrded murderers and thieves but a Runner wielding some of the same powers against them?

Perhaps he detected some part of her thoughts in her features, for a faint gleam of amusement lit his eyes, even as he maintained a steady silence.

'I see,' she murmured, unexcitingly. 'How thrilling that must be.'

'It is exhausting, dangerous, frustrating and often punishing work,' he said. 'The more so since the Wyrde comes in so many varied forms, and it is rarely possible to understand the nature of another man's Wyrde only to look at him. But I can well imagine that it may seem thrilling to you, ma'am.'

Gussie said nothing, for visions of Mr. Ballantine's working life had taken strong possession of her mind. How she *wished*, sometimes, she had been a man! To travel about the country, hard on the heels of miscreants and rogues, dispensing justice for the wronged! She had no doubt the kingdom was full of men like Theo and Lord Felix, but less retiring (in Theo's case), and rather less expired (as per Lord Felix); very much inclined to make the most of their Wyrded powers, in ways that came too much at the expense of others; of *course* Bow Street had made provision for it! Of course they had men like Mr. Ballantine!

Consumed with a sudden feeling of wistful regret, Gussie only belatedly realised she had mentally left the conversation, and abandoned her interlocutor. Her aunt had taken up the conversational slack, of course, being a well-bred woman; but Mr. Ballantine had noticed. He kept looking at Gussie, but not with offence. More with… curiosity.

'I was daydreaming,' she explained.

'Thrilling derring-do?' he said, with a ghost of a smile.

She sighed. 'Of course.'

'You have not had much opportunity to engage in daring deeds, I imagine.'

He spoke with more sympathy than she might have expected, given the dismissiveness of his earlier comments. 'Very little,' Gussie said. 'In fact, I have scarcely left the Towers in my life, except for being abducted recently.'

His eyes opened wide. 'Abducted?'

'Yes, and that is how Lord Maundevyle came to enjoy his present condition. Perhaps I had better tell you about it.'

'Perhaps you had.'

So Gussie did, mitigating the blame attributable to Clarissa Selwyn as much as she could. She did not really believe Miss Selwyn to be a dangerous criminal; she was only addicted to fantasies of derring-do, as Mr. Ballantine might put it, and somewhat lacking in judgement.

'I may have to pay a visit to Starminster,' said Mr. Ballantine, when Gussie had finished.

'Oh, no! I do not think there is any danger from *them*. Lady Maundevyle remains unWyrded, to my knowledge, and Charles is a wet blanket. All bluster and no bottom.'

He laughed at that. 'A devastating judgement.'

'Come to think of it, poor Lord Maundevyle is

something of a damp squib himself. All he does is trail about the park, lamenting his condition and plaguing the wildlife. Now, if I had been a dragon—' She stopped, aware suddenly of whom she was talking to.

'You would have done the thing with some style, I collect?' prompted Mr. Ballantine.

'And so I would!' said Gussie with spirit. 'And I might have eaten a few people, too. Only those who particularly displeased me, but still, it is perhaps for the best that I am not a dragon.'

'Only a plague.'

Gussie frowned. 'Yes. Shall I have to be put in prison? I am more of a public hazard than Lord Maundevyle, I assure you.'

'I hope not, ma'am. It would be a great tragedy to lock away so lively a wit.'

Gussie blinked. 'How charming of you. I did not at all look for such a compliment.'

Mr. Ballantine bowed. 'If you will permit me, I believe I may be able to assist you with your dragon problem.'

'How very kind of you.'

'I imagine it to be in the public interest for me to do so.'

'Yes, of course. Must you arrest him? You must find it difficult.'

'His lordship is rather unwieldy in his present state,' agreed the Runner.

He was never called upon to exercise his dragon-repelling powers, however, for several events subsequently occurred to distract every occupant of the Towers — and to resolve the Dragon Problem, albeit in ways no one could have foreseen.

The first of these was the arrival of no fewer than three fresh respondents to Lord Felix's ritual. How they came to present themselves all at once was a matter of some doubt, for they patently had not travelled together, nor would ever dream of doing so.

One was a lady of advanced years and a great many pretensions to refinement. She was elegantly dressed in a lavender gown and dark spencer — 'I am in mourning for my poor sister, whom I shall doubtless soon follow into the grave' — and kept a stock of *sal volatile* in the embroidered reticule hanging from one wrist, to which she frequently turned whenever anything the least unsettling occurred. Her name was Miss Horne, and whether or not she was Wyrded was a subject which failed to occupy Gussie at all, for she took an immediate dislike to the lachrymose old woman, as did everyone else. Since her repellent behaviour led to her being iced by Lady Werth within six hours of her arrival, her presence in this narrative will necessarily be brief.

'I am terribly sorry,' Lady Werth said later, of the lamentable event. 'Only she aggravated me so much I could not help myself.'

Three hours sooner, Mr. Ballantine might have made some objection to this misuse of Wyrded power. But even he could not find it in himself to regret the sight of Miss Horne, poised in the act of raising a phial of smelling-salts to her long nose, much more charming as an ice-statue than she had ever been as a flesh and blood woman.

'I trust she will regain her proper form in due time, ma'am?' was all Mr. Ballantine said.

'Yes,' sighed Lady Werth, with proper regret. 'In a day or two.' She added, with a slight frown, 'It is a pity she had so insisted upon taking the best chair.'

The second of the new arrivals was a pastry-cook from a town somewhere in the neighbouring county of Suffolk. Gussie was not able to catch the name, for Maud Digby arrived in a state of such high indignation, and expressed her displeasure at the summons at such a volume, more than half of her remonstrations succumbed to the echo persistent in the lofty hall and died away undeciphered.

Gussie gathered that she was An Honest Woman, and Obliged to Earn her Bread Through Her Own Labour, with No Husband to Assist Her, and that Good Positions were Difficult to Come By. Since the third eye blinking from the centre of her forehead proclaimed her most inconveniently Wyrded, and no arrangement of her bushy brown locks could possibly hope to hide it, Gussie collected that Good Positions might indeed be Difficult to Come By, and sincerely regretted that the poor woman should have felt compelled to convey herself, through means unspecified, across many miles, with or without her employer's leave.

A look of desperate appeal to her uncle revealed him to be thinking along similar lines, and in short order, the unfortunate Maud Digby was on her way back to Suffolk in his lordship's own carriage, carrying a handsome purse with her by way of compensation. She had ceased to vituperate the moment she had seen the money, though had continued to grumble under her breath about the high-handed ways of *the Quality*.

Gussie could not blame her.

It was about half an hour after Maud Digby's departure that the second dragon made her presence known.

Miss Horne (not yet iced, for that came later) went off into hysterics at once, but nobody had much leisure to attend to her, being too much occupied with the dragon herself. For she did not, as might be expected, swoop over the Towers with wings outstretched in a grand display of airborne splendour; nor did she come to a crashing and spectacular landing in the driveway beyond the great doors, and set up a spray of loose stone to announce her arrival.

Nobody noticed her appearance at all, in fact, until a great, wedge-shaped head, bejewelled in emerald-green scales, came snaking through the open door into the hall.

'Pardon me,' said the dragon. 'I am summoned to attend upon Lord Werth. Is he here?'

TWENTY

The aforementioned Lord Werth, together with his wife, his sister, his niece and his guests, gazed upon the dragon — or the dragon's head, that being all that could then be seen — in speechless amazement. One might hold an arcane ritual with the intention of summoning a dragon, but one did so without in any great degree expecting success.

And unlike Lord Maundevyle, this dragon *spoke*.

The reigning silence was broken only by the thin shrieks of Miss Horne, who, prostrate upon the floor, appeared to be trying to inhale the contents of her pungent phial, much good it would do her.

The dragon flicked out her tongue, and tasted Miss Horne's leg.

'I might eat her,' said she conversationally, 'if only to put a stop to that horrible noise. But I am afraid she does not taste at all inviting.'

'You may eat her with our goodwill,' said Gussie, recovering herself. 'No one much wants her, I assure you.'

Mr. Ballantine, roused to activity by this exchange, stepped forward. 'Ah — nobody's to eat anybody upon these premises, please.'

The dragon bowed her elegant head. 'I shall confine my dining activities to the gardens, as is only proper.'

'At least,' added Gussie, 'Pray do not eat anybody who is supposed to be breathing. If you should happen to find Lord Felix attractive as a dinner prospect, I dare say nobody should object to that either.'

'I—' began Mr. Ballantine.

Lord Werth here intervened, by stepping forward, and bowing rather low. 'Lady Margery, I presume?'

'You are Lord Werth?' she said, without refuting this, which Gussie took for assent.

'I am the present Lord Werth,' her uncle agreed.

Lady Margery looked him over. 'Hm,' she said, and withdrew her head.

When she did not reappear, the assembled Werths exited the hall in a rush, and found her curled up in the driveway. She was not quite so large as Lord Maundevyle, but the difference must be so minimal as to be immaterial. 'I declare,' she said, as the family streamed out into the sun, 'the Towers grows smaller every year.'

'Perhaps you are growing bigger,' said Gussie, but then thought better of it. 'But I would not be surprised if the house *were* to be so obstreperous as to shrink. It has been taking its cues from the Book, perhaps.'

'Is the Book, then, still in existence?' said Lady Margery, in a tone of mild interest. 'I had thought someone must have put it out of its misery long ago.'

'We have often been tempted,' said Gussie.

'Do not delay. That Book will be the doom of the Werths one of these days, I am sure of it.'

Lady Werth said, 'We keep it under strict lock and key, Lady Margery.'

'I suppose that might do.'

Nobody, it seemed, wanted to admit that the Book had been the means of Lady Margery's own summons.

'Well,' said the second dragon briskly, after a moment's silence. 'And why am I here? I see you have procured yourselves another dragon at last. I saw him on my way in. Must he crouch in the shrubbery like that? It is most unbecoming.'

'We have not been able to convey much of anything to him,' said Lord Werth. 'He is a reluctant dragon.'

'And sadly inept,' said Gussie. 'For he cannot even speak to us, as you do.'

'Not?' said Lady Margery. 'Well! That is easily mended.' With which words, she spread her great wings and leapt into the air.

Her departure signalled an immediate exodus from the driveway into the shrubbery. Gussie arrived there to find Lady Margery landed near the profusion of lavender bushes within which Lord Maundevyle still dwelt, drawn up to her full and regal height, and addressing his lordship in bracing tones.

'Come, come! This behaviour is not befitting of a dragon. You are not a Werth, I perceive, and so there is only so much that can be expected of you. But I am sure you would wish to make some address to the family, at least? To maintain such a silence is the very height of rudeness, is it not?'

Lord Maundevyle appeared electrified by the presence of another dragon, and had, at long last, drawn himself up, and out of the slumped posture he had for some time maintained. But Lady Margery's words could not please him. He made a choked, snarling noise which Gussie at first interpreted as an objection — possibly even a threat; but soon discovered to be an attempt at speech. The crimson dragon spat sounds from between his long teeth, and perhaps they were intended to be intelligible syllables, but they emerged as growls and stifled roaring, punctuated by puffs of pungent smoke.

'Oh,' said Lady Margery. 'That is the way of it, hm?'

And to Gussie's horror, she abandoned her attempts to scold Lord Maundevyle into speech in favour of a more aggressive approach. Her elegant head darted towards his lordship — her bright teeth flashed — and she retreated again, her jaws stained with blood, and a small but nasty-looking wound blooming red upon the reluctant dragon's long throat.

Lord Maundevyle said, quite clearly, 'Ouch!', the most human expression he had yet achieved; though he did lose his grip upon it a moment later, and gave a shattering, draconic roar.

'It was for your own good,' said Lady Margery, unmoved.

Gussie did not at all see what good biting his lordship could have done, though she did not blame Lady Margery for the impulse that had spurred her to do it, for a sorrier, more lachrymose creature she could not imagine.

But the next sounds emerging from Lord Maundevyle's throat comprised considerably less snarling, and something that almost resembled words.

Upon his third attempt, he produced noises as incomprehensible as before, but much more human; more the sounds the original Lord Maundevyle might have made upon dropping a heavy object upon his own foot.

'See?' said Lady Margery. 'It is the shock of it,' she said, apparently to the gathered audience of Werths. 'Everybody has the same response to unexpected pain. We all make our lamentations in our own birth-tongue, do we not?' She lifted her voice, and said: 'Underneath, sir, you are still whoever you were before, and if you had forgotten it, then I urge you to remember it now.'

And at last, Lord Maundevyle produced words, thickly uttered and without elegance, but comprehensible. 'Madam,' he said with a growl, 'after several days in a row of eating raw sheep for my dinner, I find it impossible to believe that I was once civilised, or that I ever shall be again.'

Lady Margery snapped her teeth together in annoyance. 'Why, then, have you been eating raw meat? It is an indecorous habit. I keep an excellent cook, and I do not at all see why you could not do the same.'

Lord Maundevyle stared at her in astonishment. 'A cook?' he repeated.

Finding this too fatuous to merit a response, Lady Margery spread out her glittering wings. 'If that is everything,' she said, presumably to Lord Werth, 'There is an excellent venison ragout awaiting my attention, and I believe Francois has made me a coffee-pie to follow.'

'You brought your cook with you?' said Gussie, obscurely impressed.

'Naturally,' said Lady Margery with a sniff. 'What could possibly move me to travel without Francois?'

Gussie, assailed by visions of Lady Margery putting up at some country inn, and insisting upon installing her own selected chef in the kitchens, knew not what to enquire about first.

'Wait!' said Lord Maundevyle, rearing up. 'How do I cease to be a dragon?'

'*Cease?*' Lady Margery, paralysed with horror, could only stare.

'I do not believe that it suits me,' said Lord Maundevyle stiffly.

'You are quite right,' she said, recovering herself, and casting an eye of cold disdain over his lordship. 'It does not in the smallest degree suit you.'

'Then help me to be rid of it!'

'I cannot,' she said. 'You must *rid* yourself of it, if that is your desire.'

'But how?'

She gave a draconic shrug, her emerald-scaled wings catching the sun. 'You have remembered human speech. I dare say you can contrive to remember the rest.'

She was gone a moment later, soaring into the sky without another word for his lordship, or anybody else either. Gussie's shouted questions went unanswered, and within minutes the dazzling emerald dragon was a diminishing speck upon the horizon.

'I cannot help thinking she rather enjoys herself than otherwise,' Gussie offered.

Lord Maundevyle did not reply. He had taken up a mouthful of lavender, ripped from the bush in a fit of temper, and now spat it out again in disgust.

'You have gone off course already, sir,' said Gussie. 'That was not at all a human thing to do.'

'It wasn't a very draconic thing to do, either,' said Mr. Ballantine.

'Something of the enraged feline about him, do you not think?' said Gussie to the Runner.

'Aye. Any moment I expect him to begin grooming himself.'

Lord Maundevyle's response was a glance of withering — and rather human — contempt. He spat another sprig of lavender from his massive jaws, and sat in silent thought.

'I would like,' he said shortly, 'to slam a few doors.'

'That would be excessively human,' Gussie said, by way of encouragement. 'And ill-tempered, but we shall not mention that.'

'Tear my cravat from around my throat and hurl it at something,' he continued, ignoring this. 'A wall, say.'

'Then you might find some unoffending subordinate at whom to hurl a few curses,' Gussie suggested. 'That would be very lordly.'

'I was never much in the habit of it,' said Lord Maundevyle, with a huff of smoke.

'What were you in the habit of?' said Gussie.

'Long walks in the grounds at Starminster,' said the dragon. '*Not* in search of something to eat. Mornings in the library with a book. My favourite coat.'

'Is that the dark green cutaway?' said Gussie.

'The very one. Cups of chocolate before breakfast, brought to me upon a tray in my own room. Clarissa's needling and Charles's sour remarks. My mother's lamentations about the Wyrde, and her lack of daughters-in-law. Avoiding country-dances and balls. *Pastilles au chocolat* at supper time, with brandy.'

Lord Maundevyle talked on, and Gussie listened to this narration of his personal habits and tastes with great interest — at least for a time. When she noticed that his lordship appeared to be — well, *shrinking,* she could spare no attention for anything else.

Her aunt appearing disposed to comment upon it, Gussie waved a hand in hopes of dissuading her, for Lord Maundevyle's soliloquy ought not to be interrupted.

The assembled Werths watched in breathless silence as Lord Maundevyle steadily talked himself smaller, and then less crimson, and finally a great deal more human than he had been for many days.

He did not appear to notice the alteration at first, which Gussie wondered at. But then, gesturing over his enjoyment of hunting during the appropriate season, he caught sight of the limb with which he had expressed his emphasis: no longer a red, scaled collection of claws, but a pale human hand.

He stopped.

Gussie lamented Lady Margery's abrupt departure afresh, for she might gladly have kissed the irascible old Werth. Lord Maundevyle beheld his restored arm in silence for some moments, and a bright sheen to his eyes suggested he did so in a state of heightened emotion.

Then, in a voice rather tremulous, he said: 'If it is not too much trouble to your cook, Lady Werth: would somebody *please* bring me a cup of chocolate?'

TWENTY-ONE

Lord Maundevyle experienced some further difficulty before he could be said to have gained full control over his physical state. Halfway through the aforementioned chocolate, which he downed with the gusto of a man dying of thirst, he snapped back into his draconic shape, so fast and so unexpectedly as to send the unfortunate cup flying.

The sound of its landing, and subsequent shattering, split the air, followed by a roar of frustration on his lordship's part.

This setback proved temporary, however, for within two hours he was a man again; and his impromptu and involuntary transformations did not persist past the following day.

'Your dear mama will be so relieved,' Gussie offered, at dinner upon the day of Lord Maundevyle's return to recognisable humanity.

He looked up from his plate of apple-roasted pork, but only briefly. It was his third such helping. 'What has that to say to anything?' said he.

'I am sure she has been concerned for your welfare?' said Gussie, without being sure of any such thing, but it seemed polite to say so in company.

Lord Maundevyle maintained an eloquent silence, and applied himself to a dish of fricando of veal. Only a slight raising of his eyebrows hinted at his opinion of his mother's claims.

'I hope you will accept the use of our carriage in returning to Starminster, Lord Maundevyle,' said Lady Werth pleasantly. 'Of course, you may wish to put your wings to use instead, but I cannot help thinking so long a flight must be fatiguing.'

Lord Maundevyle looked, wide-eyed, at her ladyship, and seemed uncertain of a response. 'Thank you, ma'am,' he said at length. 'I have not yet made any fixed plans as to the mode, or indeed the time, of my return to Starminster.'

If he were reluctant to go home, Gussie could not blame him for it. But nor was it within her power to extend his invitation to the Towers, and considering that the periodic intrusions of putative Werths had yet to wholly cease, she could not blame her aunt and uncle if they preferred to be rid of a difficult guest, either.

One such guest maintained a station near the bottom of the table, a vicar of the name of Cardwell, who ate with all of Lord Maundevyle's gusto without having anything like his excuse. He was as rotund as might be imagined with such habits, and very red, with a loud barking laugh and manners sadly vulgar. Nobody could imagine him at all likely to possess any genuine Werth heritage, though of course it was impossible to be certain. The greater the variety of people turning up at the Towers — and the larger the number — the more Gussie wondered whether the ritual had not indeed misfired, and drawn in an assortment of visitors who were only Wyrded, and not necessarily Werth.

Some of them were proving difficult to dislodge. Indeed, a Miss-Horne-shaped ice sculpture still occupied Lady Werth's favourite chair.

Mr. Ballantine, hitherto rather quiet, spoke up into the silence following Lord Maundevyle's speech. 'If you are not disposed to return home, yet, sir, I should be glad of your assistance.'

Gussie looked at the Runner in astonishment, as did most of the rest of the family.

'Me?' said Lord Maundevyle after a moment, surprised into a degree of incivility. 'In what way may I be of use?'

Mr. Ballantine sat back, abandoning his emptied plate, and embarked upon explanation. 'It's to do with the work I was engaged in before I... happened to arrive here,' he began. 'Being already some few days delayed, I should be glad of a swift return into Suffolk.'

'Are you asking me to take wing?'

Mr. Ballantine inclined his head. 'The distance is not so very far. If we leave in the morning, we might be there before noon.'

Lord Maundevyle glanced about, as though enquiring of himself what reason he might have to draw out his days at the Towers. Coming up with none, apparently, he said: 'Why not, indeed? Since it appears to be on my account that you were brought here, it is to some degree incumbent upon me to mitigate the damage.'

Mr. Ballantine smiled. 'I shall be very grateful, sir.'

'Being a novice dragon, if I should chance to pitch you off my back somewhere between here and Suffolk I daresay you will not regard it.'

Mr. Ballantine blinked. 'I shouldn't regard anything in that state, I should imagine.'

Lord Maundevyle gave the faintest of smiles, and returned to his dinner.

The Runner's attention moved to Theo, who sat picking at a portion of iced pudding — and then to Gussie herself. 'On a related note, I heard mention earlier today of an unusual book?'

Theo looked up, frowning, and exchanged a horrified look with Gussie. 'It is nothing,' he said curtly.

'The doom of the Werths one of these days, was it not said?'

'Lady Margery exaggerates.'

'Let us all hope that she does. Lady Werth, however, mentioned something about lock and key, I believe.'

Her ladyship looked conscious.

'I ask because,' continued Mr. Ballantine, when nobody spoke (except Mr. Cardwell, whose bluster everyone was pleased to ignore), 'I came into Suffolk pursuing the matter of a stolen book.'

Theo's eyes narrowed.

'A book?' said Gussie, with a sideways glance at her aunt. 'Is it at all a… an unusual book, sir?'

'That is rather the question,' said Mr. Ballantine. 'You see, the theft did not go cleanly, one might say. It is a spell book, or said to be such, though as to the authenticity of its contents I couldn't say. In the process of our unknown thief's absconding with it, several people were left injured in strange ways, and I've been unable to account for the nature of the wounds.'

Gussie did not much want to ask about the "strange ways". Nobody else did either, judging from the silence.

At last, Lord Werth mustered the courage. 'What ways were those, Mr. Ballantine?'

'I should say they were bite marks, if that made the least sense,' said Mr. Ballantine. 'And something else I cannot account for at all. Bruises shaped as though something long and thin had been wrapped around the limb, and pulled tight.'

Nobody spoke.

'I had thought the theft must have been conducted either by form-shifters of an unusual type, or perhaps with the help of beasts I cannot picture in my mind,' said Mr. Ballantine, undaunted. 'And perhaps it may prove to be so. However, that there might be an altogether different explanation now seems possible, and I'd be glad to hear more about the book you find it necessary to keep securely locked away.'

Gussie could not feel it appropriate to speak openly of

the Book in such mixed company, and her aunt was sure to object to the discussion of such questionable subjects as thefts, criminals, wounds and Wyrded monsters at the dinner-table. 'Perhaps we might do better to show you, Mr. Ballantine, than to attempt an explanation?' she suggested.

'I look forward to seeing it,' said Mr. Ballantine.

'No,' said Theo. 'No, you really don't.'

Mr. Ballantine, for the first time, looked faintly discomfited.

In the end, Lord Werth was obliged to take Mr. Cardwell on a tour of the churchyard, before he could be got out of the way. Gussie regretted that Mr. Ballantine had raised the subject of the book over dinner, but he could not be expected to understand why it had been unwise.

'I hope your uncle will have sense enough to show Mr. Cardwell only the churchyard, and not its occupants,' said Lady Werth, gathered at the top of the cellar stairs with Gussie, a pace or two behind Theo and Mr. Ballantine. The latter two were intent upon the door, and the stairs downward; Gussie heard Theo's voice, pitched low, as he endeavoured to impress upon the unsuspecting Runner the supreme importance of taking care below. Mr. Ballantine did not appear sufficiently afraid, Gussie thought, but that would soon alter.

'I don't know that I agree with you, Aunt,' said Gussie. 'If anybody can get rid of Mr. Cardwell it must be Lord Felix. And promptly too, I should think.'

'Very true,' said Lady Werth, much struck.

'Unless you would like to make a sculpture of the good vicar, too? He and Miss Horne might be shipped out together.'

Lady Werth was seen to blush. 'I ought not to have lost my temper with Miss Horne.'

'Nobody has in the least missed her, Aunt.'

'How true. And how sad.'

'I have not much sympathy to waste on so poor a specimen.'

'Have you much sympathy for anybody, Gussie?'

Gussie dutifully thought about it. 'I worry about Nell, on occasion. *Such* a quantity of children.'

'Is that all?'

'Yes, I believe that is all.'

Lady Werth smiled faintly. 'I am sure it is very liberating.'

'Wonderfully. Come, Aunt, you must acknowledge my upbringing to have been of some influence. The world in general has little sympathy for the Wyrded, and by extension the Werths. But none of us is at all in want of it, so what can it signify?'

'A compelling argument.'

The conversation necessarily ceased here, for Theo and Mr. Ballantine had gone below and opened the stout door behind which the Book lay imprisoned. Gussie had wanted to accompany them, but upon encountering Theo's fiercest frown, and more convincingly his arguments as to the impossibility of keeping an eye on his cousin and Mr. Ballantine at once, she had yielded to persuasion, and consented to remain a spectator. Her last visit was not forgotten. The welts on her arms had taken days to heal.

The usual sounds echoed up from below: the opening and slamming-closed of the door; a crash, followed by another; someone's yelp of pain (Mr. Ballantine, Gussie concluded). A low, ferocious snarl (possibly the Book, possibly Theo).

The gentlemen did not remain long in the cellar. Soon the door was flung open again, and Gussie heard hasty footsteps pounding up the stairs.

Mr. Ballantine came into view.

'My God,' he panted.

'I know,' said Gussie.

'Lord Bedgberry,' he said, turning to stare wildly back

down the stairs. 'He had an *axe*—'

'It is never wise to consult the Book unarmed,' said Gussie, neglecting to mention that she and her aunt had more or less done so very recently. 'Certainly not when it is roused, which it has been rather, of late.'

'Roused,' said Mr. Ballantine, somewhat recovering his composure. 'That is one word for it.' He winced as another, resounding *crash* echoed from below, and held up his right arm. The sleeve of his coat hung in tatters. Gussie recognised the pattern of red welts now adorning the exposed skin.

'Do they match the wounds you described, sir?' she enquired.

'I believe they do, Miss Werth. Thank you. You have saved me a deal of trouble, I believe.'

'I fear there remains considerable trouble ahead,' said Lady Werth. 'The Book escaped, once, in the time of Lord Werth's grandfather. It is said to have taken two weeks to subdue it again.'

'It occupied the north-west tower,' Gussie said. 'Kicking my great-great-uncle Silvester out of it — literally, we understand.'

'It was a bloody siege,' Lady Werth murmured.

Surprisingly, Great-Uncle Silvester's own voice echoed out of the darkness. 'A fine brew, I thank you. And how does her ladyship, Marlowe?'

'Exactly,' murmured Gussie. She did not waste any time searching the low-lit chamber for the grotesque; if Silvester did not wish to be found, it was futile to attempt it. Mr. Ballantine, however, turned twice in a circle attempting to locate the source of the voice.

'Who was that?' he said, when Silvester did not speak again.

'My great-great-uncle Silvester.'

Mr. Ballantine stared at her.

'If you had not already realised it, Mr. Ballantine, this is a very strange house you are come to.'

Great-Aunt Honoria choosing that moment to appear, as devoid of neck, body and limbs as ever, Mr. Ballantine received the fullest proof of Gussie's words in very short order. To his credit, he only flinched in response to the dowager countess's macabre appearance, and when she favoured him with her best and most ghastly smile, he controlled himself enough to make her a bow. 'Ma'am,' he said, and if his voice shook a very little, no one could blame him.

'I like him,' said Lady Honoria to Lady Werth. 'A cut or two above the rest of these newcomers, no?'

'He is certainly possessed of a strong stomach,' said Gussie.

Mr. Ballantine cleared his throat, and bore admirably with the reappearance of Theo, coming in a rush up the stairs with thunderous brow and one hand pouring blood. 'My stay here has been most — edifying,' he allowed.

'Damned creature has bitten me!' declared Theo.

'How clever of it to acquire teeth,' Gussie murmured.

Theo turned upon her an unamused glare. 'Clever? Aye, you *would* say that.' He had brought one of the axes with him, and now threw it down in disgust. It fell into a corner with a dull clang. 'That's it,' he declared. 'I shan't wrestle with that cursed Book again. In fact, Mama, I recommend that it be burned.'

'You know we cannot,' said Lady Werth. 'All the history of the family is in there, and who knows what more that we have missed—'

'Nothing of use,' said Theo. 'If you refer to the ritual, it has brought us only a succession of tiresome gate-crashers, and I for one am in favour of its never being conducted again.'

'It did solve the dragon problem,' said Lady Werth.

'And I, for one, think Mr. Ballantine an *interesting,* tiresome gate-crasher,' offered Gussie.

'I am almost unmanned by this encomium, Miss Werth,' said the Runner.

'Mm,' said Lady Honoria, hovering over Lady Werth's shoulder. 'Yes, I *do* believe we will keep this one.'

Mr. Ballantine's widened eyes betrayed a degree of horror.

'My aunt speaks without any intention of incarcerating you,' Gussie said reassuringly. 'At least, I am almost certain that she does.'

Lady Honoria smiled.

'I believe I must be going,' said Mr. Ballantine, with a backwards step.

'Not until the morning, was it not?' said Gussie. 'I do not know if Lord Maundevyle can be ready to leave at this hour, but I am certain Lord Bedgberry and I would not.'

'Lord Bedgberry and yourself, Miss Werth?' said Mr. Ballantine, looking from one to the other in confusion.

'What?' barked Theo.

'We are going with you,' said Gussie. 'Theo is quite the best person to pit against this spell-book of yours, as I am sure you've observed. And see, he has had the foresight to bring his favourite axe with him.' She retrieved the fallen weapon from its corner, and presented it to her cousin with a smile.

'No!' said Theo. 'Have I not been mauled enough?'

'Never *quite* enough, cousin.'

'And as for yourself, Miss Werth?' said Mr. Ballantine.

'Surely you are not going to be so unhandsome as to suggest I could not be of use, Mr. Ballantine?' said Gussie, opening her eyes wide. 'And after I defended you to Theo, as well! It is too much.'

'I—' began the hapless Mr. Ballantine.

'Gussie,' said Lady Werth. 'You cannot go gallivanting across the country with only a pair of gentlemen for company.'

'I had not thought to,' Gussie said soothingly. 'If Miss Frostell is not disposed to attend me again — and I suspect she might prefer not to — then—'

'Then *I* shall go,' said Lady Honoria, smiling again at

Ballantine. 'I am quite able to chaperone my great-niece, I believe?'

Mr. Ballantine, rather pale, stared back at Lady Honoria, and to his credit, this time he did not flinch. 'Er. Your ladyship would not happen to be in possession of a more respectable form?'

'What could possibly be otherwise than respectable about a disembodied head?' said Gussie.

To this unanswerable question, Mr. Ballantine did not attempt to respond.

'Were it too liberally rouged, that might be another matter, but Lady Honoria being a lady of impeccable taste—'

'Gussie,' said Lady Werth. 'You know there are reasons why you must *not*—'

'Are there, though?' said Gussie.

Lady Werth said, with the flexibility of a block of stone, 'Yes.'

'I believe I can promise to keep my hands to myself.'

'It is not that simple—'

'It might be that simple, but the truth is nobody knows. And I am not contented never to know, Aunt, any more than I am contented to spend the rest of my life kicking my heels at the Towers. I have been very docile up until now, I am sure you will recall, and I cannot think it has availed anybody very much.'

Lady Werth merely looked her misgivings, which appeared to be considerable.

'Would *you* want to be nailed to the drawing-room carpet for the next forty years?' Gussie persisted.

'Come, Gussie, it is not just the drawing-room,' said Theo, with ready malice. 'There is the parlour, the great hall, an entire *cottage* at your disposal, not to forget—'

'Theo, if you do not stop talking I shall release the Book myself.'

Somewhat to her surprise, Theo stopped. At once.

Gussie directed a meaningful look at her aunt. 'Do you

want to send him into Suffolk by himself?'

'*I* shall be present, Miss Werth, in case you had forgotten,' said Mr. Ballantine.

Gussie could only return him a withering look. 'Yes, and I should like to see you manage Lord Bedgberry.'

'I am quite able to—' began Mr. Ballantine, nettled.

'No, no,' said Theo, unexpectedly. 'She's perfectly right.'

After a short silence: 'I confess, Miss Werth,' said Mr. Ballantine, 'I do not see what you propose to do on what I perceive to be turning into a family expedition.'

'It is not really *you* I intend to assist,' Gussie admitted. 'But that there should be two such Books in the world, and in adjacent counties, is of some little interest to me. I never heard of another before.'

'So you are curious,' said Ballantine.

'Why, yes,' said Gussie brightly. 'Is that a problem?'

Twenty-Two

Dragonflight, Theo decided, merited a permanent place in his life. Yes, there was the utter horror of the launch into the air, and the unsteady, windswept flight that immediately followed — an experience which had Gussie in fits of screams (though to be fair to his cousin, he never did fully decide whether they were screams of terror, or delight). The rest, though, might rank among the greatest of luxuries, provided the weather continue fair, for he had space enough to make himself comfortable atop those crimson scales, and to carry several edifying tomes along with him as well. He spent much of the flight into Suffolk absorbed in a book, repelling every attempt by Gussie, Lady Honoria or the bothersome Runner at engaging him in conversation. Only when the journey drew to a close, and Lord Maundevyle began to spiral slowly down to the ground, did Theo look up from his book — and only then did it occur to him that Mr. Ballantine and Gussie were *still* talking to one another. Had they been doing that the whole time?

He consented to set the leather-bound tome aside a little before the dismount, for the view of the landscape below did at last arrest his attention. All the agricultural splendour of the county lay spread before him, networks of neatly-squared fields in shades of green and gold and brown, and bordered with deep green hedgerows. He watched in fascination as a small herd of cows grew gradually larger, and then, becoming aware all at once of what bore down upon them, went into a collective fit of hysterics and thundered off.

'A fine Wyrde, all told,' he said to his own self, but Gussie answered quite as though he had been addressing her.

'Is it not, though? I am experiencing no small amount of envy myself!'

'I don't *envy* it,' muttered Theo. 'I am happy with my own Wyrde.'

'And who would not be, indeed?' Gussie said, in that over-polite tone she always used when she was secretly mocking and imagined herself very clever about it. 'Given the choice between dragon-flight and supping upon a fresh flow of blood at every meal, who could hesitate?'

'But *is* anyone given the choice?' Ballantine put in.

'Surely you must know the answer to that,' Gussie answered. 'Specialising as you do in Wyrde-related misdemeanours.'

'I was enquiring into the arrangements among your family, Miss Werth.'

'Ah,' she said gravely. 'Because we are so splendidly Wyrded, you imagine us to possess some special secret.'

'I know you to possess a highly unusual book, for a start. That is by no means common among Wyrded families. And then there is you, Miss Werth.'

Gussie, clutching Lord Maundevyle's back with a white-knuckled grip, her hair flying upwards in the rushing wind of descent, did not seem likely to reply. But once the dragon's four feet were safely planted upon the ground again, and Mr. Ballantine had slid down without mishap, she made her own descent, eschewing any assistance, and said: 'I am no manner of miracle, Mr. Ballantine. I have no power to choose the nature of anybody's Wyrde, including my own.'

'Are you sure?' said he, and Gussie fell silent, for of course she was not.

Neither was Theo.

His attention being at that moment distracted by the appearance of a second female, most unexpectedly, he forgot whatever he had been going to say to his cousin about her Wyrde. The lady made a very odd appearance, standing in the middle of a field freshly harvested of some scrubby crop Theo neither knew nor cared to identify. Not only that, but she was of statuesque proportions and almost as tall as Theo — taller, if the astonishing height of her powdered hair were taken into consideration.

It was the hair that gave it away. 'Lady Honoria?' said he incredulously.

His great-great-grandmother paused in the process of shaking out her voluminous and outdated skirts, and smiled at him. 'Yes, dear?'

Theo swallowed, unsure what it was about her appearance that bothered him more; the fact that she had inexplicably re-acquired her full figure, from head to toe, with all the arms and legs typically thought necessary; or the fact that, despite this nearer relationship with a regular human shape, she was in no way less disturbing than usual. Her skin remained deathly-white, and while one might find it possible to pass that off as the product of the face-paints that had been popular several decades before, nothing could excuse the bloodshot appearance of her eyes, the bloodless pallor of her lips, or the maggot that crawled slowly from the corner of her mouth, and dropped silently into the mud.

Not to mention the whiff of decay, faint but noticeable, that assailed Theo's nose when she took a step or two nearer.

'Oh, capital!' said Gussie, as oblivious to proper conduct as ever. Then again, had not his own mother said the same of him, time and time again? It was not untrue. 'You look charmingly, Great-Aunt,' said Gussie, possibly sincerely, possibly not.

Lady Honoria touched the tip of one finger to her cheek, next to her mouth. A spot of grave-rot blossomed there and spread, black and neat, like a mole… a little bit like a mole. Not very much like, once Theo came to look more closely at it. 'Thank you, dear,' said his great-grandmother, smiling like a girl at her debut.

Theo turned away. 'Well, and where are we?' he said, watching in fascination as Lord Maundevyle's barn-sized and violently red physique vanished, leaving an ordinary man in its place. His lordship carefully smoothed down his coat, unsmiling as ever. He met Theo's gaze without in the smallest degree changing his expression.

'I hope we're on the outskirts of Woodburgh,' said Ballantine. It had escaped Theo's notice before, but in point of hue, his waistcoat resembled the draconic scales of Lord Maundevyle more than a little. 'The book vanished from a private library in the town, owned by one Hester Daventry.'

'Was it she who called in the Runners?' said Gussie.

'Her brother, I believe. A London gentleman.' He shaded his eyes against the strong morning sun, looking all about him, and finally uttered a triumphant, 'Aha! That must be it.'

Theo detected the signs of a settlement upon the near horizon, and regarded it with sour distaste. Were it not for the appearance of the damned Runner — no, were it not for Gussie's cursed habit of *interfering* — he might still be abed, and fast asleep.

'And have you indeed brought us straight to the right town?' Gussie was saying to Lord Maundevyle. 'How very clever of you.'

'I hope that it is,' said Maundevyle.

'I rather think you were *born* to be a dragon,' she said warmly, at which reflection Lord Maundevyle only looked appalled.

'He was,' said Theo shortly.

'In the same way you were born to be a good-tempered and respectable credit to the aristocracy?'

'Exactly in that way.'

'It is lovely to see you both succeeding so well,' Gussie murmured.

'Woodburgh!' crowed Ballantine.

Theo, having offered his arm to his great-grandmother, suppressed his next comment, being too much engaged with supporting the old lady across the muddy, uneven field. Last century's silken shoes were in no way suitable for a country walk; that and a certain lack of flexibility in long-dead limbs had given her a shambling gait, and her progress across the countryside was painstakingly slow and attended by much muttered cursing. Theo so much dreaded what might happen if she came to fall over as to put up with the unpleasant odour she exuded as they walked.

Some ten minutes brought them into the centre of the town, it being a settlement of moderate proportions. Ballantine walked up to the grandest house in evidence, a sizeable construction of stout bricks and flint, and rang the bell.

'Surely you do not propose that all of us should attend you?' said Lord Maundevyle, halted some way out in the street.

'I certainly propose to take the Werth clan along,' said Ballantine without turning around. 'I fancy I'll have need of their unusual expertise. You, though, my lord, are more than welcome to occupy yourself elsewhere. I have certainly taken up enough of your valuable time, and I thank you for it.'

Theo watched with some curiosity as Lord Maundevyle hesitated, obviously thinking the matter over. He had him down as rather a dull dog, except for the dragon-shifting; too much addicted to the maintenance of suitable appearances, and the not-being-seen to associate with those too far below his own station.

But Lord Maundevyle gave a shrug, and came up to the house, proving Theo wrong.

'Excellent,' said Gussie with one of her winning smiles. 'For we may need you, you know.'

Lord Maundevyle regarded her quizzically. 'Oh? How shall you need me?'

'You were not by, when Mr. Ballantine and Lord Bedgberry went down to the Book,' said she.

This being not especially enlightening to his lordship, Theo took pity on him. 'She means we may need you to don your teeth again and rend one or two things,' he said.

'Well, just the one thing, in all likelihood,' Gussie amended.

Theo unhooked his axe from his belt, and hefted it. 'I shall be quite able to take care of it.'

'Are we not here in search of a book?' said Lord Maundevyle, blinking. 'Surely a mere book-thief cannot be so dangerous?'

'It isn't the thief,' said Theo briefly, but was unable to say more, the door at that moment opening and the wary face of a young maid appearing beyond it.

'Is Mrs. Daventry at home?' said Ballantine. 'I am here from Bow Street.'

The maid was evidently nonplussed at the presence of five people clustered upon the doorstep, one of them wearing the red waistcoat of a Runner, another wearing the fashions of two generations past, and the other three, by their attire, clearly members of the Quality. 'Will you come in?' she said, opening the door wider. 'I'll see if Mrs. Daventry is awake.'

Theo thought the hour far advanced for a lady to still lie abed — a lady without his own habits, that is — but the matter was explained when Mrs. Daventry appeared, more than ten minutes after their arrival. The maid had ushered them into a small, neat parlour, prettily papered in floral blue, and with a great fire burning in the grate, despite the warmth of the season. Mrs. Daventry proved to be a woman in her later years, and visibly an invalid; she was thin to the point of gauntness, and her eyes held a feverish glitter. 'I am so sorry to keep you waiting,' she said upon entering the room.

Theo, perceiving the chairs to be insufficient for their number, immediately got up and crossed to the fire. Mrs. Daventry looked as though a wisp of wind would break her to pieces.

She sank immediately into the vacated chair, and regarded her plethora of visitors in measured silence as Ballantine rushed to make assurances. Despite her evident ill-health she was handsomely dressed, in a morning-gown of deep green silk and a cap of gauze-fine lace. The Daventrys were not short of money.

'Bow Street,' she said in her soft, wheezing way, echoing Ballantine's introduction of himself. 'Yes, I received word from my brother that I was to enjoy such a visit. I hope you can find my book, sir.'

'We will do our best, ma'am,' said Ballantine. 'May I introduce my associates to you?'

'Associates?' she faltered, looking from one to the other in puzzlement. When her scrutiny reached Lady Honoria, she stopped, and frowned.

'You are thinking I ought rightly to be in my grave, ma'am,' said Lady Honoria kindly. 'Indeed, you are quite right! But once in a while it is amusing to come out of it again, and an adventure is always a welcome diversion, is it not?'

Ballantine coughed. 'The matter of your book seems to extend some way beyond the ordinary, ma'am. I have taken the liberty of bringing a few Werths along, and a Maundevyle. Between them, they do seem to possess an unusual degree of expertise in the bizarre.'

'Werth,' echoed Mrs. Daventry. 'I believe I know that name.'

211

She could say this without visible recoil, which clearly heartened Gussie as much as it puzzled Theo.

'Perhaps you could tell us about your book, Mrs. Daventry,' said Ballantine quickly. 'I take it the thing was in some way remarkable?'

'Or I would not have had a Runner called in to retrieve it?' said Mrs. Daventry. 'Quite so, sir. And from the company you keep, I see you are accustomed to the remarkable.'

'A bit more so today than I was last week,' muttered Ballantine.

'Nonetheless, sir, I am afraid you may find my story *too* remarkable for credence.'

'That is in the highest degree unlikely,' promised Gussie. 'You will find us ready to believe anything.'

Ballantine cleared his throat. 'Miss Werth means to say that she is — er, acquainted — with one or two remarkable books herself.'

'It is true, then?' said Mrs. Daventry.

Nobody answered her, save with a collection of blank looks.

'Is there not said to be a legendary book at Werth Towers?' said Mrs. Daventry. 'A book of curses?'

'Good heavens, is that known so far abroad?' said Gussie.

'It is not a book of curses,' said Lady Honoria in a gently chiding tone.

'No, true,' said Gussie. 'It is itself a curse.'

Mrs. Daventry hesitated. 'The book I have lost was sold to me last year,' she said. 'It is a curse-book, dating from some centuries past.'

'Curses, ma'am?' said Ballantine. 'And did you use any of them?'

'To my disappointment, I have not been able to read it.'

'Who were you intending to curse, if I may ask?'

'No one in particular,' said Mrs. Daventry.

'Very well. And how did you come to realise that the book was missing?'

'One night, about a week ago, I left the curse-book lying open upon my reading-stand when I went up to my bedchamber. I was awoken in the night by a tremendous noise, and when I came down, I found several of my servants in various states of injury, and the book gone.'

'I see.'

'And the window of my book-room was broken,' she continued. 'Quite shattered into pieces.'

'How do you imagine that came about, ma'am?'

'I do not know. I suppose the thieves entered, and doubtless escaped, that way.'

'And now we come to the matter of the thieves. Do you know of anyone who knew you possessed the book, and might have wanted to take it?'

'No one. The sale was conducted privately, and naturally I have not been in the habit of speaking of it.'

'Its former owners, perhaps?'

'The book was sold to me out of the personal effects of a recently deceased gentleman. The seller offered it for a price far below its real worth, which I am ashamed to say I took advantage of. He can have had no idea of what he was selling, and did not appear at all interested. I bought it as one of several titles, the rest being of no particular interest.'

Gussie chose this moment to interfere. 'Did you ever notice anything unusual about the book, Mrs. Daventry? Besides the nature of the contents?'

'I do not know what you mean,' said Mrs. Daventry.

'Any — any unusual behaviour?'

'Behaviour? A book? No indeed.'

'Sounds in the night?'

Mrs. Daventry stared. 'You are aware we are speaking of a *book*, Miss Werth?'

'Perfectly, ma'am.'

Mrs. Daventry's reaction having effectively answered

Gussie's question, she abandoned the line of enquiry.

'I'd be glad to speak to the servants, if I may,' said Ballantine. 'All those who were present in the book-room at the time of the book's disappearance, and particularly those who came away injured.'

Mrs. Daventry rang the bell.

The merest glance at the welts on Robert Footman's arms, the savagery evident upon the first housemaid's legs, and the butler's ruined fingers, was sufficient to confirm the whole party's suspicions.

'It's my belief there never was a thief,' said Gussie, once the servants had been dismissed, and they were left alone in the book-room.

'No thief?' said Mr. Ballantine, disbelieving. 'You cannot mean to tell me that curse-book threw itself out the window?'

'Having seen the Book of Werth,' said Theo, 'I wonder that you can doubt it.'

'There are reasons why it was always kept in the cellar,' added Lady Honoria. 'No windows down *there*.'

'I am unsure whether to feel envious or relieved,' said Lord Maundevyle unexpectedly, having absented himself from the interviewing of the servants, and maintained a general silence since. 'There is an ancient book in the possession of my family, but it is not half so fascinating.'

'A sadly inert thing, I collect?' said Gussie. 'Not much in the habit of fomenting disaster?'

Lord Maundevyle inclined his head. 'I shall mention the curse-book to my mother,' he murmured. 'I am persuaded she will require one of her own.'

Gussie's grin was outright malicious.

'You might be right, about the thief,' said Ballantine, having ignored these asides altogether as he prowled about the book-room. 'None of the servants said anything that proves they saw an intruder. It has only been assumed, from the presence and the nature of the injuries.'

The book-room had been tidied, Theo surmised, since the event with the curse-book, for there was little sign of the tussle that had evidently taken place there. One of the large windows remained boarded-up ahead of a glazier's attention, which rendered the room rather dark. Theo received an impression of outdated but comfortable décor, with much dark wood and slightly threadbare armchairs. Since Mrs. Daventry in no way appeared short of the means to refurbish the room, he supposed it was kept in its present state out of preference, perhaps even sentiment. The smells of beeswax and book-dust hung heavy upon the air.

'But,' said Lord Maundevyle, after a moment, 'Mrs. Daventry said that her curse-book had exhibited no unusual behaviour before, and she had owned it for a year.'

'There are times,' said Gussie, 'when our own, dear Book appears quite sluggish. One might almost take it for an ordinary book, in such moments as that.'

'For a whole year together?' said Ballantine.

'Well, perhaps not,' Gussie admitted. 'But I have not been in the habit of visiting it every year. Theo?'

Theo shrugged his shoulders. 'Nor have I, but I should be surprised.'

'Aye,' said Ballantine. 'So, then. Either we are in the wrong entirely, and there has indeed been a thief, perhaps attended by aggressive beasts. Or, something has... awoken this curse-book, a few nights ago.'

'To what end?' said Gussie. 'If it did throw itself out of the window, as you so wonderfully put it, why did it do so?'

'Where was it proposing to go?' Theo agreed.

'It could be anywhere by now,' said Ballantine.

'But I doubt it has gone anywhere quietly,' said Gussie. 'Stealth does not tend to be a prominent quality with such tomes.'

215

'Then we'd better enquire about the town,' said Ballantine.

'That could take all week,' objected Theo, who, despite feeling a more than passing interest in the matter of the duplicate Book, had no desire at all to extend his stay in Suffolk past the end of the day.

'I shouldn't think so,' said Ballantine. 'Such news gets about. We've only to find the largest inn in Woodburgh, and make our enquiries. If there is anything to learn, you can bet it's to be heard there.'

'I suppose you spend a lot of time visiting inns,' said Gussie, rather wistfully.

'With one thing and another, yes,' Ballantine agreed.

'What a fine Runner you would have made, cousin,' said Theo.

'Had I been a man? Yes, I think I would.'

'Licensed to poke your nose into everything that is going on! It is a tragedy you were born a female.'

Gussie did not take this bait, but only smiled. 'Well, here is my one chance to play at being a Runner, and I can assure you I mean to make the most of it.'

'It is no game,' said Ballantine, with a frown.

'Is it not?' said Gussie, clearly disappointed. 'Why, but there are rules, and stakes, and consequences for losing—'

'No real prize for winning, though,' said Ballantine dryly.

'Save the natural satisfaction of seeing justice done,' said Gussie primly.

'That, of course.'

'Shall we go?' said Theo. 'The Book is not going to subdue itself.'

'Yes,' said Gussie, and strode for the door.

'Perhaps I shall go first, Miss Werth?' said Ballantine, mildly enough.

Gussie stopped short. 'Right,' she said.

TWENTY-THREE

The largest of Woodburgh's three inns was the White Hart, encouragingly situated not so very far from Mrs. Daventry's house. Being the premier coaching-inn besides, it was a commodious place, bustling with ostlers and grooms as well as cook-staff, housemaids and guests.

Mr. Ballantine insisted on going to see the innkeepers alone, to Gussie's disappointment.

'They will speak openly to a Runner in ways they wouldn't to a young lady of quality like yourself,' said he, in firm response to Gussie's protests.

'Or an alarming old woman?' said Lady Honoria.

'I believe you may terrify the poor souls, ma'am.'

'Nonsense! When you can see I am on my best behaviour.' She smiled.

'I shall go in alone,' repeated Mr. Ballantine.

He did so, spared further protests. Gussie was left standing in the street, Lord Maundevyle a stern and silent presence upon her left, and Theo drifting restlessly about upon her right. Great-Aunt Honoria gave a windy sigh.

'Well, I am thirsty,' said Gussie, after two minutes of this. 'I am sure one of you will be so kind as to attend me into this lovely inn, where I am sure I shall find refreshment.' Without further ado she strode across the street and entered the inn, not pausing to determine whether any of her companions proposed to join her.

She spotted Mr. Ballantine at once, though fortunately he had his back to her, already deep in consultation with a respectable-looking man who could only be the innkeeper.

A woman she took to be the innkeeper's wife saw Gussie as she entered the taproom, and came over immediately. The curtsey she dropped, and her manner, indicated that the quality of Gussie's pelisse and gown was not lost upon her. 'Shall you be wanting a room, Miss…?' said she, her gaze darting over Gussie's shoulder, perhaps in search of the companions she was doubtless expected to have.

'Werth,' said Gussie. 'No, certainly not! I would only like to order some lemonade, if you have it, and a light nuncheon. Perhaps a private parlour? And it appears I shall be dining alone, for my companions are all of them far too lily-livered to come in here with me.'

'Lily-livered?' faltered the innkeeper's wife.

'Yes, for Mr. Ballantine will frown awfully, and he is severe when displeased.'

'If you'll forgive me, Miss Werth, you ought not to be wandering the town alone,' said the innkeeper's wife. 'Not that I would ordinarily presume to say so, but you see, there's been disturbances. It's not safe to go about alone. Mr. Baker's been saying so to all as has passed through.'

'Disturbances!' said Gussie. 'Excellent! Do tell me more.'

That won her a wary look from Mrs. Baker, as she now took the woman to be. 'Two people was attacked in the street,' she said, lowering her voice, as though to speak at a normal volume might invite the attention of the attacker. 'Not a week ago. The watchman may never recover the use of his arm, they say. And—' her voice sank even further '—there's a vagrant who's dead.'

'Dead!' Gussie stared at the woman in shock. 'Quite

dead! Are you certain?'

'Fully certain of it, Miss Werth, and so I hope you will take care in Woodburgh.'

'Where did these events take place?' Gussie asked.

'Not three streets away, in Pelham Lane.'

Whether Gussie's shocked ejaculation had been heard so far away as the street, or whether hunger or curiosity had brought the gentlemen along with her, Gussie shortly found herself flanked by Lords Maundevyle and Bedgberry, to whom poor Mrs. Baker, overcome by such a quantity of gentry, quite effaced herself.

'Nuncheon for four, then?' said Gussie.

'Yes, ma'am, certainly,' said Mrs. Baker.

'Will your aunt want to take any refreshment?' said Lord Maundevyle.

She caught his meaning: only a living woman could have need of such mundane considerations as sustenance. 'I hardly know,' she admitted. 'Just because I have never known her to eat does not mean she will not wish to, I suppose? Besides, there is always Mr. Ballantine.'

'You're never here with that Runner, Miss?' gasped Mrs. Baker.

'Why, yes! In fact, I am a Runner myself, you know.'

Ignoring the widening of Mrs. Baker's eyes, and the appalled stare directed at the spectre of Lady Honoria as she drifted into the inn, Gussie marched off in the direction indicated, and took up a comfortable position in a neat, snug little parlour, there to await her nuncheon.

'If someone has actually died,' said Gussie afterwards, when a selection of cold meats and a salad had been laid out upon the table, 'then the matter is of greater urgency than we imagined.'

'I suppose it's of no use to tell you you ought not to be mixed up in it?' said Theo.

'No use at all.'

'I thought not.'

Lady Honoria availed herself of a piece of bread, took a tentative mouthful, and swallowed it down with an expression of disgust. The bread was swiftly restored to the dish. 'What a pity we did not bring Lord Werth with us,' she mused. 'He might have wrung some information out of the vagrant.'

Lord Maundevyle paused in the act of raising a forkful of meat to his lips, and set it down again. 'He is not often in the habit of raising the dead, I hope?'

Gussie considered. 'Not so *very* often, no.'

'Not so much as he used to,' sighed Honoria.

'There can be no call for any raising of the dead,' said Mr. Ballantine, storming the parlour with an expression of grave disapprobation. 'I ought to have known I'd be subject to such ideas, in choosing such a disgraceful set of associates.'

'But no, we are very useful,' said Gussie, smiling at him. 'Come now, how soon would you have drawn the correct conclusions, otherwise? You would be chasing non-existent thieves until Christmas.'

'We are not yet certain that it *is* the correct conclusion, Miss Werth,' he reminded her. 'And did I not mention something about remaining outside until I'd finished with my enquiries?'

'You did, certainly, but I did not perfectly understand why,' said Gussie, helping herself to a portion of a fine salmagundy. 'You could not be under the impression that any of us might be mauled to death in here.'

'I might be concerned about what's thought of a young lady keeping company with a Runner.'

'You are concerned for my reputation!' Gussie beamed at him. 'I pray you will not be, however. A young lady properly attended by her aunt can never be too much frowned upon, and besides, I am six-and-twenty; hardly a schoolroom miss.'

'But three gentlemen—' began he again.

'I believe I have said it before,' Gussie interrupted.

'There is nothing that can salvage the reputation of the Werths abroad in England, and I don't at all mean to waste my life in the attempt of it. Whatever my dear aunt may believe, no attention to the proprieties can possibly render *me* acceptable, and I am long past repining over it. Won't you sit down?' She waved her fork at the vacant seat next to Lord Maundevyle, aware the while of that gentleman's steady regard, unreadable as ever. Did he disapprove of her? She did not mean to be unhappy about it if he did.

Mr. Ballantine condescended to sit, though not without a degree of displeased mutterings under his breath. He did not attempt again to remonstrate with her, however, and Gussie was glad of it. His solicitude could not offend her, but nor could it please, and after all he had no right of interest in her that might justify his interference in her affairs. Since the same could be said of Lord Maundevyle and Theo, obligingly, did not care, that left her free to do as she pleased, did it not?

'We have news,' she said, once Mr. Ballantine was fairly seated.

'Oh?' said he dangerously, his frown returning. 'Do not tell me you've been making enquiries of your own.'

'No, indeed,' said Gussie. 'It was not at all necessary. Everyone is concerned for my well-being, it seems, for that good Mrs. Baker could not stop talking of it. You have heard, of course, that someone is dead?'

'*And* a watchman has lost his arm,' said Great-Aunt Honoria, with relish.

'No, was it taken quite off?' said Gussie. 'I thought it had only been savaged.'

'Perhaps that was it,' she allowed.

Lord Maundevyle definitely disapproved of her now, for his eyes had gone wide, and when he caught her looking at him he looked quickly down at his plate.

Then again, with a sister like Clarissa surely he was accustomed to worse?

'By the landlord's account, the injuries suffered by

those two men are a match for the servants at Mrs. Daventry's,' said Mr. Ballantine. 'Albeit more severe. And since those events took place on the same night, and not far from Mrs. Daventry's house, I believe we can feel tolerably certain that the curse-book is responsible for both.'

'In which case it was known to flee down Pelham Lane,' said Gussie. 'And then — where?'

'I've heard nothing else,' Mr. Ballantine admitted. 'Wherever it went after that, it has left no trail that we may easily follow.'

'Supposing it did go somewhere else?' said Gussie.

'Aye, what is on Pelham Lane?' said Theo. 'Perhaps it found something to its liking.'

'Why would it break so spectacularly out of Mrs. Daventry's book-room only to linger a street or two away?' said Mr. Ballantine.

'It's of no use expecting sensible behaviour from a Book,' said Theo.

'Quite,' said Mr. Ballantine. 'I wonder that it didn't occur to me to realise it before.'

When the waiter came in soon afterwards, bearing a fresh jug of lemonade, Mr. Ballantine bade him pause. 'Is there anything of note on Pelham Lane?'

The waiter paled. 'You don't want to go near there, sir. The most terrible things have been happening!'

'I know. I am here to look into it.'

The waiter appeared to notice his red Runner's waistcoat for the first time. 'Oh!' he said, but cast a doubtful eye over Mr. Ballantine's company, unmistakeably gentry.

'My associates,' said Mr. Ballantine. 'It makes more sense than it doesn't.'

The waiter set down the pottery jug with great care, and finally answered: 'There isn't much on Pelham, sir. There's St. Mary's church, of course, and Fletcher's circulating library—'

'A churchyard,' said Mr. Ballantine, with emphasis.

'A *library*,' said Theo.

Mr. Ballantine looked up. 'You think it's there?'

Theo's lips quirked in an acid smile. 'Where else would it make any sense for a Book to go?'

'I thought there was no expecting sensible behaviour from a Book?'

'But you must allow, there's nowhere else it could be so well hidden.'

The waiter making fast for the door, Gussie raised her voice. 'There haven't been any reports of trouble at Fletcher's, I suppose?'

'Trouble, ma'am?' said the waiter.

'Deaths or injuries,' she smiled.

The poor boy visibly shuddered. 'Not that I hear tell of, ma'am.'

'How disappointing. Thank you.'

The waiter shot her a horrified look, and fled.

'Well,' said Mr. Ballantine. 'If there's a man or woman left in this inn who won't go to bed with nightmares, it won't be for lack of trying.'

Gussie applied herself to her salmagundy, and made no answer.

Fletcher's Circulating Library proved to be a very cramped establishment, with a number of volumes and periodicals on display, and signs of a closed back room that interested Gussie very much.

Thus much had to be determined by peeping through a window, for the place was shut.

'Ought it not to be open?' said Gussie doubtfully.

'I am not much familiar with the practices of subscription libraries,' Mr. Ballantine admitted.

'Well, nor I, but I cannot suppose there is much custom to be had if one does not trouble to keep one's establishment open.'

Mr. Ballantine eyed the locked door with misgiving. 'I

hope it isn't a sign of some of that trouble you spoke of,' he said. 'But in case it is, I'd be glad if you ladies would keep away.'

'I daresay you would,' said Gussie.

'Gussie,' said Theo. 'I am sure it wasn't your intention to come along only to put Mr. Ballantine into difficulties?'

'Of course not, but—'

'Then unless you are possessed of some method of self-preservation I've yet to witness in you, I suggest you do as Mr. Ballantine asks.'

'I emerged unscathed from my last interview with the Book!' she retorted. Then, remembering the welts upon her arms, amended this to, 'Well, nearly so!'

'Different book. As far as we know, the Book of Werth has yet to kill anybody.'

'Untrue,' said Lady Honoria, polishing a spot of window with her sleeve before peering into the library. 'Or did you never wonder how your great-aunt Bertha came to die so young?'

Theo, observed to turn whiter than usual, let this pass. 'Gussie?' he said, when she made so bold as to attempt the handle. 'Please?'

She turned, shocked. 'Did you say *please*?'

'I should prefer not to have to explain to my mother why you are brought back in pieces.'

'That *would* be unpleasant,' she allowed. 'Though I do not see why Lord Maundevyle is to be permitted entry. *He* is not so very terrifying, either, save in his dragon form, and he can hardly take it on in the street.' Having said thus much, she retired to the far side of the street with very ill grace.

'Perfectly true,' said Lord Maundevyle, and came to stand beside her. 'You will permit me, I hope, to stand lookout over you instead.'

She looked up at him, unimpressed. 'I am only female, sir, not blind. I am able to perceive the rampant approach of a murderous Book just as well as you.'

224

He was expressionless, as always, but it struck her that his eyes were smiling. 'Pray humour me. My part in this adventure ended when I brought you all into Suffolk, and my pride will not bear having nothing of any use to do.'

'In that case, I am decidedly in need of a guard.'

'I am glad to hear it.'

'After all, there is no saying what my cousin may do when he grows hungry.'

'Surely he has been sufficiently sustained?'

'Mrs. Baker's comestibles were admirable, but not the sort to be of much use to Theo.'

Lord Maundevyle digested that. 'I had wondered,' he said. 'All those nightly perambulations.'

'He imagines it to be a secret, beyond the family. Pray don't disabuse him of the notion. He is like to become cantankerous.'

'I shall be as silent as the grave,' he promised.

Lady Honoria gave an eloquent, and hellish, cackle.

'I... hadn't thought,' said Lord Maundevyle in horror.

Lady Honoria patted his arm, probably in an attempt to reassure, but since the gesture left a quantity of grave-dust smeared across his lordship's sleeve, it was not much appreciated.

Across the street, Lord Bedgberry and Mr. Ballantine had given up on forcing the front door, and slipped around to the side of the building instead. Gussie caught only occasional glimpses of their activities thereafter, but she did hear the faint but distinctive sounds of a window creaking open, and witnessed a pair of airborne feet disappearing through it shortly afterwards.

'They are in!' she crowed.

'I wonder if we shall be taken up as loiterers?' mused Lord Maundevyle. 'I hope they do not expect to be very long.'

'An ancient curse-book must surely stand out, even in a book-shop,' Gussie said. 'In fact—'

She stopped, for the front door of the library swung

open with a crash, and Mr. Ballantine came barrelling out with Theo close behind him.

Gussie hurried across the street. 'What is it?'

'I believe we've found Mr. Fletcher,' he said grimly.

'Dead?'

'Let's say that I hope so, shall we?'

Gussie swallowed. 'And what of—'

The door slammed shut again, but now there was no sign of Theo.

'He has not gone back in again?' she gasped.

Mr. Ballantine swung back around, and stared at the door in consternation. He tried the handle; locked.

'Lord Bedgberry!' he shouted, and pounded upon the unyielding wood.

Somewhere behind the noise of Mr. Ballantine's protests, Gussie could hear a familiar *crash*.

'I daresay he will be all right,' she said. 'He has got his axe with him.'

Mr. Ballantine stared, wild-eyed. 'His axe? You imagine an axe will be sufficient defence against *that book*?'

'Oh, no,' said Gussie. 'But an axe wielded by Lord Bedgberry? Very likely.'

'The lot of you are out of your wits,' said Mr. Ballantine savagely, and set off around to the side of the building again.

But Gussie grabbed his arm. 'Don't! Why do you think Theo shut the door on you?'

'This is no time to hesitate! Your cousin is in the gravest danger—'

'Will you *not* listen? Five minutes ago you reminded me that my presence was like to be more of a liability than an advantage, and you must believe the same is now true for you. Theo knows what he is doing.'

'This is my duty,' said Mr. Ballantine. 'I am a Bow Street Runner. It is my job to protect the lot of you, not stand back in safety while you're injured or killed while doing my work for me.' Half this sentence emerged somewhat strained, as he was at work upon the window again. This time, Gussie could not prevent him from hauling himself up onto the ledge, and vanishing back inside.

Gussie sighed. 'I did rather like him, you know,' she said to her aunt.

Great-Aunt Honoria nodded sympathetically. 'A pity.'

Gussie paused for half a minute more, wincing at the sounds emerging from Fletcher's library. 'There must be something we can do,' she fretted. 'Theo can take care of himself, but of Mr. Ballantine as well?'

'I will find out what is passing,' said Honoria, and in the blink of an eye she was reduced once more to a severed head. She experienced some small difficulty in fitting her high-stacked hair through the open window, but soon she, too, disappeared inside.

Gussie was within half a minute of throwing caution to the winds and following them both, when she became aware of a presence nearby.

She turned.

It was not the Book, as she had briefly feared. It was Lord Maundevyle, a dragon again, and in danger of demolishing two or three houses if he should chance to move unwisely. His head rose higher than the rooftops.

'Oh, for—! Lord Maundevyle! You cannot imagine this useful!'

He ignored her, lowered his head, and bashed his face against the firmly locked door. It crumpled at once — the door, to her relief, not Lord Maundevyle's face — and he proceeded to fit as much of himself through it as he could.

This was not much, to be fair, but seemingly enough, for two minutes afterwards he withdrew his head again.

Clamped between his teeth was a furiously writhing Book.

Theo, dishevelled and bleeding, appeared at the ruined door. 'Has he got it? He's got it!' He stared up and up at the towering dragon engaged in a grim battle with a betentacled Book bent on escape.

'Can he hold it?' Gussie gasped.

For an agonising moment, it appeared as though the Book would slip through his teeth — or beat him into submission, as it strove to do — and career off down Pelham Lane, there to spread further disaster.

But Lord Maundevyle braced himself, tensed his long, muscled neck, and with an audible *crunch* bit down hard upon the Book's ancient covers.

A tearing *crack* sounded, and a thin scream, and the curse-book went limp.

Slowly, Lord Maundevyle lowered his head.

'Take care!' Gussie warned. 'I am sure it is not above a little misdirection! It may yet escape.'

But it did not. Once laid upon the cobbles of the street, Gussie saw that its covers were torn almost in two, and many of its pages severed from the spine.

Theo sagged against the doorframe, breathing hard. 'Good God,' he said. 'The thing is worse than ours.'

Lord Maundevyle was so ungentlemanly as to spit, as though something foul-tasting filled his mouth. '*What are they?*' he roared.

'I did not until this week realise there was more than one,' Gussie said. 'I have no answer for you.' Then, tearing her eyes from the grotesque sight of the fallen and savaged curse-book, she straightened with a start, said, 'But Mr. Ballantine!' and tore past Theo into the library.

He lay prone near the back of the room, surrounded by a rain of fallen volumes and the sheets of torn newspapers. Gussie ran to him, her heart pounding, but by the time she reached him he was already struggling to sit up.

'Thank goodness,' she said, dropping to her knees beside him. 'You are alive.'

'I think so,' he wheezed.

'Are you very badly hurt, sir?'

'Less so than I deserve to be,' he said grimly, putting a hand to his bloodied face. 'You were right, Miss Werth. I should have listened to you.' He caught his breath upon a half-sob of pain, and let it out slowly. 'I lasted twenty seconds, I think. It cannot have been more.'

'You could have little notion what you were facing,' she said charitably.

'Having met the Book of Werth, I ought to have had.' He rose slowly to his feet, and stood swaying slightly. Gussie hovered, wishful of assisting him, but unwilling to encroach so far. 'I'll have much to tell when I return to London. We are in no way equipped to deal with the likes of this.'

Gussie supposed that "we" meant his fellow Runners, particularly those specialising in the Wyrde. 'Then it will prove a profitable adventure, sir, and you had better stop berating yourself over it. It never does do any good, you know.'

He nodded, and condescended so far as to accept the arm Gussie offered to him. 'I take it the cursed thing has been subdued?'

'By Lord Maundevyle,' Gussie nodded. 'Those teeth of his really are impressive.'

Once outside, Mr. Ballantine stood looking down at the ruined book with some chagrin. 'Mrs. Daventry won't be pleased.'

'I shall offer to buy it from her for a fabulous sum, and she will be very well satisfied,' said Theo.

'Buy it?' Gussie repeated, dismayed. 'Theo, you are not proposing to take the thing home?'

'What else is to be done with it?' he demanded. 'I don't see that anyone else can be relied upon to keep it contained, and we cannot have it whittling down the good citizens of Woodburgh any further.'

'My uncle will not approve. Theo, I am persuaded *no one* at the Towers will approve.'

'Do you have some other notion?'

Gussie looked at Mr. Ballantine.

'I can't help you,' he said. 'As I may have mentioned,

229

we are not equipped for such a charge.'

Gussie gave a sigh. 'I wonder what has become of Great-Aunt Honoria?' she said, and wandered back into the library.

'Miss Werth—' began Mr. Ballantine.

Gussie had already stopped, having perceived what she had been too distracted to notice before: the crumpled body of a man, presumably Mr. Fletcher, slumped against one wall. He appeared as though he had been thrown there, with sufficient force to break several of his bones — including his neck.

'Oh, dear,' she sighed. 'Aunt, he is too far gone. I don't believe you will find it possible to speak to him.'

Lady Honoria acknowledged the truth of this, and abandoned her station some three inches away from Mr. Fletcher's grey and rigid face. 'I always did envy your uncle his abilities, a little,' she admitted. 'I am quite unable to replicate them.' By the time she reached the door she had once again donned her body and limbs, and was restored to as much respectability as she was capable of achieving. 'Are we for home, then?' she said.

'I presume so,' Gussie said. 'I'm afraid we are taking somebody back with us.'

TWENTY-FOUR

'Another book,' said Lady Werth stonily. 'You cannot mean... another *Book*?'

'I'm afraid so, Aunt. Theo would have it so, and to be truthful I could think of few reasons to argue with him over it.'

'Besides the incidental fact of my excessive dislike to the scheme?'

'Yes! And yours, too, Uncle,' Gussie said. 'But he was unmoved. I could almost believe him to have taken a fancy to the Books.'

Lord Maundevyle had restored Gussie, Great-Aunt Honoria and Lord Bedgberry to the Towers, leaving Mr. Ballantine to oversee the clean-up of Woodburgh, and subsequently to return to London to make his report to Bow Street. The hour being far advanced by the time of the dragon's descent into the Park, Gussie had been famished, but too weary to think much of her dinner. She had gone directly to her cottage, choosing to break the news of the second Book to her aunt and uncle in the morning.

If she had entertained hopes that Theo might have spared her that duty, she was destined to be disappointed. Having acquainted Miss Frostell with the previous day's events, she walked up to the Towers straight after breakfast, and found Lord and Lady Werth still enjoying a state of blissful ignorance as to their return.

Thankfully, there was no sign of the Reverend Cardwell, or of Miss Horne either.

Determined to get the business over with as quickly as possible, Gussie had collected her victims into her aunt's favourite parlour, and there undertaken the task of destroying their comfort.

'What can he have been thinking?' gasped Lady Werth.

'The curse-book had been badly behaved,' Gussie said. 'I believe he thought it a little too much to leave a murderous Book on the loose in Woodburgh.'

'*Murderous?*'

'It is known to have dispatched a few unfortunates.'

Lady Werth subsided into a horrified silence.

'Could not Mr. Ballantine have taken it away?' said Lord Werth, a little plaintively.

'The Runners had never even heard of such Books before, Uncle. Mr. Ballantine denied having any notion how to contain one of them.'

Lord Werth sighed. 'Theo is not proposing to put it in with the Book of Werth, I hope? I had better look in on him.'

'I am sure he would not be so foolish,' said Lady Werth.

Gussie was not so sure, but she let the matter go. Her uncle and Theo between them would see to the curse-book's suitable incarceration.

'I confess myself intrigued by them,' Gussie admitted. 'The Book of Werth seemed a mere fact of life, like childbirth, or smallpox. That there could be two such tomes is remarkable. Where do you suppose they came from?'

'I hardly know,' said Lady Werth, fidgeting in her chair. 'But I wish they had not come to *us*.'

'Do you suppose there might be more?'

At this prospect, poor Lady Werth turned very white.

'Gussie! Do not so much as whisper it! It is a terrible thought.'

And it was, for while the Book of Werth had always been temperamental, and prone to fits of indignation, the notion that it might be capable of killing anyone who happened to be within reach was so distant a possibility as to have receded beyond the reach of day-to-day anxiety. The presence of its twin did away with such comfortable notions as relative safety; Gussie thought of her own visit to the family tome only the week before, with no one but her aunt for company, and shuddered.

'Do you think you could ice the curse-book?' said Gussie, struck with a sudden thought.

Lady Werth considered. 'I have never thought to make the attempt.'

'Well, perhaps you could? Then it could not be such a danger.'

'I could ice them both,' said Lady Werth, with a smile Gussie found chilling.

'It would not be possible to consult our own Book, if it were iced?'

'I can see no occasion for doing so in the foreseeable future. Indeed, I should be happier to burn it than to read from it.' She rose as she spoke, clearly bent upon following her husband down into the cellars.

Gussie briefly considered attending her into the curse-book's presence, and decided not. She had enjoyed enough close proximity to the abominable thing for one week.

She went instead back to her cottage, to spend the rest of the day with her excellent Miss Frostell.

A letter arrived for Lord Werth some few days later, with a postscript intended for Gussie.

It was from Mr. Ballantine.

The matter of the books has caused great interest, and equally great consternation, in Bow Street, he wrote. *Your family's experience with The Book of Werth was not wholly unknown in all quarters, but the details I have been able to provide were of great use.*

I am not yet able to write with any specific information as to the probable source or history of these books, nor whether there is any explanation for their behaviour. The case is considered pressing, and I have been set to look into the matter with all possible haste.

I do not propose to wait upon you again at the Towers just yet, but I should be surprised if the course of my enquiries does not, sooner or later, lead me back into those cellars of yours. I hope you won't dislike it. Bow Street has also appealed for news of any further such books. I am sure you are joined with me in hoping that there are no more to be found.

Seeing as the case concerns your family rather nearly, I shall take the liberty of communicating to you my findings, as far as I am able. In the meantime, may I hope that Mrs. Daventry's book of curses has been suitably subdued? If its containment is likely to prove a danger to your family, I shall do my best to arrange for alternative accommodation for it in London.

He had signed it with a great scrawl of a signature in thick, black ink, and beneath that was written the following afterthought:

PS - Please encourage Miss Werth to contain her curiosity. I have no doubt the case will interest her quite as much as it can Bow Street, but I should be sorry indeed if the matter of the book should be the means of dispatching her to an early grave.

Lord Werth's response to Gussie's bristling indignation was a meaningful look, and a speaking silence.

'It is the greatest impertinence!' she insisted. 'As if I should dream of pursuing my own investigations, against Bow Street's express instructions!'

Lord Werth raised his eyebrows.

'And in the face of such obvious danger, too!'

'Of course you would not,' said her uncle.

'No. Not *alone*, at any rate. But Theo—'

'Gussie,' said Lord Werth sternly.

'If *Theo* and I were to look into it jointly, and perhaps

with Lord Maundevyle's assistance?'

'Gussie—'

'And my Aunt Honoria. And Frosty! She has a bright mind, if not any great combative prowess. Between us, I am sure we could make considerable progress, and without the smallest danger.'

'I should infinitely prefer it if we could *all* return to the general peace that prevailed at Werth before this nonsense began,' said Lord Werth.

'I am sure we shall! Now that you have got rid of the reverend Cardwell, and Miss Horne, and anybody else who has drifted up while I was away.'

Lord Werth's lips tightened.

'Poor uncle,' said Gussie soothingly. 'We have had a time of it, have we not? What with abductions and Wyrdings, dragons and Bow Street Runners, murderous Books and far more strangers underfoot than any of us could have wished for—'

'They will be gone presently.'

Gussie said, more seriously: 'It is not my intention to create further chaos, Uncle. If I say I shall do my best not to drown you in further troubles, will that do?'

Lord Werth sighed, and if his shoulders were seen to sag just a little, one could hardly wonder at it. 'I perceive that it will have to.'

And to do justice to Gussie, she said it with every intention of carrying the happy notion through. If circumstances were not to prove in her favour, she may at least be given credit for trying.

MORE FROM
CHARLOTTE E. ENGLISH

THE WONDER TALES:

Faerie Fruit
Gloaming
Sands and Starlight

THE TALES OF AYLFENHAME:

Miss Landon and Aubranael
Miss Ellerby and the Ferryman
Bessie Bell and the Goblin King
Mr. Drake and My Lady Silver

www.charlotteenglish.com

Printed in Great Britain
by Amazon